Chasing Empty Caskets

A Sharp Investigations Novel

Book Two

BY: E. N. CRANE

EDITED BY: A. O. NEAL

Dedication

Thank you to my dogs: Perry and Padfoot.
Their shenanigans, antics and behavior are the model for all
things Winnie.
Thank you to my husband, because he knows how many "people" live in my head and he's never had me committed. He also
keeps me in coffee and snacks when I start yelling at imaginary
people.
Special thanks to Jeff Neal for lending me his military knowledge. Most of this is made up, but I strive for imaginative accuracy.

Chapter One:
F.M.L.

S taring at the paperclip on my desk, I wondered how hard I would have to stab myself in the eye to die. I'd never been suicidal or prone to ideations of death, but an hour with this man and I was ready to throw it all away. Life, liberty, snacks, coffee...

Maybe I was going a little too far.

I should aim to scramble my frontal lobe to the point where I could no longer understand the man sitting in front of me. Except I already didn't understand him, and my brain was perfectly intact. His voice droned on with the same thing, the same accusations...

Instead, I should poke myself in the eardrums so I could no longer hear him.

It's sad when one has to resort to self-mutilation to make it through the day.

Mr. Figs wasn't an attractive man. I'm told in his prime he looked like George Clooney, but now he just looks like The Penguin from the Michael Keaton Batman movie. He was short, round, had a nasally voice, and he smelled like rotted garlic and onions, causing me to choke on my next breath. Another wave of the stench wafted toward me, and I tried to breathe through my mouth before I lost consciousness.

The rotary fan made another pass of the room, and the scent disappeared.

I sniffed the air, nothing. My eyes dropped to the floor and stared at my partner. Sgt. Winnifred Pupperson, ex-military police K-9 just like I was her ex-military handler. She was a snack-loving German shepherd Malinois mix, and as far as the Army was concerned, we were carbon copies of the same nightmare. The two of us had made Laverne and Shirley look like put together ladies, but we'd survived quite a bit together. Despite the honorable designation in our discharge, we had been anything but during our four years of service to the United States. There was the destroyed marketplace in Afghanistan, the crushed pretzel statue in Germany, the cow in Sweden... not to mention the attempt to blow up Florida, though I personally considered that a service *to* this nation and not against it.

A small *pooft* sound escaped and the smell came again. It was stronger with every wag of her tail, and I fanned my face.

We may not survive this gas.

"That was disgusting. How can I survive years in Florida, but you raiding the trash can at 3AM for cheese wrappers is grounds

2

for a chemical warfare treaty violation?" I said to her, and she let out a wide yawn and rolled onto her back. "Could you at least try to be professional while murdering us?"

Another *pooft*.

"Ms. Sharp, are you even listening to me?" the small man whined, and I turned back to him.

"Yes, I'm listening. I've been listening for an hour. Nothing has changed, Mr. Figs. I cannot go to your house and exorcise your wife's ghost from the premises."

"Why not?" his voice whined at the end. "Aren't you an investigator?"

"I'm not a paranormal investigator, also-" he interrupted me.

"Didn't Mrs. Margot make you promise to help? My dead wife's ghost is a problem! Help me with *my* problem, Ms. Sharp!"

He was just this side of a toddler stamping his foot and whining about how he didn't want to go to bed. I clawed at my face and hoped for a meteor or a radioactive spider. Maybe a Russian man who wanted to experiment on me in the name of science?

Nothing.

"Her ghost is not a problem," I tried again, calmly, while banging my head against the desk. "You are a problem, but her ghost is not now, nor will it ever be, haunting you because you will definitely die first."

The pot of coffee sat empty beside me. My cup beside me, declaring me a unicorn trainer, was also empty.

Mr. Figs sniffed in disdain and I found my patience was as empty as my caffeine supplies.

My office was a small room that sat beside the town's outdated public library. The wide front window, looking out onto Main street, sat beside a wooden door with an old school brass knocker. Above the office was a minimalist apartment where I lived. The apartment had a kitchen, a bathroom, and a closet. There was plenty of room for my bed, Winnie's bed and snacks for both of us. As far as closet space... I didn't have many clothes from when I was in the Army that weren't issued by the Army. After living in Florida for four years, most of the ones I had purchased were tossed due to sweat stains and weird smells. The whole building belonged to an older woman who I'd helped rid her church of imposters and crooks just over a month ago, Mrs. Glen Margot. The agreement was I wouldn't refuse help to any townsperson who asked, but I was starting to think living in my parent's basement wasn't so bad.

"She's haunting me! I can't get away from her!" he shouted again, and I stared longingly at the paperclip.

"Mr. Figs, she is not dead. She is standing right there!" I pointed at the front door. In front, leaning against an old four-door vehicle in a hideous shade of blue, was a pleasantly plump woman in a flowered dress. She had a sweater on in deference to the January air and an ice cream cone in each hand. One white and the other a shade of pink that screamed sugar rush.

"That's her ghost!" he insisted and I got up, Winnie rising beside me. "Banish her to the afterlife!"

"I am much more likely to banish you to the afterlife if you don't..."

"Ghost! Ghost!" he shouted over me and started bouncing in his chair.

"That is your wife. She is alive. And she bought you ice cream!" I marched to the door and pushed it open. Winnie scented the air and her tail went full helicopter. "Stay!"

Winnie flopped over in dismay. We both knew Mr. Figs didn't deserve his wife's ice cream, but Winnie hadn't earned it, either. The farts and the four AM alarm every Thursday when the trash men came were definitely grounds for ice cream refusal.

I glanced at the calendar; it was thankfully only Tuesday. The woman cleared her throat.

"Mrs. Figs!" I called, gesturing her in. She came closer and smiled wide, her wrinkled face pleasant and comforting.

"Good morning, Cynthia," she said, extending a hand. "Would you like this ice cream?"

"Sure," I said, taking the cone of single scoop of chocolate chip. "Thank-you."

"Of course. Why has Elmer been in here for an hour?" she asked. He was pointedly looking anywhere but at the door. At least he had stopped jumping and shouting. If he gave himself a heart-attack it would be the second time I had summoned EMS here for a client this week.

"He said you are dead and haunting him."

"He... really, Elmer? You brought Little Cynthia Sharp into this?" She was scowling at the man, and I stifled a laugh into my first bite of ice cream. At six-feet tall and a size 14, no one had ever called me little. From my blonde hair to my lavender eyes, I was much more a "Cyn" than the proper name Cynthia

5

my mother gave me. It would seem that the older folks in town didn't believe in nicknames. They also thought everyone should be addressed by their complete name- Cynthia Sharp and Sgt. Winnifred Pupperson, K-9, was the official title added below the gold lettering naming my business Sharp Investigations.

"Banish her ghost at once!" he shouted, and Winnie tilted her head. I ate more ice cream and leaned against the door frame. This was now someone else's fight *and* I have ice cream.

The day was looking up.

"Stop it, Elmer! Just because I said the Game of Thrones books are better than the TV show does not mean I am dead!" she exclaimed, and my mouth fell open. My last suspected "haunting" had been from a woman with cataracts confusing a portrait of her with her deceased husband with a mirror. She said he was always with her in her house and wanted him with her everywhere. I pointed out that it was a painting, and when I moved it she tried to beat me with her walking cane. Apparently denial is more than just a river in Egypt.

Once the bruises healed, I made a new policy to no longer make house calls.

"This is about... books?" I asked, staring between the two. I love reading, but Game of Thrones? I had been tortured to the point of considering self-mutilation over Game of freaking Thrones? While it was my opinion that both the books and the TV show weren't the greatest, I now had a whole new reason to hate the series.

As well as the people in this office.

"No! It's about taste, and she doesn't have any!"

Again, I had to disagree. Except, she married him so maybe that was true.

"The book is always better!" his wife countered, and I rubbed my temples with my index fingers.

"Books are stupid!" he shouted, and she fisted her hands on her hips.

"Books are not stupid, Elmer. You are dyslexic and audio-books make you feel old!" she countered and he went back to jumping.

"I'm not old! Audiobooks are for people who don't have TV!"

"Stop," I sighed into the silence. No one bothered to even lower their voice.

"STOP!"

"Do you want a divorce?" I shouted over both of them and their heads whipped around.

"No!" they shouted at the same time. I was both disappointed and relieved.

"Then work through this at home. I have to get to work; we're birthing a calf today." I walked over and took each of their shoulders, faced them toward the door and gave a little nudge.

"Which do you prefer?" Elmer asked as Winnie helped me herd them forward, hoping to score some ice cream.

"Prefer what?" I asked, taking my first bite of the cone now that I'd cleared the ice cream off the top. Winnie had them just at the threshold.

"The books or the show?" Mrs. Figs asked and they both stared at me seriously. They weren't walking out the door, and suddenly my brain wasn't the only thing frozen. Two Figs stared at me with hope while also ready for condemnation. They demanded an answer.

"I... uh...." Stuffing the cone in my mouth, I made a show of looking at my watch. "Late! Sorry!"

Full coward mode activated; I ran upstairs. Once there, I stared at the space. It was small, but comfortable. The couch was used but not old, a faded grey faux suede that Winnie loved to flop on. The same place I'd shared one of the most promising kisses of my life. I could still feel his hands under my shirt, his lips on mine...

I shook my head clear.

"Focus, Sharp. You need to get ready for work." I scolded myself out loud, and Winnie cocked her head. Just in case, I checked my cell phone. No missed notifications and I sighed.

Grabbing my backpack, I checked that it still had the work essentials of sunscreen and a hat. I stuffed snacks in my cargo pants pockets. Oreos and Cheetos for me, biscuits and doggy jerky for Winnie. Metal water bottle for each of us went into the bag, and a change of clothes, just in case. With a last look around, I sighed and checked my phone again.

Still nothing.

I listened at the top of the stairs and couldn't hear any voices. I crept lower and paused at the door that separated my space from the office. Still quiet. I pushed the door open a crack, and Winnie poked her nose into the room. She looked back at me, I looked at her and nodded.

The room was clear.

After opening the door, I checked that nothing new had entered my office and ducked at the sight of the Figs outside of the front window. They were still yelling. Mr. Figs was having a tantrum so loud, Daniel Kirby from the village police department had shown up. I fought back a snicker as I crawled along the floor to the wooden door. Back pressed to it, I reached up and rotated the deadbolt to the locked position. Satisfied with my immediate safety, I got off the floor and stood at the window a moment to see Officer Kirby take an ice cream cone to the face. I smiled wide, waving goodbye to Daniel as I closed the curtains on the front window and left through the back door.

Winnie and I arrived at the farm twenty minutes early. I fiddled with the radio, but all I could find were talk shows and smooth jazz. My CD player held a country music CD leftover from when Mo and her EMT had needed a four-wheel drive vehicle to explore the sand dunes on the coast. Mo, aka Mary O'Connor, was owner and operator of Mary's Muffins and More. She was one of my best friends, had been since elementary and the only person I'd trust with my Jeep. Despite being a "trip to the beach for four-wheeling", there was a lack of pictures and her bra was under my back seat. I expect they just needed a little more room to maneuver than her Nissan offered.

I was so proud.

I stared longingly at my silent phone.

Then I picked up the third of four iced coffees I'd purchased on the way here through a drive-up chain. I hadn't had enough cup holders for all four, but I took care of the problem in the parking lot by immediately drinking two and chucking the empty cups in the bin with Winnie's whipped cream cup. Cup three was gone as some guy sang about having dirty shoes. No idea why Mo thought this was romantic, because I'd personally prefer he take a shower and chill on the couch.

Without any good reason to stay in my car, I hopped out and made my way to the barn, killing iced coffee number four. I looked around at the cow, sheep, and goat enclosures, at a loss for where to start. Our newest calf would be born in the arena on the other side of the barn. The sheep milk was the last thing I checked yesterday, and the goats were just jerks. Speaking of jerks, I checked my phone again.

"You know how they say a watched pot never boils?" a friendly voice said behind me.

"Shut up, Larry," I grumbled, stuffing the phone back in my pocket.

"It's been a month, Cyn."

He ignored my request. I checked my pockets for duct tape to force the issue, but came up with only cookies, so I ate one.

"I don't know what you're talking about," I responded, but I was lying. Sgt. Ian Cruz, my K-9 training handler in the Army, had come to Sweet Pea to solve the mystery of a fake captain, a weapons theft contingent that had been working for decades, recover or destroy a mind control program, and set up the Sharp Investigations office. He was Cuban, hotter than the surface of the sun, and has now made out with me on two continents.

Then he promptly left to never be heard from again.

Most recently, he had shown me around my new apartment, and just as I was about to get my hands on ALL of him, in front of the very comfortable couch, he left. A phone call came in, he listened, stared at his shoes, and left. He said he'd be back, he said he'd call, he said I could have anything of his I wanted.

He was a stinking liar.

"Yeah, you do," Larry walked up and put an arm around my shoulders. He reached down and unclipped Winnie's leash, but she stayed with us as we ambled toward the open-air paddock where the cows usually gave birth. Better than goats.

Currently in labor was Pooh. They'd originally named her Winnie the Pooh, and then Winnie, but I called her Pooh because it helped me keep straight which four-legged friend we were talking about.

"Whatever." I stuck a hand in my pocket and pulled out another Oreo, stuffing it in my mouth.

"Do you wear cargo pants just so you have places to keep your snacks?" he asked and I narrowed my eyes at him. "I'm not judging."

"Yes, you are. For your information, these pants also hold Winnie's snacks, her toys, and a Taser for annoying childhood friends." I smirked at the last, but he only smiled wider.

"You don't have a Taser," he said smugly, and I bared my teeth at him.

"Are you willing to risk your neural pathways on it?"

"Yeah," he said, moving closer and stuffing a hand in each of my thigh pockets. While my cargo pants were loose fitting enough that it wasn't terribly intimate, my breath still caught at the intrusion.

"Hey!" but he was too quick and he had all my dog treats, snacks, and my cell phone. He held them above my head, taking small steps backward with Winnie trotting along beside him. He danced down the barn aisle and I gave chase. We rounded the horse stall on the end, collided with a fence, and landed in

11

a pile of hay with Winnie jumping on each of us in turn. She licked our faces, grabbed her treats from Larry, and ran.

"Seriously! What is this? Are you six?" I demanded, completely out of breath.

"I just wanted to see you smile." He handed everything back and I touched my face. There was, in fact, a smile on it.

"You have to clean up Winnie when she poops out all those treats," I looked over at him. He was tall, muscled in a gangly way, with dark hair and light eyes that filled me with fond memories of being a kid and building mud castles in the sandbox.

"No, I don't. I'm a doctor," he said, wiggling his brows. I punched his shoulder as I remembered the not-so-fond memory of the time he took Amber Carter to the 8th Grade Dance because I wouldn't give him my string cheese.

"Exactly, an *animal* doctor. She's an animal and you just gave her three times the recommended daily amount of treats," I crossed my arms, as though it settled the matter and I won. Unfortunately, crossing your arms flat on your back just pushes your boobs into your chin and Larry smiled bigger.

"He's missing out," Larry spoke softly, his smile going from immature to serious.

"I don't..." my mouth started but he pressed his against it, warm and inviting. It was a brief kiss, and just as suddenly he was gone. On his feet, he offered me a hand up, but I was confused and processing.

He waggled his fingers and I instinctively reached out. Taking his hand, I let him pull me up. He took a small step back so we weren't pressed against each other, but if we inhaled at the same time, we'd be touching. He didn't release my hand. and I wasn't sure if I wanted it back. The feel of his lips lingered on mine and we stared at each other.

A moment passed, and then another, neither of us sure what to say or do.

Larry broke first and the moment ended.

"I know I messed up before..." he started, and I decided I did want my hand back. His face flashed a second of hurt, but he stuck the hand I emptied in his pocket. He scratched the back of his head with the other hand, lifting the bottom of his sweatshirt. It would seem his arms weren't the only part of him that had gained some muscles, and I involuntarily licked my lips. Then I remembered his most recent "mess ups".

"Messed up?" I asked and he stared at his shoes. "Messed up like when you said you couldn't go with me to the prom because someone else already asked you, but really you decided you'd rather not go than go with me, your supposed friend? Or when I asked you to hang out on summer break my first year of college, but you said you were busy and then Mo and I saw you in the drive-thru of Chicken Palace? When we waved, you drove off and spilled soda on the employee who worked there."

"I..." he opened his mouth, but I shook my head.

"No, Larry. You were a crap friend, and honestly, I don't know if you're any better of a friend now. Messed up is far too kind for what you did. Every time we got close, you slammed a door in my face. Now, after all these years, suddenly you want to kiss me in a pile of hay and act like you're somehow better than Cruz? He never promised me anything. I recall in fourth grade, you promised to always be there for me on the way home from the zoo, and then you blew me off because of the teasing."

13

"That's not fair! It was fourth grade!"

"Yeah, and I needed you. I needed you and you were gone. Mo was the only one there. She was the only one who made time to see me and maintain a relationship. You were too busy to even grab a bucket of chicken with us, but not too busy to get one for yourself."

"I texted you to go bowling with me during those two months after college before you went into the Army, and you never even responded!" He shot back and I stared at him, head cocked to the side. Texting? In the post 2010 world? I hadn't done much texting... because...

"You know I didn't have a phone for those two months, right?" I asked him, and he switched from indignant to confused. It was as though I had told him I was from the planet Pluto and bled green goo. "And Pluto is a planet!"

"What? No... what happened to your phone? What the hell do I care about Pluto for?"

"It fell out of the Jeep in Missouri and I ran over it," I said with a shrug and he gaped. "Also, Pluto is a planet. I just want everyone to know Pluto is a planet and deserves planet status."

Great, I was rambling about Pluto. My face was warm, and my heart was racing. I could still feel his mouth on mine, and it was warm and comforting.

"How..." he started, then changed his mind. "Or rather why?"

"Don't ask. It's like the arm casts. I couldn't keep a damn cell phone to save my life then." I brushed hay off my clothes and looked toward Pooh who needed some more water. "As far as Pluto..."

I shifted uncomfortably.

"So then... how did you get in contact with people?" he was still baffled by a woman in the second decade of the year two thousand not having a cell phone.

"Same way I did before there were cell phones," I said, noticing Pooh also looked to be panting a little harder. "Time to get to work."

I turned toward the arena, ordering Winnie to stay. She and Pooh had a history of animosity. Specifically, Winnie thought she was a really big dog who wanted her snacks and Pooh thought she was a nightmare on four legs in need of a kick to the head. Neither was wrong, but we needed the calf to be born without elevated cortisol levels, so I kept them apart on principle. Just under the fence, something caught my leg and I turned over my shoulder to stare at Larry, holding my foot.

"Problem, doctor?" I asked, grabbing the rail to keep my balance. My leg ached, and I acknowledged there was a very real possibility I needed to stretch more.

"Just give me a chance, Cyn," he said quietly, letting go of my foot and taking my hand. I shook out my hamstring and popped my hip just to watch him wince at the sound.

"A chance to do what, Larry?" I asked as I popped my other hip and stretched out my back.

"To make things between us right."

"We're fine, Larry," I said, turning my back to him again. "Go get your stethoscope or whatever."

"If we're fine, have dinner with me Friday?" he said and I turned to gape at him. "If we're fine, then there's no reason not to go, right?"

My mouth worked, opening and closing, but nothing came out and he smiled.

"I take silence as a yes," and then he walked away, showing me his very cute ass. My face burned and I tried to make myself look away, but it was hypnotic. Still, a girl has to have her pride.

"I take my grudges to the grave, Dr. Kirby!" I shouted after him, but it came out just a little breathy. He shot me a wink over his shoulder and did a little shimmy for my benefit.

Stupid cute butt.

Stupid Larry Kirby.

Chapter Two:
Bodily Harm

*B eep. Beep. Bee*p.

"No!" I cried out.

Woof! Woof!

The bed shifted as Winnie jumped off. Her claws clattered along the floor until she reached the window, paws on the sill. Even with my eyes closed, I could feel her, ears up and on alert.

Beep. Beep.

Woof!

"For the love of dog, Winnie! Shut up!" I said through the pillow wrapped around my head. It was pointless. The trash truck continued to beep, the dog continued to bark, and the pillow did absolutely nothing. Switching it from being wrapped around my head to in front of my mouth, I let out a long scream of frustration. Winnie joined me and started howling.

"Winnie!"

"Ow woooo!"

Then the phone rang and I contemplated assault with a deadly weapon... I just needed to pick a target. Trash Truck? Cell Phone? Both were very tempting, but I groaned and started slapping my bedside table. I was trying desperately to make the offending electronic device be quiet. Instead, the call picked up and the raspy, high-pitched voice filled the room.

"Cynthia! What's going on?" she shrilled, and I could picture the raven-haired woman with a cigarette half-hanging out of her mouth.

"It's trash day, Mrs. Charles!" I shouted at the phone.

"I can't hear you! The trash is here!" she bellowed back.

A metal dumpster clanged to the pavement in the alley. Winnie howled and I screamed.

"Shut up!" just as the truck went quiet.

"Cynthia Sharp, don't you dare tell me to shut up!" Mrs. Charles said, but then a bout of thick, wet, hacking coughs filled the line. Winnie stopped howling and stared at the phone. Her head tilted left, then right, before the coughing stopped.

"Are you alright, Mrs. Charles?" I asked and heard her drinking. A sputter and a smacking of lips told me it wasn't water, and a long inhale told me the coughing hadn't disrupted her cigarette in the slightest.

"Of course, I am. Now, why were you screaming?" she seemed to be settling in for the night. Mrs. Charles was the sole proprietor of Casey's Bar across the street. She had been running it since I was twelve, and despite being the same age as my sister, Heidi, she wore her years like milk left in the sun.

Her first name was also Gloria and no one knew who the hell Casey was.

"Because..." the trash truck started beeping, Winnie barked loudly in response, and Mrs. Charles began coughing into the phone again. The device was still on the bedside table, not on speaker, and yet it was as clear as if she was sitting in the room with me. If this was punishment for something I'd done, I had to have cleared my debt by now. If this was pre-punishment for something I would do eventually, it better involve levels of debauchery and reverse harems only read about in erotica. I waited patiently as the truck rumbled away, Winnie trotted back to her bed, and Mrs. Charles took another two fingers of whiskey.

"It's early dear, go to sleep," she said into the phone and hung up. I stared at the phone and whipped my head back to Winnie. She was already back asleep. My phone screen was dark, and the truck began its slow rumble to the other side of town. It was like a really bad dream... that I couldn't get back to sleep fast enough to escape.

A warm, wet, slimy piece of sandpaper rubbed against my face just as Ian Cruz lost his pants and exposed paw print boxers in red, white and blue. His chest was hard muscle and his smooth skin, every inch flawless and delectable. My hands reached out to grab him but he moved just out of reach.

"Why aren't you dancing?" I muttered and the room filled with the slow rhythmic melodies of Boys to Men. He sauntered closer, hands outstretched to catch himself as he lowered down. A heavy weight settled on top of me, and I wrapped my arms around his warm back, taking a long inhale of... dog breath? The sandpaper returned and his face was replaced with Winnie's.

"Feed me, Cyn!" her face said. The man disappeared, and I opened my slobber coated eyes to find my arms wrapped around the tan and black body of my furry partner in crime... solving. We definitely were supposed to stop accidentally committing crimes after breaking a prisoner out of jail and punching one of the town deputies in the face.

Despite the burns and complete demolition of a chicken habitat, it was one of my prouder moments though it probably shouldn't be. I'd solved the crime, punched a cocky jerk in the face and nearly nailed the hot guy. I felt myself smile at the memory as the sandpaper came for my face again, and I grabbed her by the neck fluff.

"Look here, missy. We need to have a talk," I said sternly and she whimpered. "Oh no, no sad dog eyes. I need sleep. I need sleep, the naughty dreams that I missed out on in real life, and to not hear Mrs. Charles try and cough her soul out of her body and into the afterlife!"

She tried to lick my face.

"No, no apologies. Next Thursday, you are wearing the hearing protection you had for range days, and if I hear so much as a *woof* you are not getting a Pupperoni stick for a month, and there will be no Puppacino's ever again. This is your last warning, Pupperson. You wake up the neighborhood again and you lose snack privileges!"

She let out a small simper and I narrowed my eyes.

"Do we have an understanding?" She dropped her eyes to my chest and I nodded. "Good girl."

We climbed out of the bed, and I clipped her leash on after pulling on some sweatpants and stuffing my feet into slippers. Down the stairs, out the back door, and across the street, Winnie made quick work of morning business and sat impatiently on my feet while I yawned.

"Seriously, there's more to life than breakfast," I muttered, but we trudged back to the apartment anyway. Winnie fed, coffee brewing, toaster pastries toasting, I flopped onto the couch and stared at the ceiling. It was too early to be awake and too late to go back to bed.

"Alexa, play... something," I said to the robotic assistant in the corner. I saw a brief circle of blue lights.

"I'm sorry, I don't know that" she responded, and I sighed. Was it too much to ask for robots to take over all of my life decisions? Nothing major, just what to eat, listen to or read...

My phone buzzed and I picked it up off the floor, both confused and not surprised by its location.

Larry: *Can't wait until tomorrow.*

Me: *What's tomorrow?*

Larry: *A night you'll remember forever.*

Me. *A full 8 hours of sleep? Because if you could give me that...*

Larry: *I can give you something better.*

21

It seemed unlikely so I dropped the phone back on the end table. The coffee finished just as the toaster popped out my breakfast and Winnie shoved her bowl into my path.

"One breakfast per day, kid. No exceptions," I told her, moving around the bowl. Except she had planned for this and laid a trap. I moved into her spilled drinking water and slipped into the splits, screaming curse words into the rising sun. She licked my face and then nudged her bowl closer!

"Hells Bells, Winnie!" I shouted through pain and dog slobber.

Somehow, that Alexa understood.

"Playing *Highway to Hell* by AC/DC."

Kind of understood. The other song with "hell" in the title by AC/DC filled the room, and I watched Winnie wag her tail to the beat. Lacking something else to do, I sang along as I tried to put my limbs back where they belong. Slowly, painfully, I got up and poured coffee, stuffing the toaster pastry in my mouth and burning my tongue.

"Hot! Hot! Hot!"

"Playing *Hot Hot Hot* by Buster Poindexter," Alexa announced, interrupting AC/DC with a salsa inspired tune.

"Party people, all around me feeling hot, hot, hot," I sang and danced around my kitchen making coffee. "Yeah we rum bum bum bum."

At half past seven, I was staring at the curtain covering the front window of my office and sweating bullets. Just on the other side I could hear my worst nightmare.

People.

There were at least a dozen people. Audible voices ranged from screaming toddlers to the shouting of seniors who hadn't yet put in their hearing aids. Mixed in was the shuffle of house slippers not necessarily indicative of any age, but a clear reminder it was early. There couldn't possibly be that many things for me to investigate. Winnie nudged the bottom of the curtain with her nose, and I dropped to the floor.

"Winnie!" I hissed, and a sharp rap sounded on the wooden front door.

We'd been made.

"J- just a second!" I called toward the door, cursing that I hadn't pretended to have been startled into an early grave by the sudden noise.

Hand shaking, I pulled the cord on the curtain, opening it to let in the sun. Without looking outside, I slid back the door bolts that kept the masses out of my sanctuary. Slowly, I pulled open the door and braced for the onslaught of humans.

A single woman stood in the doorway.

"Are you...." She glanced down at a crumbled paper in hand. It had the look of something that had been discarded and recovered repeatedly. "Cynthia?"

"Yes?" I asked, voice going up at the end in question. I cleared my throat and tried to look professional. "What do you need from Cynthia?"

"Excuse me?" her eyes were darting around the room, but I still wasn't sure I wanted to be Cynthia today. The sounds that had permeated my inner sanctum were across the street. A line extended down the block for Mo's Thursday Turnovers, and it looked to round the corner at Maple. Mo, or Mary O'Connor, owned Mary's Muffins and More. She had taken a diner style pastry establishment in a dead-end town and turned it into a boutique bakery. In December she'd had a "Minty Monday" promotion with a chocolate mint muffin that was sneakily made with zucchini so you could pretend you'd eaten a vegetable. This month, there were inventive turnovers, and they were as incredible as the magic muffins. The January flavor was some sort of maple apple concoction that was as addicting as it was fattening. While I no longer needed to meet certain fitness standards after leaving the Army, I hated clothes shopping enough to make at least a moderate effort to keep myself in the size fourteen to sixteen range. I'd also grown accustomed to being capable of outrunning the man next to me in the event of a zombie apocalypse, and I wasn't ready to be the sacrifice.

At least I wasn't until this morning, I thought with a dark look at Winnie. She wagged her tail, and I lifted a lip, half snarling. Then I remembered I had a proper client *for the first time in forever,* I sang in my head. There was music, there was life, and I wanted to stuff some chocolate in my face. I hummed to myself and caught my customer staring. Right, Disney songs were not a form of communication to normal people, and I had no other choice than to be Cynthia for at least the next twenty minutes, which is how long I estimated my coffee would last.

"Yes, I'm sorry. I'm Cynthia, please call me Cyn. Come in, have a seat," I said and stepped back from the door. She had soft brown hair and rhinestone studded glasses. Her glasses had fogged in the cold, obscuring her eyes. Her posture was nervous and hesitant. "I have coffee?"

It felt like holding a treat out to a skittish dog, but it did the trick. She shook off the trance and came inside. As she passed, I smelled cinnamon and strawberries. She stood maybe two inches beneath my chin, making her height average. Her walk was confident, her hair flawless.

She was a woman used to being in charge.

Her posture slipped into uncertainty, back to confidence, and then she simply stared at the back wall. My guest chair was two feet to her left, but she'd stopped moving, just staring transfixed at a spot on the wall. I extended my left hand to touch her shoulder, then felt weird and pulled it back. Another minute passed where she didn't move so I cleared my throat.

She blinked.

"Woof!" Winnie said, and the woman jumped a foot into the air and dropped a hefty handbag that exploded onto the floor.

"Sorry! Winnie, place!" I ordered and she slowly sauntered to her bed in the corner. I dropped to the floor and helped her scoop change, eyeshadow, foundation in ten different shades, and at least twenty lipsticks back into the purse.

"Quite the collection," I commented as she stuffed it all back in. Her eyes darted up and pinned me in place. "Not... a collection?"

A smattering of freckles crossed her nose, her skin the color of desert sand after the rain, and her hazelnut eyes...

"It's... for work. I like options."

"Got it,' I answered and looked away first. Her fear and despair had shot straight through me, and I had a bad feeling. "Wanna ditch your coat and I'll get the promised coffee?"

I turned to the pot in the corner and poured the liquid into paper cups.

"Milk? Sugar? Creamer?" I called as I added almond milk and honey to mine. It was a strange mixture that Mo had gotten me hooked on during a short fight with strep throat.

"Black is fine," she said and I whipped around, mouth open.

"Seriously, I have everything," I said, gesturing behind me. "No request is too extreme. It's basically Burger King for coffee over here. The only place with more flavor and milk options is Mo's, but I don't have a line and I don't charge."

"I like it black," she said, shrugging out of her coat and I shuddered. "I know, it's just hot bean water, but we couldn't afford extras when I was growing up, or after I was grown, and I just got used to it."

I nodded but still blinked through the horror as I handed her the plain, sad coffee.

"How can I help you..." I started, hoping to prompt her into sharing her name. The woman was a bombshell. She had a plus size figure that sent her extra to all the places you'd want a little extra. Her hair was in a braid that draped over her shoulder in a manner that was both casual and artful. Self-consciously, I reached up and tried to smooth the frizz on top of my head. I'm pretty sure I brushed my hair this morning... probably.

"Henrietta. Henrietta Handover, and yes, my mom was a huge DC fan and alliteration was big. We all have H names, and if you want to poke fun, I will burn you with my hot bean water," she said steadily, and my face broke into a massive smile.

"No jokes, but your mom sounds like a badass, and I admire a woman with a willingness to fight. How can I help you, Ms. Handover?"

"Mrs. Handover. Believe it or not, my pre-married name was Harkness," she narrowed her eyes. She must get a lot of judgement, but I could appreciate marrying a person whose last name started with the same letter as yours. You wouldn't have to learn new initials when you signed crap. "But, you can call me Retta."

"Hi, Retta," I said, watching her drink her bean water with a shudder. "That's Winnie, Sgt. Winnifred Pupperson if you go by the window. We used to be MP's, military police, in the Army. She's trained in explosives detection and tracking... I'm trained to always follow her around, pick up her poop, point the bomb disposal guys to the bombs she finds, and stop her from stealing people's food... sometimes it goes better than others."

"Which part?" she asked, a little concerned.

"The food part. I've never once failed the bomb and poop collection parts of my job," I said, but it was only half true. Once, I didn't have a bag so I'd left her poop on the side of the road in nowhere Afghanistan.

The guilt was killing me.

"You figured out the Reverend Tim thing?" she asked, referencing my first *case*. A woman on the church board had come to me about missing Bingo money, but the money wasn't missing. What was missing was a history of seminary training on the part of the reverend and his predecessor. Also, a bunch of guns and a weird mind control program that thankfully never existed. In the process I shot off a man's hand, and I spent far too much time wondering if anyone called him "stumpy" afterwards.

Well... far too much time until I remembered he was possibly dead at Maggie's orders.

They'd given me WAY too many drugs that night.

"Yes. I had help, but yes. I heard Maggie's husband is still sitting in his chair waiting for her to come back," I said and she smiled. "I personally wonder if he was even real or just like a Stepford husband... maybe an inflatable?"

Her smile turned into a soft laugh that soothed my nerves at the memory.

"I think Larry is the only smart Kirby man, the rest were a few sticks short of a wood pile," Retta said, and I let out a startled laugh.

"Sorry, never heard it phrased that way."

"I'm sure you haven't. I decided long ago that I would make my own euphemisms because the existing ones were overused." Her hands shifted on her coffee cup, and I could sense her restlessness.

"Are you ready to tell me about... whatever it is?" I asked, sitting down and picking up a pen. Then setting it down and folding my hands. Then picking the pen back up and pulling out some paper. "I'm sorry, you might be the first person with an actual problem to walk through this door, and I don't know what to do."

It was Retta's turn to laugh outright.

"This is probably a matter for the police, but I love my job. I don't want to lose my job over speculation," she said, staring into her cup. "It's just, I have this feeling and there's a history with the place. Nothing seedy... Well, no that might not be true either. I work at Vincenzo's Mortuary just outside Dayton. I'm a cosmetician. I decided at some point during cosmetology school I'd rather put make-up on dead people than living people, and there is very little competition for the gig."

I nodded my agreement but hadn't written anything down. My stomach had started doing little twitches at the mention of dead people. Specifically, touching dead people, voluntarily, for extended periods of time. I wasn't scared of cemeteries, but fresh dead bodies... Retta had stopped speaking.

I looked up and she was staring out of the front window. A teenager stood there, maybe thirteen years old, of indeterminate race, peering in at us. A group of boys stood behind him, conspiratorial looks in their eyes.

"Winnie, window," I said and she low-crawled to the window, popped up and let out a ferocious snarl. The boy fumbled backward, slipped on the morning frost and fell flat on his butt. He crawled backward, got up, and took off down the street. I pulled a treat from my desk drawer and tossed it to her.

"Please, Retta, go on."

"What..." she was staring between the window, the desk, and my dog as though a man would pop out and shout she was being

"Punked", except none of us was famous. She blinked and I let out a low breath.

"When I first opened this office, it became a right of passage for the local junior high school boys to press their naked butts and faces against the window. I think it stemmed from friends of Daniel Kirby's kids. Most are barely walking, but some of their friends have older siblings I guess," I shrugged it off. Frankly, I was glad they chose to put their naked butts on the window and save the front show for someone else. I also refused to wash my front window so that butts and faces touched the same glass as revenge. "I'm not sure if it's a family loyalty/friendship thing, or just an excuse for idiot kids to be idiots."

"But... Daniel Kirby is an officer!" she cried out, appalled at the lack of professionalism. "Or is he a deputy?"

I shrugged, talking to him long enough to ask was not high on my list. Sweet Pea wasn't a county, but as a village saying it was a police department was a stretch. I made a mental note to read the next marked vehicle I saw.

"Yeah, but I punched him in the face before Maggie and her crew blew up Roger's chicken farm," I drank some more coffee and tried not to smile too much.

"You... why?" her mouth was agape and her beautiful skin was a shade or two lighter. Hand shaking, she lifted her coffee to her mouth, almost just to have something to do. A long drink of her hot, nearly flavorless, bean water improved her color. I checked the bag beside the pot: Chupacabra from my Geek Grind order. It probably tasted fine, even if it was boring.

"Sorry, we were in the trailer and I was trying to get Daniel out before it blew up. Larry and his cousin Mitchell had their hands full running away like arm-flailing chickens. Daniel was doing way too much talking and not enough walking, so I... gave him a twilight sleep. Like they do for dogs who need X-rays? Except he was so much heavier than Winnie, so I needed help, and then my help dumped him in a puddle of mud. Daniel couldn't do anything because Sgt. Cruz... Ian... was very somewhat heavily armed, and I had the great fur ball of teeth over there. So now I think we are in a petty game of chess... or Battleship... maybe Yahtzee?" I glanced at my phone to see if "help" had gotten back to me yet.

Still radio silence from Cruz.

"Yahtzee?" her face was torn between amusement and horror.

"Yeah... that's the game where you throw dice from a cup and hope for the best, right?" I asked and she raised a brow.

"Was it wise to start any game based on the principle of throwing things at an armed and dangerous man?" she countered and I glanced at my shoes.

"The butt imprints on my window say no, but the satisfaction in my gut says yes. Honestly, he's too lame to be dangerous, but he is armed and his wife is...." I shivered and drank more coffee. "You put make-up on dead bodies? For... money?"

"Wha- Oh! Yes, the dead bodies." I shuddered but Retta didn't notice. "There aren't any."

She stopped to drink her coffee and it was my turn to gape.

"There.... What?" I stammered.

"Well, there are some dead people, but not as many as the records say there should be," she corrected, but that somehow wasn't any better.

"Did they..." I gulped. "Walk away?"

31

Retta laughed in my face, and Winnie let out a woof of amusement.

"Good lord, you people need to let go of this whole concept of zombies." Her body shook in merriment, and she relaxed into her seat. "I went into work last week, to prepare Mrs. Michael's for her eternal slumber, and I opened the wrong drawer."

I cringed and then picked up my pen to look like the movement was voluntary. Retta missed absolutely nothing, and she shook her head at me.

"I thought you'd be tougher, what with being in the Army. Anyway, Mrs. Michaels was in drawer three, but it looked like 13. I pulled 13 open, but it was empty. So, I went back to check the clipboard and it said 13 was supposed to have a Mr. Creevy. So, I started opening all the drawers, trying to figure out where all the people were so I could correct the board... and there was only Mrs. Michaels. The other two guests, Mr. Creevy and Mrs. Granger, were nowhere to be found. I checked the itinerary to see if they'd been buried the day before and just not taken off the roster, but it showed their services scheduled for yesterday. I asked Mr. Lorenzo, and he said it was pre-filled out and the bodies were arriving later."

Retta paused and I stared at my paper. Make-up, drawers three and thirteen, Vincenzo's Mortuary, Michaels, Creevy, Granger, Mr. Lorenzo- not enough dead people.

"Your boss is named Vincenzo Lorenzo?" I asked, making a face. It was as bad a fake name as a Reverend Tim Church, the con man trading military weapons for drugs who died of a lethal dose of amphetamines and Viagra... delivered by his daughter's hench people.

Family, am I right?

"Yes..." she said and I watched her face register the same suspicion. "That probably should have been a red flag sooner. Anyway, the day before yesterday, I went in to prepare Mr. Daniels for his service today. There was a note for Mr. Creevy and Mrs. Granger, closed caskets, no services requested. I was curious, those are usually reserved for trauma victims. The drawers were still empty. Another person was listed, a D. Thomas, who was nowhere to be seen."

"Do you think someone is harming bodies or just stealing them?" I asked, trying to wrap my head around what someone would want a dead body for... and then almost immediately wished I hadn't. We were far enough from Halloween they wouldn't just be a prop, but people were into some weird crap.

Please just be sitting at a desk so a lazy person doesn't have to go to work, I pleaded internally. *Please do not let me find these bodies in a sex shop.*

"Ms. Sharp?" Retta tugged me out of my personal pleas.

"Sorry, you were telling me... what you think is happening to the bodies," I made direct eye contact to not let my mind wander again.

"I'm not sure. I just... three bodies not where they belong? It's weird and I was getting concerned, but I don't know where to start with this. I mean, they're dead so... is it a crime to misplace the dead?"

"Depends on how and why it was 'misplaced' and who knows how it got there," I said and sat back to think.

"That Thomas guy can't have arrived at all. I would have been there when he was delivered," she said, puzzling to herself.

"Did you ask Mr. Vincenzo Lorenzo about Thomas?" I asked, trying to figure out why all the missing people shared names with Gryffindors. Retta was maybe forty-five, she had to have noticed... but I said nothing so she'd explain whatever had put that guilty look on her face.

"No, but I checked the files in his office," she hesitated and lowered her voice. "I picked a lock."

I nodded, waiting for the reason she looked guilty.

Her gaze traveled the room and her hand shook. Picking a lock was her great big terrifying secret. Poor, law-abiding woman thought that was the worst thing I was destined to hear about today. Anticlimactic after dead bodies dancing away, but I tried to look a little stern.

Lock picking is bad, I tried to get my face to say but her reaction said I looked constipated so I moved on.

"You found?" I prompted.

"There weren't any files. I found purchase orders for high-end caskets. I'm talking top of the line, real wood, and satin-lined caskets. It's The Holy Grail vehicle of dead body delivery to the lord, and worth more than the building itself. Yet, the coffins weren't in the storeroom. There were no caskets, no bodies... just... payment records and invoices." Her hand shook a little, and I considered reaching for her to offer support.

Except her hand touched dead people.

"Where do you think they are, then?"

"It could be an accounting mistake, or a filing error. I just... I just have a bad feeling, but I don't want my boss to know I was in the office. Even more, I don't want the cops to know I can pick locks."

Again, the guilt over something people could learn from a YouTube video. I fought my inner skin crawlies and patted her hand. The hand was warm and soft, not in the least reminiscent of the dead bodies she touched.

I shuddered and took my hand back, trying to look like I caught a chill.

"So... you want me to find out where the bodies, the caskets, or the money are?" I asked, staring at my notes. This was definitely more interesting than paintings mistaken as mirrors, but it was a little out of my depth.

"Any of the above would be reassuring." She shifted her over-full bag in her lap and withdrew her hand. "Do you think you can?"

I tapped my pen on the desk and tried to think. Winnie let out a loud fart and jumped up in alarm at her own body functions.

"Woof!" she said to her tail, and Retta fanned her face while I laughed.

"We'll see what we can do," I said, and she headed out to get in line for turnovers.

Chapter Three:
Double the
Trouble

M y back ached and I had enough manure on my shoes
to fertilize a pasture of wheat. It was just after 1600,
four p.m., and I was slogging through muck to recover a
run-away horse. The horse was easily sixteen hands, though
that unit of measurement still meant absolutely nothing to
me. She was a tri-color palomino, another fancy way of saying she was beautiful, and she'd gotten her bridle wrapped
around a hook mounted to the barn wall.

"I'm going to take you to the pound, Winnie!" I shouted at
the dog in question. She had two paws on the fence and would
not stop barking at the palomino trying to get through the fence

but tethered to the wall. "Seriously, if you shut up right now, you can have a treat!"

I'd spoken the magic word. She trotted over and I put her leash back on, anchored to a paracord wrapped around my waist. I tossed her a treat and stared at the horse. It was on its back two legs and screaming loudly, horse speak for *I will murder that beast*, I imagine. The bridle slid up and she was free, but she hadn't realized it.

The horse and I were on the same page. Dog was definitely going down, and freedom is an illusion.

"Woah, girl. Woah," but I couldn't get closer without bringing Winnie closer and Joseph, the ranch manager, was watching from across the field. He knew nothing of animals, but his business acumen made him invaluable to the owners of the dairy. Mysteriously, no one knew their names... or rather I'd never asked. There was a portrait in the attached ice cream shop that I was convinced was a spoof of the classic farmer pitchfork couple, but it was the owners.

Supposedly.

A blur of white streaked past my right, and I turned to see a billowing lab coat floating behind Larry like a cape.

"Hey, Heather, who's a good girl?" he said, taking her bridle and stroking her face. "Who's a good girl?"

He pulled a carrot from his pants pocket, and I resisted the urge to make an inappropriate joke.

"That's a girl," he said, leading her past Winnie with her head facing away from the offending demon dog.

"Cynthia!" Joseph called out, and I shrunk into myself. We were getting fired. No way around it, we were getting fired.

"Yes, sir?" I called, starting the slow walk of shame toward him.

"My office!" He spun on his heel and stomped toward the ramshackle plywood building he'd built himself. As an office, it was better than nothing, with electricity and an oscillating fan. As a visitor to the room, it was suffocating and tragic. His desk was too big, but he refused to admit he hadn't measured properly. He always had to arrive first to not be seen crawling on all fours over its surface to get to his cushy swivel chair.

Winnie and I made the slow trek to his office, but we knew better than to keep the man waiting. I knocked once, and was summoned into the shack of business.

"Have a seat, Cynthia," he gestured to the rickety metal folding chair as though there would be room to do anything but sit. "Cynthia, we need to talk about Winnie."

I nodded and looked down at the dog in question. She had flopped over and was already snoozing.

"She's become a nuisance to the farm animals," he continued, and I had no grounds to disagree. Between Pooh, Heather the Horse, and the incident with George Goatly, Winnie had quite a bit to answer for.

"Yes, sir."

"I think she needs a job," his comment startled me and I lost balance. Looping my foot through the leg of the chair, I braced myself to keep my balance. The chair collapsed and I landed on top of Winnie, sending her into a round of howling as I tried to get my foot back from the offending folding chair.

"A job?" I squeaked from the floor. "She's... retired."

"She is a trained, working-breed canine, and there is plenty of work for her to do around here," he said, and my mind flashed through the horrors she'd already committed. Winnie had chased a herd of sheep to the back 40, spread recently sheared wool for a quarter mile in a game of keep away, and taken naps on top of pregnant cows, though admittedly the last bothered absolutely no one but it was still weird.

"You... have a job in mind?"

"Don't look so concerned, Cynthia. We'd like her to be the dairy's mascot," he said, steepling his fingers in speculation. "She can sit in front of the ice cream shop, take photos with customers in exchange for treats. She could wear a hat!"

I gagged at the thought, but Winnie would do anything for a treat. She proved this by sitting up and offering him a paw. She was fully willing to accept his job offer.

"Winnie, children are sticky!" I hissed at her, but she didn't look away from Joseph. "They're sticky, they'll pull your tail, and you'll have to wear something stupid on your head!"

Her paw remained up, an offer to shake. He accepted it, and I crossed my arms with an eye roll.

"Fine," I huffed, and they both smiled. "But don't let them give her ice cream or she farts in your house."

When I pulled behind my office an hour later, my passenger seat was full of dog costumes. Joseph had clearly been thinking

39

about this for a while and had begun accumulating dog accessories. I knew the man had daughters, but I had no idea he had such taste for the pink and fluffy. With Valentine's Day a few weeks away, he was trying out a level of branding that made the Christmas decorations in the gazebo look so... last season.

"He's going to paint you pink when I'm not looking!" I said to Winnie in the rearview, but she was still chewing on the antler he'd given her. "You'll be pink and wearing a tiara. Just like his ice cream!"

She gave exactly zero fluffs and I dropped my head to the steering wheel. Two knocks sounded on the window beside my head and I leapt out of my skin. Mo was standing there, holding a cookie.

"I need a favor," she said when I opened the door. She braced herself for Winnie to come charging out, but the dog stayed put.

"Anything as long as it isn't pink," I said and she grimaced. "Oh dog, no, why?"

"I need you to go on a double date with me," she said and my eyebrows hit my hairline. "Tonight."

"You... date? Why?" I stammered, shaking. This was so much worse than I'd imagined. "Can't I shoot off a man's hand in your kitchen again instead?"

"No," she said and paled a little. "Please, don't do that again. I had to buy a UV light just to prove to myself the blood was really gone. Chris... my firefighter/EMT friend..."

She paused on the last word and turned slightly red.

"His cousin is visiting and we had these plans, but he doesn't want to leave him out. I told him you could come with us and it could be like... a double date," she spoke rapidly and without breathing. "He said you'd hate him, I said I'd bribe you with cookies, and then he made a joke about my cookies and we stayed in bed for *a bunch* of hours and...."

Big inhale.

"Please stop. Why will I hate him?" I asked and she bit her lip. "Mo?"

"He wouldn't tell me, but he was laughing so hard I imagine you will be far more entertaining than the dinner planned for just outside Dayton," she said, and I paused. "Don't say no. I need this, Cyn. You owe me after that man in my bakery!"

"Wow, I saved your life!"

"You shot off a man's hand! Do you know how long it took to get the blood out?" she countered. "Tonight, dinner outside of Dayton."

She raised a threatening finger, and I raised my hands in surrender.

Just outside Dayton was where I wanted to visit anyway.

"If I go, can we make a pit stop?" I asked, thinking a visit to a mortuary might be drastically less creepy with a baker, a first responder, and a date I was going to hate.

"Yes! Anywhere! Where do you want to go?" she switched from threatening to excited, and it was my turn to look guilty.

"I need to check out a funeral home with either disappearing or invisible bodies. So maybe wear black?" Her mouth fell open, but she couldn't take it back now.

"Thanks for being such a good friend!" I said, giving her a hug and running inside before she remembered how to speak.

At the last second, I called over my shoulder. "Sorry about shooting off that man's hand in your kitchen!"

An hour later, I was wearing my nicest flats and a flowing black dress with long sleeves that was both warm and cute. Winnie was upstairs napping, and I was staring at a four-door Honda pilot. Chris sat behind the wheel and a small man in the back seat was looking at me like something that walked out of a freak show. Given the distance between his legs and Chris's seat, the feeling was destined to be mutual.

"I thought you said she was cute!" he hissed at his cousin and Mo gave me wide, apologetic eyes. "She's the Jolly Blonde Giant and I didn't bring any green beans!"

"Shut up, man," Chris said, giving me an apologetic look as well. "She's probably armed."

"Of course, she's armed! I bet she needs a damn spring-loaded grip to put on gloves. What am I supposed to use to shake her hand? A freaking extension cord?"

"Sit tight, I have something upstairs you can use instead," I growled, and Mo jumped out of the car.

"I thought the Army took all your guns back?" Mo hissed and I narrowed my eyes at her.

"I bought one. It's legal," I replied through gritted teeth as I heard him compare me to a human growth hormone experiment on females gone horribly wrong. He was one comparison to "oversized load" vehicles away from being shot and having his pieces fed to Winnie.

"In the car, Cyn. In the car, we don't want to be late!" she squeaked, and I growled a second time. She handed me a cookie

42

and I stuffed it in my mouth. "Cyn, Robbie, nice to meet you both!"

"Is this like feeding the bears in Jellystone?" he sneered, and I turned around again. Mo spun me back toward the car with another cookie in my mouth.

"I'm going to need a million of these," I muttered, and she patted a two-gallon handbag. She shoved me toward the door and I dug my heels in. She forked over another cookie. Then another as a thought flitted across her face.

"You haven't even seen him standing yet," she grimaced and handed me another cookie as I climbed into the backseat. It was a tight squeeze, even with Mo moving her seat forward. Folding myself, I climbed in sideways, maneuvering my excessive legs to try desperately to get them into the damn mini SUV. A cramp caused my left leg to spasm, and I stretched it out to shake the pain.

"Cramp! Cramp!" I hollered as Mo climbed into the seat in front of me.

"You can't put your feet on my side of the car!" he whined. "Where will I put my legs?"

"You barely have legs, dude. You can spare a little foot well," I said, hoping to sound kind enough Mo would give me a cookie. She didn't and I crossed my arms pouting.

"But I want all the leg room!"

"Your legs have plenty of room! I just need to borrow some of your extra," I spat through clenched teeth and Mo handed me a cookie. Apparently acknowledging his legs was more cookie worthy than insisting they didn't need the full foot well. Chris turned the engine over and pulled down Main Street. He pointed the car toward Dayton as I shifted and tried to tuck my skirt under my leg to keep it from touching any of the obnoxious, vertically challenged man seated beside me.

Leaning against the window, I counted to ten as he started yipping like a small dog at the park.

"Your leg is touching me!" His voice sent my nerves on end, and Mo handed me a cookie.

"Her arm is touching my part of the armrest," he insisted. I moved my arm, and Mo gave me a cookie.

"Don't give her anymore cookies or there won't be any room *on* the seat *or* in front of it!"

Then I punched him in the face.

Mo did not give me a cookie.

Chapter Four:
Death Boxes

"Sorry, again," I said to Mo, sitting beside her at the restaurant, Mi Asiago Prego, middle America Italian with no resemblance to the real thing. She'd made the reservations at New Year's when Chris said he needed an insurance policy that she was serious before he kissed her at midnight. It was gag-worthy cute and now it was ruined. Chris was with his cousin in the bathroom, trying to get the blood out of his "one good shirt" before it set. Mo was on her second glass of wine, and the third was on deck.

"I'm not saying he didn't deserve it, but I wore my good underwear, Cyn!" she slurred through her buzzed state. A few men at a neighboring table looked over and I gave them my best side eye to look away. "Next time you punch someone, you better plan to screw his brains out afterward in apology."

"Maybe you don't need this," I said, trying to take wine glass number three away. She snarled, and I took my hand back while it was still attached.

"You can only punch a man after you screw his brains out, Cyn!"

"I will keep that in mind, Mo. But maybe don't yell about screwing quite so loud," I said, giving apologetic eyes to a passing senior couple collecting their coats. I grabbed my phone out of my pocket and did a quick search. The mortuary was within walking distance, and Mo was now describing her good underwear in detail to the men at the neighboring table.

"Maybe you shouldn't..." but she waved me off so I gave up. "OK, fine. I guess I'll be back."

I took a bag of cookies from her purse and got up from the table.

"Where are you going?" she cackled and the men at the neighboring table leaned away from her. "You are on a date!"

"No, you're on a date. I'm on the verge of being brought up on battery charges," I said, patting her hand. "Just drink your wine, I'll be back. You three, if she goes missing, I have similar skills to Liam Niessen in Taken except my guns are real."

They did not look impressed, but I left Mo to her own volition anyway when she started caressing the knife on her table. Nobody wants an angry drunk woman at a funeral, but no one wants a crazy drunk woman with a knife either. It was fifty-fifty she'd either get abducted or arrested for their murder.

Feeling guilty, I snagged the waiter on my way to the door. The woman had a crown braid and wavy hair flowing down her back in a charcoal cascade. Her age was somewhere between twenty-five and forty-five, and I envied her genetics. Her high cheekbones and laugh lines showed a life of merriment and beauty.

"Here's twenty dollars, switch her from wine to grape juice and I'll give you twenty more when I get back," I said and she smiled wide. Even her teeth were perfect.

"Teetotaler?" she asked and I nodded.

"Big time. After those three glasses of wine, tonight is going to be a fuzzy mystery," I confirmed and the potentially younger woman nodded. "Also, I dropped a mint in her third glass so they're all going to taste weird, and she'll probably send that one back, but I'll pay for it."

"I'll keep an eye on her. Any men I should worry about?"

"The ones at the next table were very interested when she started shouting about her underwear." I glanced behind me at the table and caught a flash of someone tall from the direction of the bathroom with a much, much shorter man. "But she was also a little too interested in her knife, so I'm not sure who needs your protection more. Those two should handle it, though."

Britney, according to her name badge, took in the residual blood drops on the short man's shirt and raised a brow at me.

"Would you believe he walked into the car door?" I said, stuffing my hands into the pockets of my dress.

"Sure, and I'd be interested in learning where these creepy, man hitting doors are," she laughed, and I passed her another twenty dollars and the bag of cookies. "You don't have to buy my silence. I'm not the fuzz."

She passed the money back but kept the cookies.

"Are you old enough to know what that means?" I asked and she laughed, opening the Ziplock bag. Britney pulled out a cookie, popped it in her mouth, and handed one to me.

"Are you old enough to know?" she countered and I shook my head.

"But I'll Google it on my millennial technology and get back to you."

She winked, and I exited the door just as Chris and Robbie arrived at Mo's table. It took Chris several seconds to save Mo from showing the neighboring table her "good underwear", but he looked much more capable of following through on *Taken* threats than I did.

Even if he had zero combat or arms training.

Men are such chauvinistic jerks.

It was a brisk night out, and I checked the map on my phone as I shivered. Ridiculously, I still wasn't accustomed to winter in Ohio, and I was once again outside without so much as a sweater. Vincenzo's Mortuary was two streets over in the middle of the block. Both sides of it appeared to be paid parking, but a small black box on satellite view led me to believe there was prime, free parking for the grieving family.

At least, family members of the bodies that didn't get up and walk away.

Quickly, I set off at a power walk, passing a half-dozen couples strolling hand in hand. Thursday was a popular date night in these parts. Which begged the question what people did on Friday and Saturday night.

Dead bodies, my brain answered, and I faltered in horror. My face smacked into a flower pot hanging from a light pole, and I shouted curse words, oblivious to the happy couples. My foot caught on the curb and I took a dive into the street, stopping my face from crashing into the asphalt mere centimeters before they met forcefully.

"You OK, lady?" a man in rags who smelled 100 proof asked, and I pushed to my feet, eyeing my scabbed knees. Definitely wearing pants on tomorrow's date.

Ugh, I have a date tomorrow, I thought and tried to ignore the excited flutter in my stomach.

"Yeah," I said and stuck my hand in my pocket, pulling him a ten from my wallet. "Thanks for asking, but maybe use at least part of this to get something to eat? I'm not trying to tell you how to live your life dude, but I have a gallon of paint thinner that smells just like you."

He looked confused.

"I don't..." he stammered, but his hands betrayed his mouth. Both darted out and snatched the note with ragged knit gloves missing fingers. Guiltily, I dug through my purse for the leather ones I carried but never actually put on and handed those to the man as well. He'd probably actually use them. My eyes scanned the area, taking in the lot and the building beside it before glancing at my map.

I had arrived at my destination.

"Do you usually stick to this area?" I asked, seeing I was in the lot beside the mortuary. The walk had gone quickly, and I hadn't paid attention to any of it. I was impressed that I hadn't gotten lost or hit by a car, less impressed by the building I was looking at.

"Yeah, thass my spot," he gestured to a shrub in the corner of the paid parking lot to the east of the converted house serving the community's deceased. I saw a tarp and a neatly packed rolling suitcase. He kept the area clear of trash and the parking attendants waved at him. I noted the bathroom with a key hanging beside the door and the electric heater with the cord through the window aimed at his camp. They knew he needed help, but they also knew he wouldn't get it until he was ready so they did what they could.

"Have you noticed anything weird or... unusual at the mortuary?" I gestured my head toward the building next to the lot and he furrowed his brows.

"That what that is?" he asked, and I noticed his teeth were nearly flawless. Straight, a little off-white, but all of them were there. "Thought it was some sort of banquet hall. Lot of men in suits goin' in an' out. Big black cars, but not too many death boxes."

"You've seen the... death boxes?" I asked, following his line of sight to the rear of the establishment. I was now only calling them death boxes henceforth and furthermore.

"Not too many. Not enough for a death box house. Ju't an occasional one, thought may'e they did death box demos," he said, rubbing his palms together in the leather gloves, still clutching the note. Death box house was now replacing mortuary in my vocabulary as well.

"Thanks... sorry, what's your name?" I asked and he blinked at me. Despite the alcohol, there was a tangible sadness mixed with something darker. He drank to forget.

And he succeeded.

"Mos' people call me Paddy," he said and shrugged. "Gets a little blurry."

I nodded and handed him a paper with my cell number.

"Can you call me if you see them bringing in death boxes?" I asked and he stared at the paper. "If you remember. No pressure. I'll bring you some food, OK? Also... when you want help..."

He shuffled away and I wasn't entirely sure he'd remember me tomorrow any more than Mo would remember her date. I was one dog away from being that man myself, I noted when I saw the war medals hanging from the bag beside the tent. He'd had a life once, but whatever he'd seen had taken that away.

Shaking my head, I stared at the two-story atrocity painted in mustard yellow with brown trim. There was no sign out front beckoning in mourners. The porch was dark, as was the second floor and most of the first. A single light bulb illuminated the back lot, and I strained my senses to detect... something. A car drove past and washed the whole area in LED headlamps, and my eyes fought through the explosion of spots.

Cautiously, I walked closer to the death box house. It was eerily still and silent, but I located a lower window that was illuminated and set a course for there. The parking lot Paddy lived in was mostly empty, but I still had to pick my way carefully. I did not want to walk into any cars or potholes filled with water from what I hoped was last night's rain and not Paddy's morning home brew. The window was to the rear of the building and I found a small opening that led into the neighboring lot. Beneath my feet, the sand crunched and I decided removing my shoes would be better for stealth. Tiny rocks poked the skin of my feet, but the result was a much quieter approach. A foot from the window, I heard voices and pressed my back against the wall, trying to listen.

"Boss said..." a man began and another interrupted.

"I know what *your* boss said, but it's not possible!" the second man said, giving the impression of clenched teeth and a scowl.

"Boss won' be happy," the first man said again, and I dropped to my knees to peer into the window. Inside was a sterile room with steel tables and a drain in the middle of the floor. A bank of freezer drawers took up one wall, and a sink sat beside each table.

"I don't care about your boss. You can't use this as an interrogation facility!" the second man hissed back at the first. Passing the window, I reached the corner and tried to look around the corner without appearing around the corner. "Come on, you shouldn't even be here, Andy."

Two men were there, as advertised. One was short, large, and breathed through his mouth. The second, probably the hisser, had a pointy face and slicked back grey hair. His nose held wire-rimmed circle glasses, and his frame was an unhealthy skinny that whispered illness or addiction.

"But you have the drains!" the first pressed the issue in his deep baritone, and I held my breath. "You made the deal, pops. This is what you signed up for."

"You can't shoot people in my prep room! I won't allow it and neither will your mother!"

I gasped and pressed my back against the wall, hoping they hadn't heard.

"What's that?" the grey-haired glasses man asked, and I picked up the steady thumping from halfway down the backlot.

"He's in the trunk. I told you, the boss said…"

"Get him out of here! I will not have murder in my mortuary," he hissed and the man cracked his knuckles. "Don't try and intimidate me, it won't work, son."

"That ain't the plan," he said, and headlights washed over the lot from the parking lot. "I ain't your son, either."

"Hey!" A man shouted, and I turned to see Paddy waving the paper at me. "Hey! Tha's the guy who bring the boxes!"

I pressed my fingers to my lips, but Paddy was shuffling over. He still had the ten in his fist and he waved it at me.

"Lady, that's the guy!" he shouted, and I heard the men around the corner approach my end of the building just as my phone rang. I tugged it out of my pocket and took off along the building at a sprint.

"Yeah!" I asked into the device, breathlessly getting to the corner. It was a poor time to take a call, but it never hurt to have a verbal witness to your murder that was sober. I tried to listen for footsteps chasing me, but I could only hear my pounding heartbeat.

That and the man on the other end of the phone.

"You need to get back here, miss!" a male voice shouted but I didn't recognize it. I looked at the number and saw a Dayton area code.

"Who-" I started, but glass crashed in the background and I heard Mo shout.

"You don't deserve my friend, you hobgoblin troll with hairy knuckles!"

"I'm on my way back," I said, stuffing the phone in my pocket and sprinting up the street back toward the restaurant. Bursting through the door, I saw Britney holding a cookie and looking like she was having the best day ever. Robbie was on the floor, Mo's foot in the center of his chest. She had an empty wine bottle above her head, upside down and held aloft like a magic sword.

"I have conquered Robbie the Rapscallion and I shall claim that man as my prize!" she shouted and held her arm out toward Chris. He took her hand and moved her off of Robbie, then stared down at her with a look of lust and confusion. Robbie was on the floor crying when the suited maître de approached me from behind.

"Ma'am, we require shoes in this establishment," he spoke, and I turned to look down at the middle-aged man who was having as good a night as Britney. "Though if you are here for them…"

I stared down at my naked feet. They were red and filthy from running here sans shoes, and I felt my face burn.

"I'm so sorry," I started and looked around. In one hand I held my cell phone, purse slung on the elbow. In my other hand… was nothing. "I… lost my shoes. But I'm here to…"

I gestured toward my good friend, her conquest, and her prize.

"Drive them home."

"Very good, please handle it immediately," he said, and I handed him all the cash in my wallet.

"Spread it around," I muttered and went over to pick the small man up from the floor and usher the lip-locked love birds toward the back door and the Honda Pilot. I fished the keys out of Chris's pocket and earned myself an invitation to join them from Mo. Passing, I unlocked the car and nudged them toward the door. When that failed, I shoved.

"You're insane! You're all insane!" Robbie was shouting, and I gestured to the passenger door.

"Get in the car, loser. Or walk home. Your choice," I closed the door on the mostly contained couple and got a good look at Mo's good underwear.

She'd earned this.

"Can you even drive?" he exclaimed, and I narrowed my eyes on him. "I mean, won't your tree trunks get in the way."

"Again, you can walk," I offered and he sniffled his butt into the front seat. I smacked my head against the car frame, hoping to kill just enough brain cells to not drive this car off a cliff to rid the world of Robbie. Without any luck, I climbed into the car and checked that everyone was buckled in.

Mo was on top of Chris in the back and they were not buckled... or clothed... best to avoid that.

"If a bra hits me in the head, I'm going to charge you a bra collection fee!" I muttered into the back seat, and she flipped me off in the rearview mirror.

Aahh... friendship, I thought as I put my bare foot on the brake. Backing out of the lot, my eyes traveled over toward the mortuary. The area was still dark, but I could just make out a silhouette standing in a doorway. I shook off the visual, knowing I was too far away to have seen anything of the sort. A single pop rang out through the night, and I flinched, hoping it was just a car backfiring.

Hoping I hadn't just walked away and cost a man his life.

Chapter Five:
Visitors

I pulled the Pilot behind Mo's bakery and climbed out without turning around. I dumped the keys in the cup holder and split before anyone could notice I was gone. Robbie was asleep. Mo and Chris were... practicing gymnastics. Nothing would ever convince me they were doing anything but practicing gymnastics. I started to walk out of the alley when I saw a light on in the house diagonally across the street.

Larry was up. I looked at my bare feet and the slightly dirty dress and wondered what he'd say. Wondered if he'd let me in. Wondered if he knew any gymnastics... a howl filled the night and I shook my head.

Dog motherhood calls.

Carefully, I picked my way across the street and bumped into Mrs. Charles on a smoke break from the bar across the street.

"Getting home a little late, Cynthia," she said, raising a shot glass in salute before shooting it back. "And without shoes. Must have been a good night."

My eyes glanced back across the street toward Larry's house. It could have been... it really could have been.

"Goodnight, Mrs. Charles," I said, waving her off to head in the side door to my apartment stairwell. I heard the patter of Winnie paws on the landing and emerged onto the hard surface floor to see my best friend.

Holding a demolished bag of Family Size Mission Tortilla chips.

"Seriously, Winnie?" I said, stuffing my feet into some fuzzy boots and walking down the stairs to let her release the kraken... or corn chips as it were. "You're going on a diet!"

We circled the block and she made two steaming piles of poop. I avoided eye contact with Mrs. Charles and got back upstairs, chucking the filthy dress on the floor and trying to decide if I wanted a shower or coffee first. I looked at Winnie as though she held the answers to life's mysteries.

Winnie let out a long fart that filled the whole apartment and I threw open a window.

"We are all going on a diet!" But then I ate a handful of Goldfish and we both knew I was bluffing. I also decided to skip both a shower and coffee to just go to bed.

"Nooo!" I shouted, Winnie's bark drowning out my cries. Red and blue lights invaded from every window and my phone was having seizures beside me. The dog had her nose pressed to the window and was losing her fluff at the light show. I tried to listen for sirens or some sort of chatter, but it was impossible to hear anything over my cell phone dancing across the nightstand.

"What?" I grumbled into the device.

"Someone was murdered, Cyn!" Mo stammered into the phone.

"Are you OK?" I asked, slowly opening my eyes. She sounded shocky, but not especially hysterical.

"Yes, but someone was murdered near the restaurant we were at tonight!" Her voice was high and breathy, but dampened. She was already feeling her hangover. Also, she was not near a murderer, making this a problem for *after* sleep.

"OK, but like... it's early," I mumbled and the bell rang. "Can't you get back in bed with Chris?"

"No, I mean yes, but I called because..." the bell rang again, and I staggered down the stairs to the rear entrance. "Seriously, Mo, I need sleep."

I pulled open the door and a uniformed officer stood there, but I didn't know him. My eyes weren't opening wide enough to read nameplates or patches, but he had a haircut and a build that screamed *cop*.

Also, a gun belt, but anyone could have one of those and it looked a little light.

"Mo, weird police are at my door, I gotta go," I said, ending the call.

"Weird police?" the man said and I squinted at him through sleepy eyes. He had dark hair and green eyes, circular wire-framed glasses on his face. He looked familiar, but I couldn't place him.

"Do I know you?" I asked, and he gave a lewd smile.

"You could in that outfit," he offered and I looked down. Short shorts and a tank top with fuzzy Crocs.

Crap.

"Look, dude, it's early... or late..." I squinted at the sky. "It's dark. What do you need from me? Professionally."

I qualified at the end. A flash of amused disappointment crossed his face, but he got down to business.

"Do you know someone by the name of Andre Gatton?" he asked, and I blinked at him.

"Probably not, but I'm crap with names. Do you have a picture?" I asked, listening to the telltale click of paws on the upstairs wooden floor landing. The fur missile was inbound and I was too tired to intercept. "Also, are you afraid of dogs?"

"What does..." he started as 90 pounds of furry horror leapt from the last stair and planted two paws into his chest. The officer staggered back, landed on his ass and let out a small scream. "Get it off! Get it off!"

Winnie licked his face, peed by the dumpster, and wagged her tail while he flailed like a flipped turtle.

"Winnie, place!"

She trotted beside me, taking her spot to my right and slightly to the rear. He was still flailing around, fighting an attacker who was no longer a threat. Not that she ever had been, but he looked uninterested in the truth.

"Are you done?" I stroked Winnie's ears and stared at Officer Drama Queen.

"What the hell is that?" he sputtered from the ground and he lost more than one potential hot guy point. His face was all over the place. Not just alarmed, but also intensely studying both of us.

Was he faking all of this?

"Dog," I answered and offered him a hand.

"What the hell is wrong with that dog?" he demanded, ignoring my hand and getting up on his own. Officer Sleep Thief Drama Queen was rude *and* he expected me to help him. "It's a menace! I'm going to call animal control!"

Again, the eyes and vocal inflection weren't matching.

"Shows what you know, there is no animal control in Sweet Pea. Also, technically, we are both still property of the US Government, I think. Something about reserves came up, but I got the impression we weren't ever going to be asked to answer the call." I rubbed my arms against the breeze, strategically covering my chest in the process. "It's cold, officer. Either in with the menace, or out with the trash? I'm not freezing to death for small talk."

The unnamed officer scanned the alley and eyed Winnie suspiciously. Harry Potter, he looked like freaking Harry Potter... if he were American, obsessed with fitness and... this guy. His lopsided smile came back and he puffed his chest.

"Does it bite?"

"Me or the dog?" I asked, half joking. His chest deflated a little.

"Either?"

"Yes, but only when ordered to or attempting to steal snacks, for both. If you have any food in your pockets, put it in the car or you're liable for any and all tooth marks incurred," I warned using my best legalese. I stumbled back up the stairs and bumbled around my kitchen while he returned to his car. I got the pot in the coffee machine, but then remembered it needed water. The machine was on when I realized I hadn't added coffee. Once I added the coffee, I started to move away but the sound of sizzles indicated I hadn't put the pot back.

Officer Home Invader Sleep Thief Drama Queen re-entered, slamming the door behind him, and walked up the stairs. The Harry Potter clone looked far too comfortable walking into a stranger's home. Comfortable, that is, until he caught sight of Winnie on the couch, and he faltered. It was then I noticed his utility belt was suspiciously lacking in utilities.

His eyes weren't scared of Winnie, but they didn't trust her.

Was he hiding something?

"You put your snacks in the car?" I asked, and he nodded, eyes never leaving Winnie. "Then you're probably fine. We've both been given a treat."

I tried to put the pot back in and touched the plate.

"Fu-" I cried out, but then the hot coffee started dripping and I was too scared of losing any to finish cursing. "No! Coffee! Stop dripping! I'm so sorry!"

"Are you normally this..." the officer started but I gave him a warning finger. His eyes had switched from Winnie, who hadn't so much as twitched her tail, to me. I was running my fried hand under cold water and the other was eyeing him like he had grown a second head in the past 20 minutes. He held up his hands in surrender. "Sorry, it's just, four AM isn't that early, not for an Army chick."

"Call me a chick again and you'll be a eunuch, buddy," I growled at him and he clutched his man bits. Or at least I thought he did... he could have just wanted his hand closer to his empty gun belt.

"You're cranky."

Again, the voice and tone didn't match the face.

"It's early! Who are you?" I squinted to try and read his name badge, then I realized he wasn't wearing a uniform. It was a dark blue button-down shirt and dark blue pants with black shoes. "And why are you dressed like a police officer but not in uniform?"

"Right, Detective Harpole," he said, extending a hand. "I don't have any actual uniforms right now, but it was a bit of a drive to wear a suit, so... I improvised."

His hand hung in the air for a minute, but when I didn't shake it, he placed it casually at his side. Easy confidence, no hesitation, and again I got that sense that he was playing dopey while studying everything. Even without the coffee, something was wrong with this man.

I looked around and saw my apartment was a normal color. Detective Harpole apparently decided it was safe to turn off his emergency lights as well as stash his snacks. There was a cup of coffee in the pot but my hand still hurt so I popped a coffee pod into the Keurig and pulled out the heavy cream, honey, and the sugary creamer I sometimes needed when forced awake at unsafe hours.

"Are you... making coffee while waiting for your coffee?" he asked, and the judgment in his eyes was the stuff of mommy group legend. It was equal parts superiority complex and mother knows best, and I wanted to throw something at him, but I was fresh out of options so I settled for glaring.

Glaring... and studying... if this was a game, I'd play along. You learn more being part of the story than asking about it.

"Why are you here, *detective*?" I tried to sound offensive... or at least condescending, but I was two-pints short of life-giving liquid so it probably sounded like my mouth was filled with saliva.

"Where were you last night?" He pulled a notebook from somewhere but seemed to have forgotten a pen. I gestured toward the cup by the door filled with pens. My first cup of coffee finished, and I doctored it before drinking half in a single swallow. He stared at me, and I searched my vicinity. Nothing was on fire, and I was definitely still wearing clothes. Detective Harpole inclined his head toward my mug. I turned it around. It had the silhouette of a woman leaning into a dog silhouette, appearing to whisper and saying "My Dog and I Talk Shit About You".

I shrugged and took another drink.

We would definitely be doing that when he left.

"Last night I went to dinner with my friend Mo, Mary O'Connor, her... EMT Chris and his cousin... Skid Mark. We went to Mi Asiago Prego, aka the Midwest's most insulting homage to Italian cuisine. Skid Mark and I had a disagreement in the car, and I was interested in... avoiding him. I left for some air and walked past a mortuary... I heard some men talking, and I thought they were weird so I ran away. The restaurant was... *grateful* someone sober arrived when Mo treated Skid Mark as a vanquished dragon and Chris was her prized damsel. Then I drove them to her bakery and left them all occupied in the car and walked home."

"The man's name is Skid Mark?" he asked, risking his life coming into the kitchen and pulling out a cup from my cabinet. Without permission, he poured himself a cup from the now ready pot before he caught me trying to murder him with my eyes. "May I?"

"It's four AM, that's not that early for a police... male chick... rooster?" my confusion cost the insult its effect. He smiled, too cute-like, so I took his cup and dumped it into mine. "Also, it's rude to take things without asking first. Worse to just go through a woman's cabinets. Do you have any manners?"

"Mother, may I have coffee, please?" he said with an eyebrow wiggle and I rolled my eyes, handing him his cup back. I was tired, grouchy, and sore, but I wasn't a monster.

"Whatever. No, his cousin's name was Robbie or something, but he *is* a skid mark," I finished the coffee I'd stolen from him and poured myself another one. "If I had my way, he'd be a skid mark on the highway."

"What was the disagreement about?" he inclined his head toward my slightly discolored knuckles and I put a kitchen towel over my hand.

"Expectations of space and physicality," I said in an offhand manner and he tilted his head to the side, removing the towel but not mentioning the evidence of an altercation again.

"Care to elaborate?"

"Not even a little," I said and he moved a little closer.

"Did you see anything while you were... walking past the mortuary?" he asked, snaking the cream for his newly replenished cup. "I assume you mean Vincenzo's Mortuary on State?"

"I met Paddy, he lived in the lot next door. I also heard the aforementioned two men arguing and what sounded like a man in a trunk," I shrugged at the end. As though I hadn't been obsessing over his fate until I fell asleep. "I thought maybe I was confused and it was actually like an escape room. So, I left and went back to the restaurant."

Detective Harpole studied my face, but I couldn't read his expression. As I watched him, the coffee in his hand started tilting sideways.

"You spill it, you die," I said, and he righted his cup.

"Why did you think a funeral parlor was an escape room?"

"They were talking about drains, there was a man in the trunk, and the homeless guy, Paddy, said not enough death boxes went into the death house," I explained but he wasn't looking passive anymore.

"What do you mean there was a man in the trunk?" He set down the mug to have pen and paper ready. His teasing air had shifted... his body language matched his eyes now.

"I don't *know* there was a man in the trunk. I just heard something banging from the trunk of the car. A large man and an older man with grey hair and glasses," I tried to drink my coffee casually, but my hand trembled. "What does this have to do with... Andre Gatton?"

"So you *do* know him?" His face was showing too many teeth.

"Know who?"

"Andre Gatton!"

"No, you asked if I knew him when you got here," I countered. "Also, it's an unusual enough name I'd remember if I'd heard it before."

"What were the two men you saw arguing about?" He changed tactics and my stomach clenched. Pretty sure I was going to jail for this one. I had meant to call someone; really, I had... but by the time I got home it was too late to call, just not too late to obsessively wonder about it until midnight.

"Disposal locations?"

"Disposal locations of... what?" His brows were at his hairline, and I drank the rest of my cup of coffee to fortify myself.

"Murmur Ictions," I muttered into my cup.

"What?" he asked, and pushed my cup away from my face.

"Potential, hypothetical, murder victims," I responded defensively, crossing my arms. His eyes widened, and I remembered I was still in pajamas... and no bra. "The older man said something about interrogation, and there was a thing about drains, and maybe shooting people."

"Why didn't you call the cops?" he was staring now, and not at my chest.

"I... got distracted," I shrugged and he just kept staring. "What?"

"Do you think it's normal to hear people talk about murder?"

"I don't know. Maybe? I mean some people are super into serial killers and true crime. Why not pay for the mortuary interrogation escape room experience? Also, I was in the military! We once put an annoying private in the trunk of a car for two hours just to not hear him anymore."

"Are you confessing to a crime?"

"No, I'm confessing to... enjoying quiet. We gave him AC and a magazine."

"You thought... it was all a game?"

"Maybe? People are into weird stuff. I went home with a man I consider an underwear stain and a woman who thought he was a dragon that she vanquished," I tried to sound like I believed it... also Mo really needed to keep to a two-drink max. "Who is Andre Gatton?"

"The man who was found shot in a parking lot," he watched closely for a reaction. The room swam a little, and I had to sit down.

"Who... was he?" I asked and Harpole opened his mouth with a facetious smile. "Besides Andre Gatton, dead, and standing near a morgue."

His humor faded.

"Still waiting on prints, but gut says organized crime. Weird for Ohio, but not impossible, there's a lot of low-level wannabes running around."

"Running around doing what?" I asked, trying to figure out if whoever Andre was had died because of the missing bodies, or died because he was into something less disturbing but more illegal.

"Crime stuff. Do you know him?" He grabbed for more coffee, and I gave it willingly.

"Why would I?" I asked, rolling my eyes. "I live in Sweet Pea. Before that, I lived in Florida. Freaking FLORIDA, man. It was hot, humid, and Florida. How would I know some random guy who messes with organized crime near Dayton?"

"Found this on him. That's you, isn't it?" He pulled a paper bag from his coat and pulled a piece of paper out, laying it on the counter. It was a small sheet, ripped from a notebook with my number on it. I moved closer and then took a jump back when I realized it wasn't just a paper with my number, it was a paper with my number like two dozen others I kept in my purse in lieu of buying business cards.

The most recent one I had just given out tonight.

"Oh god, it wasn't Paddy was it?" I fought back tears and looked Detective Harpole over for signs this was a joke. There were none.

"Who wasn't what?" he asked, still studying me.

"The homeless man, who smells like paint thinner and lives in the parking lot, Paddy? Please tell me, not him..." a sob escaped and a single tear rolled down my face. "I gave him that."

"When?" He was back to writing in his own notebook, his face half-obscured in shadow.

"Tonight... Last night? I fell in the street and he helped me up. I was asking him about the death house and the death boxes, that's what he calls them, and I asked him to call me if he saw more death boxes," I rambled on through tears and my nose was running. "Was it him? Please tell me it wasn't him."

"Was *Paddy* five and a half feet tall wearing a suit and built like Donkey Kong?"

"No, he was a little homeless man! I gave him my gloves!"

He nudged the paper closer, and I took a step back. Detective Harpole still hadn't answered my question.

"Did you write everything on that paper, Ms. Sharp?" He was all business. "It's important."

I started to nod, before I saw something else. Something in a smaller, neat printing, beneath the number.

WE'LL CALL YOU

"I didn't write that," my voice was thick with tears and snot, but I pointed at the second line.

He pulled out his phone and turned it toward me with a picture. Most of the man was covered in a sheet, but his face was visible, lying on the asphalt of the alley that ran behind the lot and the mortuary.

"Andre Gatton," he stated, and I leaned in.

"I think," I wiped snot off my face and tried to move closer. It had been dark, but the single bulb had made everyone look eerie and suspicious. This man looked like an overgrown Dave Bautista without any of the endearing qualities. "I think that's the man who had a guy in his trunk."

"What type of car was the trunk man in?"

"I don't know, there were four cars back there. All sedans or similar in size," I said and he pulled up another picture of the parking lot on his phone. There were only three cars in the lot, the whole image was tinted blue with the police lights. Despite the lighting, it was evident the scene was filled with crime scene people moving around. I could just make out the corner of the tarp that sheltered Paddy.

"Where was the fourth car?"

I pointed to the corner closest to the driveway. It had been parked right beside the gate that would have prevented access to the lot... had it been closed.

"What color was the car?" he asked, still staring at his notebook while flipping through images on his phone.

"Dark colored. Blue, black... It wasn't exactly well illuminated back there."

"Could it have been an SUV and not a sedan?" I shrugged at his question but he wasn't looking. "Ms. Sharp?"

"It could have been anything with four doors. It definitely had four door handles because whatever the make or model, they were chrome plated," I thought back on how odd that was. Who wants shiny door handles?

"Why?" our eyes met and I gestured for him to continue. "Why would someone have chrome plated door handles?"

"Why would someone own an outfit that looks like a police uniform but isn't? People are weird," I made a face and he made one back. Deciding he'd won, Detective Harpole saluted me with my own coffee mug.

Wonder if he knew it said "Coffee Whore".

"What did the man's car he was arguing with look like?"

"The car wasn't arguing with anyone," I said, grabbing his cup and sniffing for hallucinogens.

"Not the car, Ms. Sharp, Andre Gatton. What did the man he was arguing with look like?" His cup was empty so I took it and put it in the sink. My hospitality limit was one cup, if he wanted more he'd have to wait for the Mud Hut off the highway back to Dayton to open.

"Slicked back grey hair, glasses, Mr. Rogers sweater," I answered, and he turned the phone toward me, again. This image was a sterile DMV image of the pointy nosed man who wouldn't let the dead guy in for "interrogation".

"Yeah, him... is he also..." I made a slice gesture across my throat.

"No. He knew this man?"

"Well enough to argue with him," I answered and studied his face. "What happened to him?"

"Let's get back to that. Who is Paddy?" he said, checking his notes again.

"He's a homeless man with a drinking problem. Lives in the tent just off the lot."

"Here?" he showed me another image of the neat little camp. Except inside the tarp tent was nothing more than a chair and a small TV.

"That's where he pointed..." I tried to zoom in, but Detective Harpole pulled the phone back.

"No one was staying there when we arrived. Nice set up for a homeless man." He was skeptical but I was still trying to figure out where Paddy's bedding was. I'd seen it... hadn't I?

"So who is the old sweater man in all of this?" I went back to my original question, brain starting to hurt from all of the things I didn't know, lack of sleep, and strangers drinking my precious coffee.

"As of now, he's just missing. He called in the dead guy and now... no one can find him," Harpole said, tucking his phone back in his pocket. "He owns the mortuary as far as we can tell... but it's weird..."

"What's weird?" I asked, hoping it wasn't the same fact I'd stumbled on earlier.

"Who names their kid Vincenzo Lorenzo?" he asked, and I nearly dropped my coffee mug.

Chapter Six: Wet Cement

"Are you ready for our date tonight?" Larry asked and I stifled a yawn. The investigations office hadn't opened this morning, and work had been one endless reminder that walking was stupid and coffee was life.

"No," I stretched my jaw to its max opening. "Can I take a rain check and trade our date for an early bedtime?"

"Why not both," he said, rubbing a hand on my shoulder. Involuntarily, I leaned into the touch and felt my eyes drift closed. "Where's Winnie?"

"Her highness is holding court," I said, gesturing to the ice cream parlor at the front of the property.

"She... what?" He stopped rubbing my shoulder, and I moaned.

"Go look for yourself." I certainly didn't need to see it again. My brave, honorable, military canine... was in a tutu with fairy wings. There wasn't even a holiday associated with the choice. She just picked the damn costume, and there was a line of kids around the building, dying for a picture with her.

Sticky handed, very loud children who had startled more than one of the horses whose hooves I was trying to clean today.

I watched Dr. Kirby walk away and truly appreciated that he wasn't wearing his lab coat... and that he chose those pants.

"Am I paying you for that, Cynthia?" Joseph asked, and I nearly leapt out of my skin when I looked at him.

"What the hell are you wearing, man?"

The leather-skinned farm man was dressed in green tights, a green romper, and a hat with a red feather. It was the first time I was able to appreciate how much tone his legs had... and how many beers he drank daily to get that round in his center. I may not be a small woman, but even I knew when it was unhealthy to keep drinking. Yet, there was a new cardboard box from a twelve pack of Bud in his trashcan daily. I knew it was different because I'd taken to marking them for a week.

Also, I'd seen his liver enzyme tests and blood sugar results.

"It goes with the theme! Today's featured flavor is Green Fairy Freeze. Winnie inspired it," he was shifting like a man with a wedgie he was too proud to pick. His eyes darted to his office trailer, and I added getting him help to my list of unpaid and unsolicited projects.

A man should feel confident picking his wedgies.

"That is not a child-friendly flavor, Joseph!"

"What do you mean? We couldn't call it Tink or anything because of copyright..." he shifted from boot to boot. "But... she's a green fairy and green fairies are a popular search engine term..."

"Yes but the green fairy..." two barks sounded and I heard a little girl scream. Joseph stared at me and I held up my hands. "Fly, Peter, this was your idea."

"Yes, but..." he started and I shook my head. He shuffled his cowboy boots and waited, hoping whatever the incident was had ended... Then something crashed, two more barks, a scream, and then a stampede. At the front of the chaos was Tinker-Winnie, chasing after a little boy clutching what appeared to be a cone of peanut butter ice cream.

"Giddy-up, Pan, this was your bright idea," and turned back to shoveling manure. No way was I going to rescue anyone dumb enough to bring peanut butter ice cream to a meet and greet with the Wicked Witch of the Snacks.

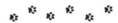

I was showered, shaved, and staring at my closet... or rather the metal rod I'd hung in my bedroom and pretended was a closet. Winnie was passed out on the couch, still dressed like a fairy. When I'd tried to take her wings I'd nearly lost a finger, so the entire outfit was staying on until she took it off herself.

Unlike Winnie, I had nothing to wear.

Last night's dress was filthy and I only owned the one the dress. Slacks and a camisole were a little too business, and everything else was jeans and shirts with more than one mystery farm stain. To add insult to an already dire fashion emergency, I only had my boots from the army, work boots, and sneakers. My one pair of flats were set to be disposed of by the kind people of Dayton PD.

My phone buzzed and I stared at a text from Larry.

Larry: *Where do you want to go tonight?*

Me: *Anywhere pajamas and coffee are acceptable.*

Larry: *Not really a date. Try again.*

Me: *I don't have date clothes, let's reschedule.*

Larry: *Not a chance. Go raid Winnie's closet.*

I made a face at his wink emoji...

Larry: *I saw that.*

"He didn't see that," I said to Winnie who thumped her tail on the couch. Just in case, I stuck my phone under a pillow. "He's just assuming."

A thunderous knock sounded, and I pushed open the curtains to look down at the street. A boy had his face pressed against the glass, and when I pushed open the window, I could hear him crying.

"What's wrong?" I asked, afraid to get too close. His hands and face were smeared in something dark, and I watched his skin peel off the window.

He was dirty and sticky, as advertised.

"I need help! Please?" he sobbed, and my heart melted.

"Stay right there," I said and closed the window. Grabbing jeans, a T-shirt, and the sneakers, I threw them on and hustled down the stairs. I moved the curtain, just a little, and the little boy was standing alone on the sidewalk. He had curly blonde hair and bright brown eyes. The jeans were new-ish, his sweatshirt green with some sort of animated frog upon it. The dark smears were chocolate, and not the blood of his mother as I suspected. Risking my life, I cracked the front door.

"What help do you need?" I asked, eyeing him like a chainsaw on legs with a full tank of gas.

"My- my..." he burst into tears, and Winnie pushed past me to get to him. I snagged her collar in the nick of time, but she may have gotten one lick of the chocolate covered boy. "My Nana!"

"What's wrong with your nana?" I asked, closing and locking the door.

"She's stuck!" he bawled, and I looked around for someone stuck in something. There was construction on the far corner of Main and Spruce, but no one looked alarmed. "Please!"

"Winnie, seek," I said, letting her lead me. She was following the boy's scent back the way he came and I followed her, grudgingly taking the sticky hand. It was small and somehow both wet *and* freezing. Children were a terrifying medical anomaly, and I suddenly understood why the ladies in mommy groups were nuts.

"Stay with us," I said, but I half hoped he'd run away.

We crossed a street at the crosswalk so his mother would be proud. After a jog through the alley, we ended up in farm country, and I was certain his nana had fallen in a plow hole. When we passed a farmhouse, I started hoping she hadn't fallen down stairs. I'd grabbed my cell phone from under the pillow, but reception out here was crap.

The little blonde boy kept sniveling, but he took delight in watching Winnie lead the way. He kept trying to grab her tail with a chocolate covered hand, crying out *doggie* so often, even Winnie was over it. As we got closer to a well-kept farmhouse, I tried to slow my breathing to listen for cries of pain and distress. I started to direct us up the front steps, but Winnie detoured toward the crops and continued on. The air was heavy with insects, buzzing and making sounds. It felt too early for them in January, but as we kept going further and further into the vegetation, I discovered why visually mere seconds before I discovered physically.

Rain drenched fertilizer had been piled beside the crops.

I went face first into a cow-pie puddle as the sneaker slid through the mud and my toe caught on Winnie. Sgt. Pupperson, for all her rank and newfound photo poser life, promptly plopped into the puddle and rolled on her back.

"Doggie!" the boy squealed delightedly and clapped his hands.

"Kid, where is your nana? There is nothing out here but mud, manure, and this mashed banana," my voice betrayed my irritation. I needed another freaking shower.

"Nana!" he cried out, plucked the mashed banana from my hand, and stuffed it in his mouth.

"Don't eat that! Spit it out! Spit it-" but his throat contracted and he swallowed the filthy fruit. I shuddered and fought back vomit until my brain caught up with his words.

"Is nana a person?" I growled and he shook his head, pointing at his mouth.

"Nana! Thank you," he beamed and skipped off back toward the house.

"Are you freaking kidding me!?!?"

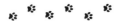

"Ma, for the last time, I have plans!" I shouted into my phone. Winnie was walking beside me, but I hadn't grabbed a leash for her, so it was blind faith keeping us together. By blind faith, I meant her hopefully being blind enough to not see all of the potential distractions and ruin my faith in her.

"With who? Mo is more than welcome to come to the party," she spoke back, voice matter of fact.

"No, I have... a... date," I choked on the last part.

"Bring him, too," she declared delightedly. "I think more men should participate. Is it that Cruz fellow?"

"No, it's..."

"Cyn!" A woman I vaguely recognized called from a doorway. We were still three streets north from Main and a block from the office. It had been a much faster trip to the "nana", but the slogging, muddy walk back was taking forever.

"Gotta go, ma!" I said into the phone and could hear her shouting as I ended the call. The woman who had shouted for me came from the doorway and was closing in fast.

"You didn't have to..." she started, then held her nose as the manure hit. "What happened to you?"

"Satanic offspring," I grumbled and realized it was Debbie when she got close enough to make out. Debbie was the local veterinarian who also volunteered and ran the local humane society. Unlike Larry, she didn't treat livestock or farm animals; she was strictly domestic pets and amphibians. I'd passed the shelter a few times, and it always sounded empty, which I attributed to her being very good at her job.

"Not *this* one?" she asked, reaching out to ruffle Winnie's ears.

"Not that one... this time," I shot a warning glance at her, and she dropped her tongue out of the left side of her mouth. Cute, innocent, derpy Winnie was not fooling anyone, but Debbie pulled a treat from somewhere and rewarded the canine.

"I'm sorry to bother you, but I need your help," she said, absently petting the fur missile and staring intently at something in the distance. "I was going to call, but then you walked by and..."

"Did you drop a banana in the mud?" I asked skeptically and her eyes snapped to me.

"What, no, I-"

"Are you in an argument about book versus movie/TV Show? Do you think a painting is the ghost of a loved one? Have you, in the last 48 hours, consumed a hallucinogenic substance that would lead you to believe aliens and/or mer-people are sending you messages?" I ticked off possible options on my fingers, deciding just this moment that these will be permanent screening questions.

"Are you kidding? Is everyone in this town nuts?" she asked, and I just stared at her. "Well, I mean... no. I need your help, but it's embarrassing."

"*The Sweetest Thing* Armageddon song embarrassing or tucking your skirt into your underwear embarrassing?" I asked, knowing if it were the first I'd have to move. Clearly, there was not a male part lodged in her throat, trapped with a piercing, but that didn't mean the chamber of secrets level weird wasn't just beyond the threshold. She was the only vet in town besides Larry. If she had a naked partner chained to her bed and needed my help getting him or her to poop out a key or something equally sex-game disturbing, I would never be able to bring Winnie in for a vaccine or a tooth cleaning. Which left Larry, and he and I had a whole different set of problems that could make him unsuitable to care for Winnie.

"I just need your help reaching something... technically someone..." she was still staring off into the distance, and I shook my head.

"I have no paranormal communication talents of any kind."

"No, jeez. Do you talk to normal people?" She wanted me to reach a *someone*, but I was the person talking to weirdos. "It's Mrs. NoraBelle, my cat."

"Oh! Yeah, where is she?" I said, moving toward the house and stopping. Mud squished out of the sides of my shoes and manure caked my jeans. I turned back to Debbie, but she still looked completely lost in thought. "Debbie? Mrs. NoraBelle?"

"Right!" she shook her head clear. "You can come in. I have to clean anyway."

Gesturing for her to lead the way, she pushed open the door to the den of disaster. Boxes were stacked three high, four litter boxes sat stacked and empty, there was one in use somewhere if the smell were any indication. Fifteen bags of cat food were stacked in the corner, and there was a fortress of cat scratch posts surrounding the food. Each post had a cat in the lofted turret and at least three more arrived to circle my feet. Winnie followed me into the house cautiously, scented the air, turned tail and ran to the porch where she flopped over and refused to look inside the house.

"Do you... are you... a hoarder?" I was hissing, and trying to maneuver around a broken alarm clock, twenty dog leashes, and an assortment of rhinestone collars.

"No... not on purpose," she sighed and picked up a cat that was about to leap from a post onto the unsuspecting bags of food. "It's just... people keep donating things. It's nice, and maybe we *might* need them, but we don't need them now. The shelter is stuffed with the generous gifts of the community... So now, so is my house."

"But... the cats?" I snagged one trying to leap onto an unsteady box tower. Setting the cat down, I lifted the lid and saw towels.

"It's so hard to get cats adopted," she sighed. "So... I adopt them."

Gently, she stroked a cat's head. It was all black with white paws and a diamond patch of white on her chest.

"I don't know how to tell you this... and I certainly never thought these words would leave my mouth, but you can't adopt all of these animals. They need a proper home... and this..." I stared in horror. "Donate it to another rescue group."

"Can I do that?" she looked far off and away, and I sniffed the air. Marijuana? Gas Leak? Carbon Monoxide... something was seriously wrong with this woman.

"Yes! Spread the wealth... but also your house freaks me out. Where's NoraBelle?"

"She's... aloft," Debbie answered and gestured to a ledge under the large window set into the front wall of the house. My eyes tracked to the left, then to the right... but it was just a window, set into a wall, twenty feet off the ground, near absolutely nothing.

"How?"

"I don't know," she answered, arms wrapped around her torso. "I would have used the ladder, but... I... don't have a ladder."

"I'm fairly certain if you did, you'd never find it. Step stool?" I asked, eyeing the much shorter woman and assuming she probably needed a step ladder to see the top shelf of her own fridge. She shook her head.

"I... don't like heights," Debbie answered, and I resisted the urge to bang my head against the wall.

"Hang tight," I said, pulling out my phone and calling Larry. "I need a ladder."

"You... what? I was just on my way to pick you up," he said, keys clattering as he collected them from the bowl by his front door. I could picture it from my sleepovers a few months back while I was healing from a broken arm.

"I'm not at home. I'm at Debbie's house, and I need a ladder. Do you have one?" I asked and I heard him hesitate.

"Yes... but..." he sighed, and I could feel him shift from foot to foot over the phone.

"Larry, there is no 'but', you either have a ladder or you don't. Which is it?"

"Yeah, I have a ladder, it's just..."

"Bring it to Debbie's house," I ordered and hung up the phone. Turning to Debbie, I watched her pick up a poop scoop, put it back down, and pick it up again. The silence stretched on, none of the cats made a sound.

Debbie sighed.

"Problem?" I asked, instantly regretting asking when she turned to me with tears in her eyes. Why was everyone crying today? Not trusting my voice, I walked over and patted her awkwardly on the shoulder. "There, there."

"I miss sex!" she cried out and I jumped a foot back. "I can't bring anyone here because of the cats, and there are boxes everywhere. My last date was allergic to cats and now... now..."

A single knock tapped on the door frame and Larry walked in, wearing a face mask and holding...

"Why is your ladder covered in Pikachu stickers?"

"Daniel needed a babysitter," he turned the ladder around and the whole other side was pink. "I'm lucky this is the only one of my tools they could find."

Debbie let out a shuddering sob and I winced. Bad time for him to mention his *tools,* but I was not going to tell him.

"Cool. Cool," I took the ladder from him and set it up under the window. "Why don't you help Debbie with the boxes, call some shelters, see if they need some donations. Or... a cat."

Debbie wailed and I shrunk in on myself.

"I can't..." he said, leaping back from a grey cat with pale grey eyes. "I'm allergic."

"To boxes?" I adjusted the ladder, hoping the cat would just leap over and climb down on her own. The feline eyed the ladder, eyed me and then turned to look back out of the front window, grooming a paw.

"To cats," he hissed, jumping as a tabby streaked across the floor in front of him. "That's why I went to school for commercial veterinary."

Turning, I just stared at him.

"Figure it out, Kirby. I need to play cat paratrooper," and I scurried up the stepladder. My height put me even with the cat and the window, but I needed to brace against the wall to feel steady. Heights had never bothered me, fast roping was my favorite method of entry into a combat zone, but this was horrifying. Mrs. NoraBelle's window was set back farther than I'd thought. There was easily a half-foot sill beneath the window, giving Spider Cat plenty of space to lie. Her back paws were tucked beneath her, tail swishing, as she flexed her claws.

"Hey, Nora," she switched to grooming her tail. "I don't know how you got up here, but it's time to come down now, OK?"

The cat continued to ignore me.

"Alright, I'm just going to..." I slid a hand under her belly, and she launched herself at my face. Claws digging in, she raked two paws down the side of my face before climbing down the ladder and disappearing into the chaos below.

"Mrs. NoraBelle!" Debbie squealed, and I slowly climbed back down. I could feel blood dripping down my face and mixing with the mud and manure. "Mrs. Nora!"

Debbie took off into the house, and I stared at her back until it disappeared. Winnie poked her nose through the open door, and Larry asked a question with his eyes behind the facemask.

"I guess we're done?" I said, trying to find Debbie using echolocation, but nothing. "Grab the ladder."

He nodded and we went outside, loading the decorated ladder and Winnie into his pick-up. He climbed in after shutting me into the car and sniffed.

"What's that smell?" he asked, and I shook my head. He turned over the engine and dropped it into gear. "It smells like cow..."

He trailed off and leaned in for a sniff.

"If you want a date to happen, you'll shut up now."

"Got it," he said, rounding the corner by Spruce and pulling to a curb. "This is closer to your office. I assumed you'd want a shower?"

My phone started singing Circle of Life, and I rolled my eyes.

"Hey, Heidi," I said to my sister. She was a doctor, settling into her late 40's with a few teenage kids I'd never met and a few below the age of ten that I had. There were pictures of all of them on my phone, but I mostly just stared at them and wondered how anything that size came out of my sister's body and didn't rip her to shreds like Winnie with a bag of corn chips.

"Mom said you won't go to her party," Heidi was known to get straight to the point.

"I have a date," I said, slamming the door to Larry's truck and starting toward the office.

"Do I need to remind you of the 'date' you had where I drove to the police station from college, three hours, to pick you up because you refused to call mom and the deputy was my ex's ex?"

"Not really..." I started walking down Main, trying to think of all the wonderful shower options the world held... and regretting that another outfit was probably headed to the trash. Winnie pranced beside me, she was relaxed and ready to show off her new mud mask.

"With Jared? You remember Jared, don't you?" she was sneering into the phone and I could hear it.

"Jared the guy who drove mom's car into Lake..." I started and then I froze as realization dawned. "You wouldn't?"

"I would. She still thinks one day someone will bring that car back, Cyn. Twenty minutes." I felt like I was sinking into the pavement as my sister blackmailed me.

"You should go if you care so much," I muttered.

"I am. Now, the man you're bringing..." my body felt like it was getting shorter and shorter as my sister, the woman who gave my parent's erotica, started blackmailing me. Because of her, our childhood bedroom was a grown-up playroom. There were riding crops and handcuffs, but no jockeys or police officers. Winnie had destroyed a ball gag and a dildo from that room, and I was still making payments to my mom for the destruction.

"What the hell, lady!" A man shouted and I looked down at my feet and hoped to avoid another ridiculous request. Except... my feet were gone. "Seriously, lady, I literally just did that!"

Staring down, I sighed and hung up on my sister.

"Sorry," I offered, trying to tug my foot out of the cement. "I wasn't..."

"I spent all day on that lady!"

"I'm sorry, I..." tugging hard, I loosed a foot. With leverage I got the second and stared down victoriously at my feet... which weren't wearing shoes. I wiggled my toes in their green unicorn socks. Taking hold of a sneaker, I tugged, but it stayed put.

"Get outta there!" he nudged me away.

"I just want my shoes," I said, trying to tug on the other one.

"You can't get those shoes, what are you crazy?" He was waving his hands, and I watched Larry sneak past with his ladder. "They're in there until I can jack-hammer them out. You ruined a whole day's work."

"If you'd just..." I began.

"There's a sign, lady!" the man was shouting at me as I stood there in green socks, stuck dumb at the whole thing. I stared at my shoes, the man, and then finally at the sign: Wet Cement.

An omen if I'd ever seen one.

Chapter Seven:
New Management

"What are you wearing, Cynthia!" my mom demanded as we stood at the doorway. "Hello, Larry, dear. Please come in."

I looked down at the slacks with a nice shirt I'd unearthed from the bottom of a bag. It was wrinkled but suitably dressy enough for a date with a low scoop neck and a bit of a shimmer. What my mom was looking at was the tan boots I'd worn in the Army finishing off the outfit.

"Hi, ma," I said, giving her a hug.

"Seriously, didn't I teach you..."

I held up a hand to staunch the flow of maternal accusations.

"My only other footwear was caked in cow manure. It was a calculated risk, but I stand by my decision until Stella's Shoes opens tomorrow," she pursed her lips at my words but stepped aside to let us in. Larry took my hand, it was sweaty and shaking... no, that was mine. His hand was calloused, dry, and warm.

"Nineteen minutes," I whispered to myself. "Nineteen minutes."

Larry chuckled beside me and leaned in to whisper in my ear.

"If I can finish the job faster, do I get a prize?"

I elbowed him in the abdomen and gave him a dirty look.

"This is *so* not the place for that..." I started, but stopped when I walked into the living room.

Seated around the room were two-dozen women and three men. All of them had paper snack plates and were talking amicably, wine and liquor flowing freely. All the car keys from the guests were in a bowl in the corner, but over half of the guests lived within walking distance, so the bowl was fairly empty.

What wasn't empty was the coffee table in the center of the room. Suddenly, Larry's statement was no longer inappropriate.

"Oh, my dog, ma!" I whirled back to her and tried to run back out the door. One of the items was humming and dancing across the table, and two of the men were now having a sword fight with some of the others.

"Sit, Cynthia. We were just getting started," she said and I shook my head, eyes wide.

"Are you kidding? I am not staying for this!"

"Why? Don't you think it would be a benefit for Larry to learn..."

"No, ma. I don't think Larry needs to know what my pleasure toy preferences are!" He shook with laughter beside me, and

I elbowed him again so he wandered toward the snack table. "Where are you going?!?"

"I think I need a snack," he winked and picked up a pretzel stick, a carrot stick, and a red vine, quirking a brow in question.

"I can kill you!" I shouted and the whole room went silent. Debbie was there, deep in conversation with a woman who was wearing a flowing skirt and top covered in cat hair. Her wild curls held from her face with a scarf. They were sitting very close and examining something on the table intently... or had been until I shouted.

"Cynthia! Come! Sit with us!"

I panicked, Larry smiled at the word *come,* and I bolted out of the house. Immediately pulling out my phone.

"You invited me to mom's sex toy party!" I screamed into the phone at Heidi, and her voice came through the phone and the door of a car that had just pulled up.

"I thought you could use something to help you relax. Clearly, you are not..." I held up a finger in warning, stuffing my phone back in my pocket.

"Have you seen our childhood bedroom? I did not need to see my mom, her friends, and Winnie's vet on a date. I needed even less to see them shopping for dildos on the coffee table where I did homework! Is there no decency left in the world? What sort of sister and mother sell sex toys together?"

"The kind who are educated and mature enough to know the value of pleasure," she responded, closing the car door.

"This isn't a..."

The door opened behind me, and I felt Larry's warm presence beside me. Relieved I wouldn't need to go back in for him I turned and looked him over.

"Your mom said... hey, Heidi. How's Gregory?" he asked and I turned to her, then back to him.

"Who's Gregory?" I furrowed my brow. "Isn't your husband Lance? Or Jimmy.... Mark?"

"The goat is good, Larry. Thanks. Cynthia, my husband is none of those and you better remember his name before you see him again or so help me... What brings you here, Larry?" She quickly moved on from me and I made a mental note to check out her Facebook.

"There's not much in that room for you unless you changed teams..." she trailed off as he put his hand on my lower back and my face flushed red. "Really?"

She clapped her hands and bounced on her toes in delight.

"You have my blessing to continue your evening, I'll make your excuses," she waved us away and paused to whisper something to Larry that sent his face flaming bright red, so we at least matched but he recovered quicker. She patted his shoulder and walked into the house, closing the door behind her as a squeal went through the assembled party.

"What the hell was that?" I asked, as he took my hand and led me back to his car. He'd traded his truck for a newer two-door sports car. We were standing there holding hands, and I fought my impulse to make sure my mom and sister weren't watching from the windows. He hesitated, rubbing his thumb on the back of my hand, chewing his lip.

"She said she'd give me a hundred dollars if I could take the cranky out of your pants," he whispered and I gaped. He opened the door and nudged me into the car. "Two hundred if I can get you to scream loud enough to wake up the neighbors. She has a standing bet with Mo."

"Did you tell everyone about our date? Did the mailman weigh in?" I wanted to glare but he was very close.

He leaned in and kissed my nose.

"I told her I'd do what I could for you," and a flutter went through all of my good parts.

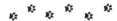

"Where are we?" I asked with a yawn. I had fallen asleep on the car ride and didn't recognize anything outside of the car window. There were too many buildings to be Sweet Pea or Yellow Springs...

"Just outside Dayton, I thought we'd get something besides burgers," he said, pulling into a lot.

"What were you thinking?" I asked and looked through the window. We were on a street filled with pedestrians, planters hanging from the light posts. Larry opened my car door and tugged me out.

"Italian. I heard this place is really good," Larry said, and I turned around to see Mi Asiago Prego, still as underwhelming as yesterday.

"Not... I might not be allowed in there," I shifted from foot to foot. He stopped and looked at me.

"Why? Have you been here before?"

"Yes."

"When?"

"Yesterday."

"By yourself?" his face registered something between jealousy and anger.

"No, with Mo and Chris and his cousin... Skid Mark," the last came out as a growl and he raised a brow.

"A date?" he asked and I waggled my hand. "With... Skid Mark? You saw his underwear?"

Jealousy was definitely winning now.

"Mo tricked me... or bribed me. I needed to see a funeral parlor, and she said she'd give me cookies if I didn't murder him. Which I didn't but then I punched him in the face, and when I came back from the mortuary Mo was wasted and playing Knight Vanquishes the Dragon to win the Damsel and... stop laughing! The cops were called!"

"Is this why your building had that car with the lights in front of it this morning?" He'd walked back to take my hand and tug me toward the restaurant.

"No... that had to do with the dead guy," I shrugged, my eyes flashing toward the mortuary. I still hadn't heard from or about Paddy. Sure, my number was in police custody, but maybe he'd... or someone had... "Can I order something extra if they let us in?"

"For the dead man?" his voice dead pan, I shook my head.

"Homeless man I met before I saw the not-yet-dead, dead man." We were standing at the door and I peeked through the window. Britney was working at the hostess desk and I took a step back. "You know they have tacos two blocks over. Tacos are so tasty. Wouldn't you rather have a taco?"

I wiggled my eyebrows, and he paused before shaking his head.

"I have a reservation here," he said, opening the door and nudging me through it. "Buck up, Cyn, it can't be that bad."

"I see you do, in fact, own shoes," the middle-aged man standing beside Britney spoke, and I studied his suit. It was a new one from yesterday, but still perfectly pressed. "Though those might be more inappropriate than not wearing any at all."

My face flamed and I stared at my boots.

"Reservation for Kirby?" Larry said, tucking me slightly behind him as though it would protect me from the little man's scorn.

"We got you," Britney said, gesturing toward the dining room. "Nice job trading up."

She gave me a double thumbs up, and my face was somehow redder and hotter.

"Can I... get both of you drunk so you forget yesterday?" I begged while Larry shook with laughter at her remark, and I hoped so hard that he would never, ever hear the whole story.

"Not a chance, friend of dragon slayer. That was my best day ever working in this place." She smiled and sat us at a table in the corner. "In fact, I'll get you a drink."

She sashayed away and I shook my head.

"I think she's hitting on you," Larry whispered, and I shivered as his lips brushed my ear. "Should I leave you two alone?"

"Jealous?" I asked, squeezing his leg.

"Only if you flirt back," he put his hand on top of mine and laced our fingers together. "Then I'm going to need you to let me watch."

I rolled my eyes and shoved him back in his chair. The bartender brought us two glasses of red wine.

"Just wanted to shake your hand," he said, taking mine. "Last night was epic. This bottle is on me."

"No, please," I begged but he just smiled. Shooting a wink at Larry, he walked away and I dropped my head to the table. "Why me? Why can't I go somewhere without being memorable?"

Larry snaked his arms around me and pulled me up right.

"Because then you wouldn't be you," he nuzzled my neck and pulled his menu over. "What did you have yesterday?"

"A heart attack," I groaned and he pulled my chair closer to his. "Seriously, I didn't get food, or a drink. I lost my shoes. Like freaking Cinderella except she at least got to have a pumpkin flavored carriage."

"Did she eat that?"

"Does it matter?" I downed the wine brought to us by the bartender and then took Larry's. He looked to consider maybe stopping me, but changed his mind.

"Feeling better?" he asked, draping his arm around me again.

"Why are we on the same side of the table?" I asked as the wine started to calm my sense of panic and dulled the ache of my skinned knees, cat scratched face. and the image of my mom selling sex toys.

"Social distancing," Larry said, and I decided it made as much sense as anything else. A new server came by and we ordered the facsimile of Italian the place served and I sent a silent apology to the people of Italy. At least two other people who were working last night brought us drinks, and by the end I was three sheets to the wind.

"Larry... Larry!" I whispered and he covered my mouth. "Why is it called two sheets to the wind?"

His hand stayed put and he turned my face, pushing in my cheeks so I looked like a fish.

"Three sheets, Cyn. I don't know why, but you're cut off. What do you want to order for the homeless man?" he asked and I pointed at my demolished spaghetti and meatballs. Larry ordered it and something with chocolate in the name, and I gave him googoo eyes.

"You... ordered me chocolate?" I reached to give him a hug but ended up face planting in his lap. "Also, how are more sheets in the wind any more sense making? Why sheets? Why the wind?"

Though how much he heard is unknown, since I was speaking to his head that didn't have any ears.

"So, so very cut off," he whispered into my hair and ruffled the fluffy ponytail. "But you have to get your face out of my lap before they really don't let you back."

"Nom, nom," I mouthed at the apex of his pants like PacMan.

"Geez, Cyn," he hissed and shifted me out of his lap. "Seriously, we are in public."

"Blah, blah, bor-ring!" I slurred as the cake arrived and I smiled. "Cake!"

Or at least that's what I thought I said before my face planted into it.

"You never disappoint, Cyn the Determined," Larry said in his car, wiping frosting from my forehead. He stuck his finger in his mouth and smiled. There was cake in my hair, in my lap and I hadn't gotten to eat a single bite of it... except what I licked from my face.

"Did you bring Paddy's pasta?" I asked and he tapped the container beside me. I gave him directions, pointing to the turns. As we approached the building, I saw it was lit up like Christmas, and a man stood out front, shaking hands with the mourners. Larry pulled to the curb, and I staggered out to search the tent for Paddy. There were three parking attendants instead of yesterday's four, but one recognized me and pointed to the corner.

"Cyn!" Paddy said, smiling. I held out the container and the plastic utensils.

"Hey, Paddy," I said, trying to stay upright but weaving from side to side. "I thought you might be hungry."

Taking the container, he lifted the lid and sniffed.

"Smells good, thanks!" he said, and I gestured toward the mortuary.

"What's going on over there?"

"No idea! Heard there was quite the ni't las ni't. Missed it goin' on meh rounds, and cops wouldn' leh me back after," he dug into the pasta, and I noticed the parking lot guys watching. Probably thought I was trying to poison him or something. I waved non-threateningly, and a glob of chocolate cake fell out of my hair.

"You doing OK?" I pulled a water bottle from my bag and handed that to him as well, wishing I'd brought a second one as my head started pounding.

"Better 'en you, it seem," he said, showing me again that despite his lifestyle, he'd retained his teeth. "You fall over?"

"Something like that," his smile widened and he picked a chunk of cake off of my shoulder.

"Tha' your man o'er there?" I followed his gaze to Larry who was leaning against the side of the car. The three attendants were watching him, and if my brain wasn't throbbing so much, I might say it was menacing. Chances were good it was all imagined, but the parking attendants seemed much more sinister today than they had yesterday.

Probably just the bright lights and booze headache.

"Don't know yet," I said with a sigh and looked back over his home. "You good? Can I bring you anything?"

"Nah, go find out if he's your man," Paddy said and waved me away with his fork. Scanning the lot behind the mortuary, I noticed that three of the four cars I'd seen were exactly where they'd been the night before. The fourth car was still MIA, making me wonder where Vincenzo Lorenzo parked if he was gone but most if not quite all of the cars were still present.

Slowly, I walked back toward Larry, studying the building as I went. It was much brighter tonight, more house party, less morgue... which probably was better suited to a mortuary, but death doesn't have to be depressing. I got even with the front, waving to the suited man on the porch who gave a curt nod and dashed back inside.

That's weird, I thought, studying the building. A large banner across the front declared "Under New Management" and the guy who ran inside looked like the fourth parking attendant from last night.

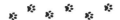

The sun arrived in the sky far earlier than I had prepared for.

Winnie had her nose pressed against my face, demanding food. I couldn't feel my left arm, the throbbing in my brain reminded me of my poor choices last night, and my service boots on my feet reminded me that I needed to go shopping today.

"Rise and shine, Rocky," came a much too loud male voice and I groaned. "I have coffee."

The smell reached me before the man did, and I held out my hands like a desert dweller being offered a ladle of water. He took my elbow, moved me to sitting and over the mug. Four gulps later It was empty, and I opened my eyes.

"I don't live here," I said, noting the strange angle of light, the open floor plan, and my dog on a second couch I certainly did not own.

"Wow, awake and coherent. So quickly," Larry said, tilting my face up to give my eyes a quick check for signs of continued intoxication. "Water and pain medicine are beside you."

He took my coffee cup and I gulped the water and popped the medicine.

"Why am I not at my house, and still wearing shoes?" I grumbled, Winnie putting her nose in my crotch to investigate. She must have smelled nothing interesting because she went back to complaining about food. "How did Winnie get here?"

Larry returned and passed me my re-filled coffee cup which conveniently read "Trust Me, I'm a Doctor".

"Would you like the short version or the long version?" he asked, and I pressed a palm to my temple.

"Either as long as you do it quietly," I answered him, and he scooted onto the couch next to me.

"'That's not what you said last night," he whispered into my ear and I jumped in surprise. The sudden movement sent my head swimming, and I tried very hard not to throw up on his couch. "Sorry. You weren't steady. I tried to take you to your apartment but you were defeated by stairs. Winnie came down, and I decided I'd take both of you to my house. When I got you here, you face planted on the couch, and when I tried to remove your shoes, you tried to punch me, so I let sleeping Cyn's lie. Winnie was very comfortable in my king size bed."

I started to nod, but that was a terrible idea, so I gave him a thumbs up.

"I need to go to Stella's," I muttered, trying in vain to stand.

"Because you are the first person on record to encase their own shoes in cement after donating a pair to the dead?"

"Yup. Feed Winnie?" I passed him my house key and he gave me a brow raise. "What?"

"Vet, have dog food. Sometimes patients stay here."

"Right..." I shrugged but didn't take the keys back. He pressed them into my hand.

"You're going to want to shower and change. I'll bring Winnie to your apartment in an hour?" he offered, and I gave him another thumbs up. He took my empty coffee cup and helped me to my feet. "Should we have a second date where you stay sober?"

A third thumbs up. I was the queen of communication today.

I stumbled through the front door and hissed at the unfortunately bright sunshine, prepared to quit when something slid onto my face. Sunglasses, good man that Larry. He patted my butt and I tried to work up a good right hook, but it seemed excessive.

He did give me coffee and sunglasses.

Stella's Shoes was off of Main St, like everything else. I slowly ambled north, taking note that it was directly behind the sidewalk repaving I'd... happened upon the day before. The shoes remained, laces permanently flopped into the cement and the tongues pushed back so my feet could escape. It would probably be a perfect mold of my feet in there. Stella's Shoes looked different and I squinted at the notice in the window.

UNDER NEW MANAGEMENT-

GRAND RE-OPENING JANUARY SIXTEENTH.

It was the fourteenth, so I walked in and blessed Stella's air conditioning and soft lighting. I walked to the sneaker section

and grabbed the same pair of sneakers I'd purchased the last time I was home. Then toward the flats and replaced the ones that were barely a week old. Dumping both pairs on the counter, I stared at the flamboyant man with bright green hair and an eyebrow piercing working the register.

"Stella sold?" I asked conversationally, and he gave me a dry look. I handed him my credit card and stared at the back wall. There was the start of a letter A in a nauseating shade of glitter beside the rest of the new name: Shoe Ambrosia. Beneath the new sign appeared Stella, a woman of modest size and exceptional fitness.

"Cyn!" she beamed and walked to the sales counter looking down at my purchases. "Interesting choices. I saw a pair just like this stuck in the sidewalk earlier."

Her eyes twinkled at me, and I tried to smile innocently.

"That's where I saw them and felt inspired," I offered and she looked down at my boots, brow raised. "Yeah, OK. Those used to be mine. So, you sold the store to an A who thinks shoes are ambrosia?"

The cashier sniffed and pushed the bagged shoe boxes to me, tossed my credit card on the counter and huffed away.

"He's... new," Stella said, looking after him in disapproval. "He came with the store's new name and the new... look. It was good to see you, Cyn."

She extended an arm and gave me a hug, patting my shoulder before walking back into the storage room. Gathering my shoes I waved goodbye and stared in confusion at the cashier talking into his phone on video mode. A strange cackle came from the device that was vaguely familiar... I started to speak and my stomach rolled over.

Right, I need food. Later, I would look into the mysterious A who offered the ambrosia of comfortable shoes in my size.

Chapter Eight:
Basket Case

T here was a basket of rocks in front of my office.

Not pretty rocks, or click clacks, but rubble. Demolished previously larger rocks in a pink wicker Easter basket without a note that I could see. My brain still had a pulse separate from the rest of me, and Larry had dropped off Winnie an hour ago. I was supposed to be open. A lone young woman stood out front checking her phone, beside the pink basket of rocks. Her phone case was also pink, as were her nails, shoes, and the tips of her hair.

"What's with the rocks, Winnie?" I asked her, twitching the curtain closed just as the woman looked up from her phone. "Do we take payment in rocks?"

Winnie tilted her head left, then right and let out a loud fart.

"You think we should?" I asked, heading to the door and unlocking it. Winnie gas trapped indoors was more dangerous than a potentially volatile basket of rocks. She let out another *pooft* and I pulled the door all the way open and propped it open. Hands on hips, the not-as-young-as-I-thought woman stormed in, not grabbing the basket of rocks. I peeked down at it... definitely used to be concrete.

"I thought you opened at ten?" the blonde woman said, eyes bulging from her artificially taut skin and inflated lips. She looked like a *Karen*, so I declined to comment and considered the rocks, the door and then the smell. Prioritizing the last, I walked to the other side of the room and grabbed the oscillating fan, placing it by the door and turning it on full.

"What are you doing, it's freezing out!" she whined, looking around the room, appalled. Winnie and I were not living up to her expectations and I still had a hangover. Her voice was too high to be comfortable for Winnie's ears, but the dog was sitting beside my desk and had zero thoughts on the woman I named The Pink Karen.

TPK for short.

"I like the cold. Also..." but I didn't need to finish the statement as she walked through the Winnie gas cloud and sputtered. Clutching her chest, she started coughing and hacking, so much the *drama queen*.

"What..." cough cough "the hell is that smell?"

She really was going for an academy award with this performance. I'm talking *Rose telling Jack she'll never let go*. I glanced at the source. Winnie was panting, her mouth open, and it looked like she was laughing.

107

"What smell?" I asked. Feigning confusion so convincingly the dictionary would put a picture of my face beside the definition of the word confusion. I gave a gentle sniff, and I had to turn away so she wouldn't see my confusion turn to horror.

"You're on a diet starting now," I hissed quietly at the dog. Turning back to my guest, I eyed her.

The Pink Karen coughed another minute, missing my comments to the dog. Her eyes were streaming tears and frankly I would have applauded if she wasn't upstaged. Winnie let out *another* blast that could have rivaled an aircraft breaking the sound barrier. TPK clutched her hands to her face and eyed the door. She looked back at me and then again at the door. I shrugged at her and went to make coffee, hoping she'd leave and take the basket of concrete with her. I heard nothing and turned around clutching my cup that delightfully announced my status as a sharp-shooter in the Army, and master marksman.

It was TPK's turn not to care as she stared, hands on hips.

"Is this about the rocks in your basket?" *Or the stick up your-*

"No! My dog is missing," she choked and I stood up straight. This changed everything.

'When did you last see the dog? Is there a collar or a microchip?" I asked and she gave me an exasperated look. I started rifling through the papers on my desk until I found a pen and started scribbling on a receipt for take-out. "What color, breed? Have you put up fliers? Or posted on social media? The residents of this town need both."

She started clicking and I stared at her, pen poised for info. She was shaking her head, looking irritated and impossibly condescending and calm for someone whose dog was missing.

"Ma'am?" I asked and she gave me a look of disgust that rivals mine when children approached me with sticky hands. "I need to know this to start. Last known location?"

From a massive pink purse, TPK produced a small, rhinestone studded urn.

"My dog has been dead for two years, *ma'am*," she snarled the last word, and I just stood with my pen poised on the paper. "Someone stole her."

"Is that... how she died?" I asked, not daring to set down my pen and startle the woman. "Was there a ransom you just found or something?"

"What? No, she died of leukemia, but she had a full life," her pink tipped fingers waved at the air. I cocked my head to the side. I checked with Winnie, her head was similarly tilted. We were at a loss so I gestured for TPK to continue. "She passed, and was cremated, and her ashes were in here."

She shook the rhinestone urn and my eyes widened, terrified it would crash to the floor. I still hadn't purchased a vacuum.

"Maybe you could be more careful to keep them... in there," I gestured, and she shook it more vehemently.

"She is not in there!" and slammed the urn down on my desk. I was relieved to hear it was metal, but the vein pulsing at TPK's hairline was as alarming as not having a vacuum in the event someone threw ashes on your floor. Carefully, I walked over and lifted the lid, glancing inside.

It was ashes.

"There's... ashes?" I asked, trying my best to sound calm and reassuring.

"That's not her!" she screamed and threw her bag on the floor.

"What... who are they then?" I asked, putting the lid back on and taking a step back. She stared at me and then at the urn.

"How should I know? I'm not an expert on ashes, I just know it's not Muffie!"

"You say this because?" I prompted and looked at Winnie. She blinked at me.

I grabbed the urn from the desk and held it out to her. She sniffed. Once, twice, and then went to the woman, first sniffing the bag on the floor and then carefully moving to the pink converse on TPK's small feet. She sniffed her and wagged her tail, looking at me.

All three smelled the same.

This woman was just nuts.

"I know Muffie. Muffie has an aura, and that jar has no aura," she said, giving Winnie a dirty look of accusation. Apparently, her confirmation of ownership was an offensive blight to the woman, and she stepped farther from the desk and dog in question.

"She... has an aura? In death?" I asked, holding the urn to the light. Winnie pawed my leg, so I let her sniff again, and she tilted her head. "What color is it?"

"The urn is pink!"

"I meant Muffies... Aura. What color was her aura?" My patience was wearing thin.

"Dogs can't see color!" She threw her hands in the air, sending the plastic beads on her wrist down her slight forearms. The plastic clatter made Winnie wag her tail and another *pfoot* escaped. I tried to study the colors on TPKs wrist. Perhaps my dog needed meditation beads to find inner peace... like, in her bowels.

"Can... *you* see color?" I asked, looking over her shoulder at the pink Easter basket full of stones. Maybe she didn't know everything was pink... maybe someone said it was something else.

"What is that supposed to mean?" she fisted her hands onto her hips and jutted out a lip in a pout. My eyes drifted back to her and then to my new shoes. They looked exactly like the old ones, just cleaner and a little stiff. I counted to ten. Then I looked at the ceiling and counted to twenty.

"It means that if you could see... Muffie's aura, then you could see its color. Even color-blind people have an aura color," I was totally making the last part up, but it didn't seem like she was at full human intelligence wattage.

"Right... her aura was..." she looked around and her eyes landed on the basket. "Pink. Her aura is pink and this jar is blue."

Strange that with her nails, hair, shoes, and bag, it was the basket that inspired her. Also, that the urn went from no aura to a blue aura. Maybe she just wanted to get a new dog without her old one seeing. Her eyes lost focus for a minute and she looked around the office like she'd just arrived. I stared back out of the window, but there were no camera persons or men with butterfly nets...

"So?" She startled me back to looking at her. "Why is it blue?"

Because you just decided it was blue, I thought with an internal eye roll.

"I'm sorry... Karen?" I asked, trying to find out her name so I could add her to my list of people to avoid and hide from at the grocery store.

"What? Why would you call me that?" she huffed and I shrugged.

"I thought you said that was your name and it seems... fitting."

I shrugged again and she blinked at me.

"My name is Terri!"

"Right, Terri. Perhaps it's a shift in color based on her proceeding into the next phase of re-incarnation, and now Muffie has a blue aura and this urn serves as a vessel of her essence that transforms with her through each incarnation," I offered, placing the jar back in her hands. This time I physically wrapped her palms around it and let go.

"Maybe take it home and use the opportunity to get to know the Muffie she has become."

"I don't want a new Muffie! I want Muffie the way she was!" She cried out and a subtle tap on the office door frame drew my attention.

"Can I come in?" Detective Harpole asked and Terri immediately perked up. He was smiling with his hair flopped over his eyes. I switched from thinking he was in his thirties to late twenties. His body was all sultry flirt.

Except his eyes, which were once again more serious than his face or body suggested. I glanced at his hair... had it been that long yesterday? Was he part werewolf?

"You can come anywhere you want," she chirped and my head throbbed with the whiplash. "What's your name, hot stuff?"

Detective Harpole smiled wide, but looked around Terri. His face looked like it always did, but the double entendre gave him an extra sparkle. He puffed his chest and flexed his arm, totally peacocking and pretending he wasn't.

Again, I looked through the window.

Again, I was not on a candid camera show.

It was very possible it had become a group civilization for the mentally ill in my absence. Perhaps the detective was a Shutter Island detective and his gun was fake, as was his badge and his supposed dead body next to a mortuary.

Except I'd seen the body, the mortuary, and the dead guy looked pretty real... and pretty dead.

His gun had yet to be seen.

"Detective Harpole, I'm here to speak with Ms. Sharp. Is that your basket?" he asked, gesturing to the front door with a flex and she blinked at it.

"No, why would you think that?" she pouted again and he looked her up and down, back to the basket.

"No reason," Detective Harpole was smarter than I thought. "Have you concluded your business?"

Creepy way to say *business*, but maybe he was lonely. I searched his face, flirty smile, flirty posture... serious eyes.

"No! She needs to find my dog's ashes! If Muffie is gone and it's whoever she is in her new life, then I don't want them!"

She slammed the urn on my desk, scooped up her bag, and stormed out of the office, kicking the basket as she passed. It didn't move as much as an inch, but her scream indicated she hadn't missed. Terri grabbed her pink shoe and began to wail, drawing a crowd of onlookers.

"Geez... why?" I muttered and then remembered I had coffee, so I drank that instead. No need to wonder about stupidity when there is coffee.

"Is that... accurate?" he swallowed hard and I looked down at the cup. It declared I was a master marksman in the Army. My Drill Sergeant had given it to me after I successfully shot a fake bird out of a tree at 200 yards.

Except it turned out not to be fake... and there were baby chicks in the tree. I was a murderer and he was very impressed.

Or just scared... hard to say.

"Yes."

"Do you... have..." he made finger guns and I raised a brow at the sweat beading down his face in my 50-degree office. I drank more coffee and remained silent, watching him. "Never mind, it's not important. Were you at the mortuary again last night?"

"I was in the parking lot. I thought Paddy would like some pasta." Turning back to the coffee cart, I tried to decide if I wanted to brew a whole pot, make another single cup, or go back to bed.

If I made another pot I would have to share... so I popped in a new pod and stared at the man.

"Paddy? Your 'homeless' man that no one else sees?" Harpole asked and I turned.

"What? Did you ask the parking lot attendants?" I gripped my skull; the shouting had been a terrible idea. "They keep an eye on him."

"Parking lot attendants?" His face matched mine when TPK was standing in his spot.

"The attendants who work in the lot next to the mortuary? There's..." I trailed off. Remembering my drunken revelation that one of the men from the lot appeared to be running the funeral home now. "What did you need?"

My brain had started to hum and I had no real idea why I was involved in this. Yes, missing dead people were weird, and seeing a man under a sheet in police lights would probably haunt me, but Henrietta wasn't concerned anymore once Mr. Lorenzo went missing.

"It's... what I didn't see. Do you know a... Henrietta Harkness Handover?" He asked, pulling out his phone to verify the name and presumably show me a picture.

"Why?" The pulse in my brain quickened and I wasn't breathing. He turned his phone and Retta appeared on the screen in a staged photo, likely from the DMV.

"You know her?" I nodded, still not breathing. His eyes were guarded and all semblance of playful had faded. "How?"

"She..." I inhaled slowly. Long exhale and repeat. "She lives in town."

"And?" he asked, not looking away.

"We've met. Is she...?" Spots burst in front of my eyes and I found my hand reaching for my chair and grabbing a Winnie head. I rubbed her ears and practiced breathing. "Dead?"

"Right now, she's just missing. What do you know about her?" His voice was still serious, eyes flashing interest mingled with something else...

"She..." my hand shook as I reached for my coffee and I tried to steady it for a drink. The liquid sloshed along the sides, and I set the cup back down without having any. "She came in the other morning. Bodies were... unaccounted for."

"What do you mean?" He took my cup, sniffed it, gulped, and set it back on my desk with a grimace. "What is in there?"

My eyes were far away, trying to remember Henrietta's every word.

"She said that there were bodies for which caskets were purchased but no body existed. Retta, Henrietta, thought they were misplaced or... worse," I trailed off and then looked at my cup. "The caskets were paid for, but there were no records of the people."

"Why didn't you mention this yesterday?" He demanded, looking around my office for something stronger. "This would have been helpful to know yesterday!"

"Because she had to pick a lock and she didn't want anyone to know she could," I snapped back. Panic at the idea that this was my fault clogging my throat until I worried I wouldn't be able to breath again. I grasped for something, anything, and grabbed my coffee, staring at its dark contents. "Did you drink my coffee?"

We stared at each other in silence, my heart fighting panic his face registering confused resignation. I was not nearly as helpful as he thought I would be and he was not as effective or intuitive as he should be... or he was acting... badly.

Someone cleared his throat and we both directed our gaze to the open front door.

Daniel Kirby stood there, with his police uniform and mirrored shades, looking like a midwestern reject from the cast of CHiPs.

"Cynthia." He drawled, and I rolled my eyes.

"Idiot face," I answered and Harpole looked between us.

"You two... a thing?" he asked, brows wiggling. The moment of seriousness had ended and Daniel made a face that must have mirrored mine in disgust and horror. Harpole laughed and the mask slipped back over his face. "So... what is this then?"

"Sibling rivalry," I said. Harpole raised a brow and Daniel made a face.

"We aren't family," Kirby spat, and I smiled wide.

"After last night's date I had with your brother, don't be too sure," I winked and turned back to Harpole as Kirby stood a moment, jaw hanging in the breeze, before turning on his heel and storming out. He made it as far as the sidewalk before he tripped on the basket, knocking it over and face planting in the process. The crowd TPK had drawn was still present, as was she. Half the town had watched Daniel Kirby fall face first into the sidewalk and at least two people had cell phones out.

I laughed so hard I gave myself hiccups.

Harpole looked like a kid whose parents misplaced him at Disneyland: not quite scared, but nervous and entertained. Daniel Kirby looked out for blood and the detective wisely gave him a clear line of sight to me.

"You can't leave crap on the sidewalk, Sharp!" Kirby shouted, face red while I gasped for air. He tripped on something else trying to right himself and fell into TPK's voluptuous cleavage.

Excited, she wrapped her arms around his head and tried to climb him like a jungle gym.

I collapsed on the floor in a fit of humor while he extracted himself, noting that no one helped or offered him access to the jaws of life. The officer's face was more purple than my commander in Florida when I chased a car through a brick wall that he was on the other side of. The car caught fire, was full of fireworks, and the wall was around a fuel yard, so frankly Kirby was just over-reacting.

It's not like we started a brush fire again and tried to burn down Florida.

"It's not mine!" I called from the floor and he picked something up and started waving it.

"Well it's got your footprints!" he shouted and threw the concrete encrusted item into the office. With better luck than the first time, he took off again down the street, and Winnie sniffed the rock.

"Is he... stable?" Harpole asked, looking at his phone for help. "I mean... usually?"

The Dayton detective decided to move on. Apparently, I was now a resident of Shutter Island or someone reasonably associated with a collection of basket cases. Oh, how the tables have turned.

"The last time you talked to Henrietta was when she came in to ask you to help her find the dead bodies?" he asked and I bit my lip. "You called her when I left?"

I nodded and he sighed.

"I wanted to let her know that her boss was missing. She wasn't too broken up about it." At a loss, I stood and walked toward the piece of concrete laying on my floor. It was a unique shape for concrete, but not unfamiliar. "She was content just to go back to work. One of the few people I've met in my life who enjoys and cares about the quality of her work."

"Well... she went," he said and I turned back to him. "She went and the last anyone saw of her, she was getting into the passenger side of a dark-colored four-door SUV out front of the mortuary."

I nudged the rock over and saw... my shoe. The workers had jack-hammered my shoes out of the sidewalk. I nudged the rock-cased shoe with my toe, curious if I got the rest of the cement off the shoe would it be salvageable? Something slid across the bottom of the shoe and I squatted beside it, Winnie coming up beside me to sniff furiously. Her head disappeared inside, coming out with a paper stained red.

"Winnie, out!" I ordered and she tried to dance away but I grabbed her collar. "Out!"

She dropped it and stared at me in distress. Releasing the collar, I leaned in to stare at the paper, the red stain smelling...

"Garlic?" I asked no one in particular. Harpole appeared beside me and picked it up. He gently teased apart the stained and slobbered on paper. The detective's eyes were wide and curious, as though finding a treasure map amid a pile of rusted swords. There was a smiling man on the front, in two images set side by side: young and serious beside wrinkled and smiling. The red stain was in a pattern of small X shapes and chevrons. Beneath the image was yesterday's date, the mortuary address. and a hand scrawled note. The writing was loopy but neat, with a single line.

SHE'S GOING TO CATCH YOU

Beneath that, a second line in perfect block letterings.

I HAVE A CASKET READY AND PAID FOR.

Chapter Nine: No Shoe Unturned

"Go away!" I shouted down the stairs. When Detective Harpole left with my cement encased shoe and the garlic note, I declared my day over. The door locked, curtains closed, I climbed back upstairs to my apartment, pulled a blanket over my head and refused to come out.

The knock came again, followed by a grumble from Winnie and then the sound of a door opening.

"I said go away!" I shouted at whoever had opened my door. The list of people with keys was as unknown as whether or not I had bothered to lock it. Footsteps came up the stairs and a male voice called out.

"I have pizza?" he shouted, a note of hesitation. Winnie's lumbering footsteps clattered Scooby style, until a man said *oof*, a woman laughed, and another man tried to gain compliance.

"Winnie, no," he said but I could hear her rolling her eyes from beneath my blanket. Someone walked into my kitchen, someone walked toward me, and someone was on the ground getting mauled.

"Rise and shine, Cinderblock," Mo said and stuck a paper cup of coffee under my nose. A low growl escaped my throat, but I propped myself on an elbow to take the coffee anyway.

"Get out," I grumbled between the two gulps that emptied the cup.

"Can't," Mo chirped, taking the empty paper cup and replacing it with a new, full cup. "We urgently need your services!"

Her smile was full of sunshine and sugar cookies, and I was torn between laughing and squishing the happiness out of her.

"Doesn't Chris handle all of your *services*?" I asked, taking a small drink from the new cup. The man who'd tried to correct Winnie, Chris himself, let out a very masculine chuckle and high-fived the man pulling dishes from my cabinet. I kept drinking until it was nearly empty while Larry touched my dish towels, my sponge and my paper towels.

"Stop touching everything!"

Larry turned around and wiggled his eyebrows at me.

"If I do, who will handle your *services*?" he quipped and the two men did another high-five.

"Ignore them, I need help," Mo said, and lowered her voice. "I think... I think Mrs. Charles is in trouble."

"Why do you think that?" I asked in a normal voice. My apartment was maybe four hundred square feet, no way to be discreet and it felt unnecessary.

"You know the police that were at your building the other night?" Chris said, bringing a plate with pizza on it to Mo while Larry carried one for me. It was then my guests learned that I did not have a table, chairs or a place to sit beside the couch and the floor. "Where's your table?"

"What police?" I asked, eyes wide. Or they would have been, except Larry tried to sit on the floor with his legs under the coffee table and was immediately trampled. Winnie was on his shoulder, head dangling toward his slice of pepperoni. "If you let her have cheese, you're taking her home with you."

Another six minutes of chaos followed where Winnie was bribed onto the bed with her own kibble dinner topped with some wet food and a sprinkle of bacon crumbles. Mo and Chris were tucked into each other on the couch, and Larry had discovered my bar stool. Not interested in joining the love fest, I decided to eat my pizza standing in the kitchen.

"Mrs. Charles?" I asked, patiently waiting for everyone to stop chewing and explain the intrusion.

"She was super nervous when the police were here. Chris and I were headed home... to his..." She flushed red, and he tickled her side. She erupted into giggles, and they wrestled on my couch for a minute.

"Quit being cute or get out," I said, taking another slice of pizza.

"You know, you'd be happier if you hadn't-"

"Can it Kirby," I warned, and he gave me an appreciative once over. I glanced down- tank top, shorts... no bra. "I repeat, Mrs. Charles?"

The second part came out so loud, everyone but Winnie jumped. She just wagged her tail and I remembered her trampling the man who'd shown up in a not-quite uniform, unarmed... with police lights.

"Right," Chris took over. "So, we saw her in her upstairs window. She was whispering into her phone and shaking. When we waved, she jerked the curtains closed, but we could see her moving behind them. Then, she didn't open the bar today after the Dayton guy was at your office again. She put a sign in the window that said 'Closed for Inventory'. Mrs. Charles lives for that bar. Why would she close?"

"Maybe she ran out of alcohol?" I said, but my mind was trying to build a timeline. She had been standing outside her bar Thursday night, congratulating me on satisfaction I hadn't received. Her demeanor was perky, her glass full, and her cigarette lit. Have I seen her since?

I tried to picture Mrs. Charles's window when Harpole was here but there was nothing.

"How did she know he was a cop?" I asked and they all looked at me. "Did he have a police car?"

Everyone shrugged.

"How did you know the police were at my house and then the office?" I asked again and Chris puzzled while Larry ate more pizza.

"Mrs. Charles had asked us if we'd seen the cop," Mo said, gently nibbling a corner of pizza crust. She was nervous. "I'd called you that morning because Mrs. Charles had found me and Chris and said he was looking for you."

"So... he asked her where I was?" I asked, but they were still clueless. Probably they had still been "practicing gymnastics".

"She still could have run out of booze," I shrugged. "She drinks like a fish."

"She just got a delivery on Wednesday," Larry countered, and I stared at him. "The truck blocks my road, so I have to time my departure to accommodate the unexpected street closure. She might drink a lot, but she doesn't drink *that* much."

"Wednesday night, the guys and I were in and she was showing us this new stuff she had in stock. It was imported and the label was a little suspicious, but she was smiling excitedly about it," Chris confirmed. The guys must have been his fellow EMS/Fire personnel because I'd never seen him hang with anyone besides them and Mo.

"Can you describe the bottle?" I asked, biting into a third slice and handing the box to Larry to hand to the love birds.

"It was cool, like a green wine bottle, but I think it held hard liquor and the label said something in Italian... or at least it looked Italian. It had a picture of Italy on it," Chris said and shrugged. Mo had set down her pizza slice and was chewing on her thumb nail.

"What, Mo?" I asked, knowing the guilty look on her face. The last time I had seen it was when she said she couldn't give me a ride home from prom because she had something else she wanted to ride.

"It's... a really strong potato vodka," she said, eyes darting around before whispering. "It's moonshine!"

"Why are you whispering?" I whispered back and she looked around in alarm.

"The cops were here!" Her voice was even lower. I fought a laugh at her innocence.

"Do you think they're hiding under the bed?" I whispered back, creeping slowly toward the furniture item in question. I dropped suddenly, lifted the overhanging sheet and shouted.

"Boo!"

Winnie jumped to her feet, barked, and let out a loud fart.

I started laughing, and when she saw me on the floor, she jumped on top and started attacking my face with her tongue.

"Winnie, off!" I said, except there were pizza remnants near my mouth so what it sounded like was Werwe Roff, and I got a lot of dog tongue in my mouth.

Like a lot.

A pair of shoes appeared, and Winnie was momentarily airborne before being set on the floor beside me. Larry stood over me, extending a hand. Reluctantly, I accepted, letting him pull me to my feet. Just like in the barn, he didn't take a step back. My body betrayed my mind and pressed against the length of him. Larry was comfortable, warm, and fit against me perfectly.

I wrapped my arms around him and he pulled me closer. We shared airspace and I forgot where I was. It was just me, Larry, and his very warm hands. Winnie yawned and I inhaled the man against me.

"Like the outfit," he whispered quietly against my cheek. "Maybe after you wash your face, I can show you what services I provide."

A shiver of excitement ran through my body, and I pushed him back. It was bad enough that I wanted the man, but now I was losing myself in his arms. Like some kind of romance novel heroine. Discreetly, I grabbed a sweatshirt and pulled it on so he couldn't see how excited I was at the idea. His eyes stayed where my nipples had been prominently displayed, and he licked his lips.

My mouth let out a groan and I slapped my hand over my face, turning away from the man toward Mo and Chris.

"Moonshine?" I prompted Mo, but she was staring at me and Larry with her mouth open. Chris was giving Larry a very male look and Mo had doe eyes. Chris turned his look to her and stroked a finger down her arm and then gestured toward us.

"This can wait," she said, jumping to her feet and trying to grab her purse. The bag tipped, a bag of cookies burst open, and Winnie tried to beeline for what looked to be dark chocolate, chocolate chip cookies.

"Sit!" I ordered and Winnie sat. Mo sat, Larry sat, and Chris looked uncomfortable since he was already sitting. I scooped up the bag of cookies and put them on the counter, taking one out and stuffing it in my mouth while I started a pot of coffee. The assembled party shifted awkwardly, uncertain if they were permitted to stand or not.

"Speak," I ordered the group while the coffee maker did its thing.

Mo opened her mouth, Winnie barked.

"I... I needed something to help me with the edible metallic paint. The store was out of vodka at a strength necessary for cake decorating. Too much water and the frosting will lose its integrity, so it has to be higher alcohol so the evaporation effect..." I held up a hand and she closed her mouth. "Right, so, I went to Mrs. Charles yesterday to see if she had anything stronger she could spare. She seemed nervous. Jumpy and all over the place, she wasn't even smoking. When I told her what I needed, she gave me four bottles and said not to mention where it came from. The bottles looked just as Chris described, but she wasn't excited about it and she couldn't give me the box fast enough. I tried to pay her, but she said she just wanted it out of her bar. I carried the box back to the bakery and a Ziplock of powdered sugar fell out. I called to tell her, to find out if she needed it, but she wasn't picking up. I put it on the shelf in my pantry beside the bottles, thinking I'd give it back if she missed it."

"She... didn't answer? Was her car still there?" I was thoroughly confused and not just because moonshine came with powdered sugar. Mrs. Charles was an old school booze hound. If she'd been alive during prohibition, she'd have probably had a speakeasy and made zero effort to conceal it when the bobbies showed up.

"Moonshine, Cyn. There was moonshine and you were drawing attention to the street!"

"Because a cop was outside my building? Mrs. Charles wouldn't have given a crap about Harpole... Daniel Kirby is in there nearly every day," I stared out the front window toward the eerily dark and quiet bar. "Why would Harpole be different? Was his car even marked?"

"Everyone knows Daniel's not a real cop," Chris said. I glanced back to see him give an apology look to Larry who grinned wide. It was common knowledge after all. My eyes drifted back to the street, the bar, and the window to the apartment above. No lights were on above, the curtains drawn, and a group of forlorn looking alkies stood lost in front of the building.

"Did anyone call her?"

Not waiting for an answer, I grabbed my phone and pulled up her number from the call history.

An automated voice immediately advised that the number was unavailable and not in service.

"That's weird..." I said, and double checked the call log. Maybe I'd dialed the wrong number... but no, the trash had come by at four forty-five AM. The number in question had called at four forty-seven. No other calls came in before or after that one until after the sun had come up.

I pushed the call button again and held my breath.

Still no answer, no voicemail and no service.

"Do you still have the bottles?" I asked Mo, pressing my face against the window.

"Yeah, at the bakery." She started to rise and then looked at me for permission.

"Can we go look at them?" I asked, stuffing my feet into shoes.

"Yes..." her voice was reluctant. "I mean, they're just bottles."

She stood fully, Chris and Larry followed suit.

"Bottles and powdered sugar," I said and she shrugged, leading the way to the stairs.

"Only a Ziplock bag's worth... I didn't open it. Maybe it's baking soda?"

Her assertion reminded me that I should show her some old school cop shows, because no way was it either but it would freak her out if I told her she probably had drugs in her pantry.

Best to tell her when she didn't think cops were under my bed.

We trooped down the stairs and across the street. We entered an alley between two buildings to see Mo's kitchen door propped open.

"Did you leave that open?" I asked, moving in front of everyone. Mo shook her head, and I peeked around the corner. The light from the display case was the illumination, the air silent and still. Crouching down, I crawled in on hands and knees, waving for the others to stay back.

Only Mo was smart enough to listen.

The two men were on all fours beside me, looking uncomfortable and confused.

"Why are we on the floor?" Larry whispered against my ear, and the tickle of his words made me grateful for my sweatshirt, but very aware my ass was in the air.

"In case someone was planning on shooting whoever came in," I answered, standing up and switching on the light. If anyone was in there, they'd already heard us. The kitchen was immaculate. All Mo's tools were clean, shiny, and standing at the ready. Disinfectant smell mingled with rising dough, and I was torn between inhaling deeply and gagging. I walked carefully through the kitchen, recognizing tools I'd never use with ones I'd only use in combat. Her expensive appliances were still in place; knives, cookware... even the cookies she put in a container were still on the counter.

"Is anything missing?" I asked, grabbing the container and pulling off the lid. Inside were red velvet frosted cookies that had the consistency of cake. I held one toward her for permission and she nodded.

"Not that I can see," she answered the first question and spun in a slow circle. I watched her inventory her kitchen with the same air a king would survey his kingdom. Mo walked toward the pantry, an alcove without a door just to the side of her walk-in oven. Though as far as I was aware, no one was actually supposed to walk into an oven, so I considered the name a carry-over from the fridge.

"Cyn!" she shouted and I ran, grabbing a knife from the counter on the way. I rushed into the room, prepared to defend and... I slipped on the floor, sliding from the entryway across the small room and running head first into the wall, dropping my knife along the way.

"Oh my god, are you OK?" Mo asked, appearing beside me and studying my skull for... who knows what. I wasn't a cookie or a cake so probably she didn't know either. "Are you... broken?"

"I don't think so. Why does it smell like..." I stopped and took a long sniff. "What is that?"

"It's the moonshine. Someone... someone dumped the moonshine," she was looking around and I saw the green glass fragments littering the floor. "Or... dropped it I guess."

Rising back to her feet, Mo surveyed the shelf and shook her head.

"The rest of it is gone, too." Her hands were frantically patting the shelves just over her head. Feeling guilty, I pulled myself to my feet and peered at the shelf four inches above her head. Chocolate, big empty space, and then containers of white powder.

"Was it in this big empty spot?" I was rubbing my butt, and the smell of alcohol was a little disorienting in such a small space.

"Yes!"

"Is this the powdered sugar she gave you?" I asked, poking the bag by the empty space that once held the alcohol. If the fumes from the floor were any indication, it was probably for the best that she'd never gotten around to serving it in the bar. Only Paddy could walk home after something like that.

"N.. no," she said, looking at the bags. She stood on tiptoes and nudged the bags around the shelf. Exasperated by her vertical limits, she climbed on the bottom shelf and stood at eye level with the empty space that previously held moonshine and "powdered sugar".

"Are you allowed to stand where food is stored?" I asked, starting to get light-headed at the smell.

"You can if you keep canned goods on the shelf where feet go and nosy friends keep their smug height advantages to themselves," she glared down at me, but there were two of her. "The powdered sugar is gone, too!"

"Cool, maybe we can talk out of the pantry?"

She wobbled on her shelf and nodded. Just in case, I pressed a hand to her back as she climbed down to keep her steady, but we'd probably both crash to the floor if she lost her balance. We both swayed and I nearly tossed my cookies, trying to nudge Mo through the doorway.

I looked down to avoid slipping, and my eyes caught on a large piece of the broken glass. It had the label Chris had mentioned, a crudely drawn Italian boot, half of the name of the bottling company, M.A.P. in Dayton, and the name of the alcohol itself.

"Non fa niente?" I said out loud and Larry tilted his head.

"It's alright? Who says their own product is 'alright' in its name?" he asked and I shrugged, curious when Dr. Larry Kirby had learned Italian. Carefully, I turned the glass piece back over and stared at a pattern of X's and Chevrons.

"Why..." I started, and then pulled out my phone. The very last picture I'd taken was of the note, stuffed into my shoe, and there in red garlic sauce was the same pattern. "What?"

I looked up, but Mo was wrapping her arms around Chris who was leaning against the far wall by the door. He was talking into his phone, presumably to some sort of law enforcement. Larry was tracking my every movement and I drank in his appearance. As though sensing potential, he leaned against a prep counter, crossing one leg over the other. His arms hung at his sides, inviting... a step closer... maybe another.

I froze staring at his shoes.

One toe was tilted up and I could see...

"X's and chevrons?" I asked, reaching down and grabbing his leg. He yelped in pain, and I decided it would be easier to look at his shoe off his foot. He reached the same conclusion, shoving my hand away and tugging off the sneaker. "Where did you get these?"

"The shoes?" he asked, rubbing his hamstring. "I ordered them online. Non-slip shoes designed for being on your feet all day."

"Why online?" I asked, comparing the shoe to the glass and the picture while he peered over my shoulder.

"The local store doesn't carry anything designed for multi-surface work. These are popular in hospitals, for custodial workers, in restaurants... anywhere fluid could theoretically coat a surface." He was giving me a sales pitch, but it didn't sound like he was getting a cut.

Mrs. Charles would definitely need slip-proof shoes in the bar. Though why not just ask Mo for the bottles back? She had to know Mo would think the drugs were powdered sugar, she could have just asked. Breaking in was just so extra... Mrs. Charles was too old and intoxicated to be extra.

"Anywhere advertised besides restaurants and hospitals?"

I was looking for any indication that the room had anything of interest to a boozehound that bought alcohol from possible drug dealers.

"They had a picture of a dude near a coffin," he mentioned and I lost focus thinking.

My eyes traveled again between the picture, the piece of glass and Kirby's shoe, his stocking foot, his pants, and landed on his bright eyes, searching for an answer to the question in my mind. Was M.A.P. Mi Asiago Prego? Was the restaurant selling drugs... was the mortuary?

How the hell did Vincenzo Lorenzo know Mrs. Charles and Retta?

Chapter Ten: After Dark

"**G**et that thing out of my back!" I hissed at Larry.

"It wouldn't be in your back if you'd turn around or get off," he hissed back and tried to adjust both of us.

"I just need another inch..." I moved a little to the left and tried to get a better angle. Larry had his hands on either side of my waist, trying to get comfortable but not succeeding. "This is stupid. Let's just go inside."

"No. That's illegal." He repeated for the tenth time, and I sighed.

"Seriously, why didn't you go home?" I muttered, leaning back against him. He was warm and comfortable, but I needed answers. "This isn't exactly 'monsters after dark', I don't need a diversion, and there won't be a show. If you want a show, you'll have to follow Chris and Mo back to their place."

Larry and I were in my Jeep, parked behind Casey's Bar. There was no light coming out of the bar and given that it was the primary beacon for the block, nothing was penetrating the interior either. Before Larry's brother could show up at Mo's, I'd slipped out the back and Larry had followed. After a brief debate, we'd gone to my car and moved it behind the bar as a compromise to Larry's "let's just go back to my place" and my "let's break into Casey's Bar and see if Mrs. Charles owns the same shoes as you".

Needless to say, neither of us was satisfied with this situation.

Larry had insisted on bringing a flashlight, but I refused to let him give away our position by shining it at the windows. He kept it in his pants... pocket, but now the stupid thing was trying to dislocate one of my vertebrae. I'd climbed into Larry's lap to get a better view of the upper windows as well as the police officers busy at Mo's. He had the perfect vantage point, and he couldn't care less.

"Do you think Mrs. Charles knows where Retta is?" I whispered, shifting in his lap to see what his brother was doing.

"I think I'm very aware of where *you* are." His voice was breathy and strained. I looked down and saw that my knee was inches from his favorite body part.

"Sorry," I moved my knee. "I'm going in."

"Cyn-" he started to argue but I'd already opened the door and climbed out.

Mrs. Gloria Charles, Casey's Bar owner and resident, had living quarters identical to mine only in structure. Her bar sat beneath her apartment with a back door that led to an interior apartment door and the rear of the bar. Unlike my office, she had a door between the rear entrance and the rest of the bar.

I pressed my ear against the door leading to the bar and listened.

Nothing.

A warm hand wrapped around my waist and tried to pull me back.

"Bad idea, Cyn. Bad idea," Larry whispered and I wiggled against him.

"Let me go or I'm taking you down, buddy," I snarled and he nipped the side of my neck. A moan escaped my mouth and he did it again. "Cheater!"

"Let me take you home, Cyn." His lips brushed my ear and my nerve endings sizzled. The stairwell was dark, and he felt good pressed up against me. I turned around and he moved me against the wall, full body pressed against mine, and slowly lowered his mouth until another breath would bring our lips together. "What do you say, Cyn?"

His hand slid under my sweatshirt, making slow circles on my ribs and my lady parts hummed with anticipation. My mouth watered and he moved closer, gently brushing a kiss against my lips. My hips brushed against... not his flashlight and my brain went strangely blank as I slid my hands into his pockets. He crushed his mouth against mine, searching every inch in massaging circles as his hands repeated the motion up my ribs until they were sliding over my breasts and I panted into his mouth.

"Come on, Cyn," he said, tugging me against him and toward the door.

"Uh-" something fell and rattled the floor above us, shaking me from my hormonal trance. Shoving Larry back, I took the stairs two at a time and pressed my ear against the apartment door. Another thud, softer, and I tried the door handle.

Locked.

"Let's go, Cyn," Larry said against my back and I shook him off. Assuming Mrs. Charles spent as much time drunk as she appeared to, there was probably a key around here somewhere. Reaching for the top of the doorframe, I mentally scolded myself. The woman couldn't manage that sober. On the ground were a doormat and a fake plant that had two-dozen cigarette butts stamped out in it.

The key was under the plant.

Slowly, I inserted the key and turned the lock, listening.

"Breathe quieter," I said to Larry and he poked me in the stomach.

"That's your breathing, and if you'd give me another five minutes-"

Another thud came from inside and I shoved Larry away, threw the door open, flipped on the light and tried to look everywhere at once.

"I know you're here!" I shouted, eyes too wide. My heart thumped loudly in my chest, and I wasn't sure if it was from the intruder in Mrs. Charles apartment or Larry's hand on my waist working its way lower in my shorts.

"This might work," his mouth was against my ear again.

A loud crash came from the bedroom and he moved away, cursing. Quickly, I grabbed a knife from the kitchen and pushed open the door to Mrs. Charles bedroom. It was over twenty steps across the room and it was alarming how much bigger her space was than mine.

So many more places for the bad guys to hide. I flipped on another light, knife hand at the ready.

"What are you... Oh my dog!"

Spinning around, I ran head first into Larry's chest and knocked us both to the ground. He was holding a spatula.

"A spatula?" I hissed at him and he shrugged against me.

"You took the knife."

"There were more knives!" I shifted against him and discovered where all his blood was as his eyes registered exactly how exciting he found this whole situation.

"And you said I wouldn't see any 'after hours' shows," he snickered, and I groaned into his chest.

"I hate you."

"I can change your mind," he wiggled against me and I licked my lips. Maybe he could until...

"Cynthia, what are you doing here?" my mom asked, and I felt all happiness leave my body as I squeezed my eyes shut tighter. I could not un-see her, naked, on top of my dad. Sex may have been ruined forever. I needed to go to a nunnery... or monk school. Larry shifted beneath me and I reconsidered.

Maybe just a nice warm shower with company would cure me.

"Cynthia, I asked you a question."

The warm feeling was gone again. .

"I was looking for Mrs. Charles," I spoke with my face pressed into Larry, feeling him shake underneath me. Nervous, I checked my hands, but I'd dropped the knife when I covered my eyes. I patted his torso and didn't feel any blood or injuries. He definitely had not been stabbed.

He was just laughing... at me...again

Now I needed my knife again.

"She's not here," my mother informed me, and I nodded.

"I can see that. Where is she?"

"Mrs. Charles is part of our..." she started and I slapped my hands over my ears, humming, while Larry laughed and shook both of us. He tapped my shoulder with his spatula and pointed over my shoulder. I shook my head and he pried my hands off my ears.

"Did she answer the portion of the question I wanted to know about?" I said to him and he nodded. "What was it?"

"She needed to go out of town but asked your parents to house sit," he summarized and I nodded.

"Is she still naked?" I whispered and he shook his head *no*. Feeling braver, I climbed off Larry and offered him a hand before I turned to look at my mother, clad in a partially sheer robe. "When did she ask you to house sit?"

Mrs. Charles's building was a full lot, whereas the building I lived in was a quarter of the library's lot. Her front door opened to a small entryway, then a kitchen, living room, dining room and a bedroom off to the left as you stared at the glass double doors leading to the upper balcony of the bar. Initially, it had been added just to give the old-time saloon look from the exterior, but one particularly profitable year before I was born someone made it accessible through a speak-easy style secret door.

"This morning, is that a problem?" She fisted her hands on her hips, and I resisted the urge to inform her that the movement negated the function of her robe. It was impossible to maintain eye contact and even harder to not maintain eye contact. This was my future. One day... many years from now... I would look exactly like that. Except taller, and then because I was taller would there be more effects of gravity?

My eyes darted to my mom's chest.

Please, gravity, no.

"Cynthia," her stern warning voice. "Is there a problem with us housesitting?"

"N-no. I just... we were worried. It's not usually dark in here," I stammered. "Shouldn't you house sit... your own house?"

"Heidi and her family are in our house, and it is date night." Very matter of fact. As though I was the one found naked in a place where neither of us lived. As though I should have assumed my parents would be getting jiggy in the apartment across the street from me, and where the one known resident hadn't been seen. "What, again, are you doing here?"

"Cyn needed to borrow some shoes," Larry said, nudging me toward the bedroom and its closet while carefully looking at my mom's left ear. He either also realized this was my future and didn't want to skip ahead, or he wasn't into the mommy daughter thing.

Maybe both.

"Mrs. Charles is six inches shorter than you!" she exclaimed, and I stomped on Larry's foot with my massive one. We would never wear the same size shoes unless her second career was as a circus clown. "What's really…"

The whole building shook, accompanied by the sound of something slamming closed… maybe slamming open?

The floor shook again.

The trap door!

I scrambled toward the window and tripped on my mom's discarded bra.

"Are you kidding me!" I cried out, but I righted myself and noticed the discarded weapon.

"What the hell, Cynthia!" my mom shouted as I went to the dining room double doors, scooping up the knife. The upper balcony of the bar was just outside her doors. The secret door was standing open, the chairs and tables that usually sat in a haphazard collection were neatly stacked. A shadow moved and I kept fighting the lock to push the door open.

"Wait!" I called, but the figure moved like smoke, grabbing the railing and lowering down to the wrap around porch on the ground level. I dodged the open door and the tables, but got snagged on an upright nail. I collided with the railing and hunched over, reaching.

My hand just barely missed taking hold of theirs. I watched and waited, watching them run down Main. It wasn't a big drop, so I swung my leg over the rail and dropped. I hit the ground on my ass, but jumped up and searched the inky blackness of night, not hearing so much as a footstep until a horn sounded. The figure had run up the road, and I caught sight just as the figure was sliding into the driver's seat of a four door, dark colored SUV. The engine rolled over and the SUV roared to life with the driver flooring it.

"Wait!" I called, but the blinding headlights flew past me and I saw nothing through the window but the flick of a lighter. Desperate to see something, anything, that would help me find Retta, I took off after the car at a full run, regretting not bringing Winnie. Knowing I'd never catch it, I shifted priorities to observe and report. The back plate was missing. Someone had taken off the insignia for the make, the model... it was an anonymous black SUV, completely untraceable, I thought.

Just before I went face first to the ground.

"What-" I started and then the smell hit. My shoe had caught on a trash bag outside the deli, sitting next to the overflowing and leaking dumpster. A leaking dumpster that had created a pool of meat juice and discarded deli salads. A pool I landed it in, soaking every stitch of clothing I wore in a briny concoction of meaty mayo rot.

"You OK, Cyn?" Larry trotted up beside me, but he didn't sound the least bit out of breath.

"Did you run here?" I asked, accepting his hand and limping to my feet. A large scrape covered my left calf and my right knee was skinned. My hands had road rash, and there would definitely be bruises in the morning. He slipped an arm around my waist and helped me walk back toward the saloon.

"What's that?" I asked, pointing to something on the ground. The SUV had been parked two car lengths from the saloon porch, and whatever was on the ground would have been right beside it. With Larry's help, I moved closer and stared down.

Being near the new A's Shoe store, it was covered in litter from the construction site, but this was different. The cigarette butt looked somehow cleaner and newer than the other debris nearby. Bending closer, I saw the cigarette butt had a neon red lipstick stain... just like all of the cigarette butts in the fake plant outside Mrs. Charles's door.

I crouched low, not sure what I needed to see but certain there was more. There needed to be more than just a ladies cigarette butt in the gravel dirt surrounded by... small X's and chevrons.

"That..." Larry nodded and started pulling out his phone. I reached for mine and accidentally activated the flashlight app, the light catching on something shiny beside the tire tracks left by the car. I walked over and stared down at a small, compact mirror with HHH engraved in fancy script gracing the cover. I turned back to Larry just as he ended his call. "I need to call... someone?"

"I called my brother." He lifted a shoulder without much commitment.

"Probably I should call Harpole and... you?" I was staring both at and through him as trash juice dripped down the back of my leg and sent my skin crawling in the forty-degree temperatures.

"Me... what?"

"Could you take Winnie to your house?" I pulled out my keys and he nodded, taking them from my hand with a little too much eye contact before leaning in. He brushed a kiss across my lips and then let out a breath.

"Only if you sleep there as well. I'd feel better if you were with me. Just... shower when you get in, please?" he asked, and I punched him in the arm. "Taking that as a yes."

Two hours later, I crept into Larry's house. Harpole hadn't answered and Kirby had decided to contact a person he knew "personally". She was tall, smart, and way too good for him, so I was pleased when she looked more interested in the evidence than the man. No one had wanted my statement, but no one had wanted me to leave.

They also had no knowledge of Henrietta being missing or a dead man in Dayton.

After being dismissed with a cursory "we'll look into it", I was turned loose.

I crept into Larry's bedroom, taking in the sight of yet another potential future. Winnie was paws in the air on Larry's bed, the man himself completely comfortable with a tail across his face. Heeding his advice, I bypassed the bed and stripped in the bathroom. Pile of meat trash clothes kicked into the corner, I showered and walked out in a towel.

I hadn't brought clothes.

A small pile sat on a chair by the door and I leaned in close. Larry had brought me underwear. I pulled them on and snagged one of his T-Shirts from a pile. It wasn't oversized and baggy like I'd hoped, but fit tight across the chest and looked mildly scandalous with the underwear he picked out.

Whatever, I thought. I was way too tired to care what I looked like. Larry looked more moveable than Winnie, so I shoved in next to him and she scooted at his nudges. He rolled over and pressed my back against him.

We were nestled together like three crunchy taco shells and I prayed to dog Winnie wouldn't fart and ruin it.

Chapter Eleven:
Sunday Mourning

With the sunlight warming my face and the warm man pressed against my back, it was the perfect morning.

Until the sound of a dog hacking drew me back to reality.

"What?" I asked, trying to drag myself to a seated position. Winnie yacked again, sputtered, and smacked her lips. The unholy terror was at the foot of the bed, paws wrapped around something white that she was chewing with the ferocity of a Kong. It was hard to make out, but it didn't look like a dog toy.

"What's that?" I asked, moving away from Larry, his three-day scruff and his bare-chest sleeping body with a sense of dread... Crawling to the edge of the bed, I stared at my dog sitting dead center amid chaos and destruction. "Seriously?"

A shoelace hung from the left side of Winnies mouth. Beside her were the remnants of a rubber sole, and she was working her way through shoe number two. Beside that were the shorts I had been wearing, ripped to shreds and just two threads left of my socks.

"Out!" I commanded, reaching for the shoe between her paws. She picked it up and ran.

"Winnifred Pupperson, get your fluffy butt back here!"

Her tan tail disappeared around the corner and a blanket was wrapped like a tentacle around my leg.

"I'm serious, you little monster!" I tugged my leg hard and connected with Larry. "Sorry!"

Free from the bed, I took off after her, stumbling into the doorway as my limbs woke up. She'd made tracks to the couch and was curled around the shoe defensively. Larry's couch was a hideous brown leather monstrosity and I quietly wished she'd have picked that over my brand-new shoes, but there was nothing to be done about it now. Sneaking up on her slowly, I held my breath hoping to not make a sound. I was inches away when she scented the air, turned her head and jumped. Leaping off the couch, she streaked past me into the kitchen, and her toenails clattered on the tile floor.

"Get back here!" I hollered and about-faced to follow her. She was between the fridge and pantry, laying down in Sphinx pose, shoe between her front paws, tail twitching.

"Winnie," I warned, taking my first step into the kitchen. Her tail thumped the ground. Another step closer and she leaned her head closer to the shoe. "Bring it here."

I took three more steps and slipped in a puddle she made beside a now empty water bowl.

"Argh!" I screamed, as I slammed my elbow into the cabinet on my way to the floor. In my periphery, I saw Winnie jump to her feet. She had the remnants of my shoe hanging from her mouth, tail wagging. Her lips were half parted, and her tongue was hanging out of her mouth, laughing.

"You're going to the pound," I told her, and she moved closer. "You're going to the pound, and I'm donating all of your treats to the dog rescue that you are not at because you are in the pound."

Winnie dropped my shoe on my face, licked my arm, and trotted back to bed as Larry appeared in the doorway. His eyes went a little wide, and I scanned my body to see if I was bleeding. I was not, but the shirt I'd commandeered had worked its way up to bra size and I was more or less naked on the floor of his kitchen.

"She booby-trapped the kitchen!" It came out as a whine, and I tried to look badass laying in a puddle of dog water to make up for it. "Care to join me?"

"I... uh... have a bed?" He offered, not taking his eyes off the paw print underwear he'd picked out for me. Winnie hacked again and we paused. Another hack followed by wheezing and Larry shook his head. Reluctantly, he tore his eyes away and went back into his bedroom. "I'll go check on the spawn of Satan. Maybe you should put on some pants."

Twenty minutes later, we were at his office.

"How did she swallow all *that?*" Larry asked with a mixture of amazement and alarm as he looked at the X-Rays of her abdomen. There was nearly a completely assembled toe of my sneaker on the screen. Beside it was something else too dense to be food and an unchewed shoelace.

"That's what *he* said," I snickered and watched his eyes flash heat. "Sorry. How do we get it out?"

He grinned and opened his mouth.

"The shoe, Dr. Kirby. The shoe, how do we get it out of the canine trash compactor?"

Larry went back to staring at the X-Rays, and shrugged.

"I guess we open her up and take it back." He answered, looking down at my stocking clad feet. "You might want shoes for this."

I looked down at the pink flying pig socks on my feet.

"Can I borrow some?" I asked, looking around for random shoes lying in his office.

He shook his head.

"Sorry BigFoot, nothing I have will fit you." He handed me his car keys. "Go back to your apartment and I'll call you when you can come pick her up."

"Don't you need help?" I asked, just as Brianne walked through the back door clutching coffee and wearing grey scrubs. Her eyes were only half open.

"I hate you both." She greeted the room.

"Have help," he said, and I stared at the pink-haired pixie with a nose ring inserted between her two nostrils. Despite her declaration of hate, her eyes softened when she saw Winnie on the exam table. Turning back to me, Brianne took in my shirt, socks and borrowed basketball shorts with a brow raise.

"Walk of shame?"

Dr. Kirby laughed and I shook my head in dismay.

"More like a walk of lame. The good doctor fell asleep on me, so I stole his clothes." I winked at her, and she gave me a high-five.

"Cyn," Larry warned, and I smiled pure sugar at him.

"Yes, dear?"

"If you keep this up, I'm taking my clothes back without waiting for you to get more," his voice held laughter, but his eyes were liquid fire.

"If you insist." I started to pull his shirt over my head while Brianne doubled over in laughter. He grabbed the shirt and pulled it back down over my torso. Despite the fact he was dressing me, his body seemed inclined to go the opposite direction if his pants were any indication.

"Go home, and if you're a good girl I'll bring you snacks, coffee, and..." he rubbed his pelvis against me.

I gulped.

"I definitely like the first two..." I stammered, staring intently at his scrub pants. They left so little to the imagination, and there was quite a bit to not imagine. Brianne's cackle brought me back.

"I'm going to go prep your dog for surgery. If you need a quickie, try and keep it down. Sabrina's Bull Terrier is cranky in the morning." She shot me a wink and strode to the back room where Winnie waited in twilight sleep. I'd seen the bull terrier resting in the back and I wondered who watched out for her at night.

"I have an overnight employee who hangs out with the animals," he said, reading my mind. "Some are more comfortable staying in the last place they saw their owners."

I nodded, wrapping my hands around his waist.

"So... that chair?"

Larry dropped his forehead to mine, wrapping his hands around me and pulling me close. Our eyes met and he kissed me, long and hard.

"I'm not quick," he sighed, and snaked a hand up the borrowed shirt for a quick grope. "Call you when she's ready."

I nodded and stared at his pants.

"My eyes are up here, Cyn." He snapped his fingers between us in irritation, but he was smiling.

"I've seen your eyes, this looks more interesting," I couldn't tear my eyes away from the string holding up his pants. It was so very easy to access all the treasures hidden beneath scrub pants. All men should wear scrubs. "Winnie's eaten shoes before. She'll be fine..."

My hand reached out, trying to get to the red lace on the green pants.

Larry swatted my hand away and dropped a kiss on my forehead.

"Out!" he pointed at the door, and I pouted. "I'll take care of you later."

"What will you bring me?" I asked, still staring. It was rather impressive.

"Ding dongs and di-" Brianne cleared her throat and we both flushed red. "Later."

He turned around and I stared at the rear view.

It was almost as good as the front.

"Didn't I sell you these shoes yesterday?" The cashier sneered, and I winced at his tone.

"Yup," I passed him my credit card, but he didn't swipe it.

"Where are the shoes I sold you yesterday?" he demanded, arms crossed.

"Half of the first shoe is on Larry's floor, and the other half is getting removed from a rogue retired canine," I answered, and picked up my card. The Square insertion device was at the top of the iPad register, so I just inserted the chip and waited. He raised a brown eyebrow, and I considered telling him he should dye them green to match his hair but then I remembered he was unpleasant.

"Larry Kirby? The veterinarian?" His face was so smug and know-it-all, I wanted to push a pie into it. The iPad chimed and I removed my card and collected my new shoes.

"Do you know any others?" I asked and tilted my head. Key lime pie for sure, I wouldn't want the pie not to match his hair.

"No, but quite a few women have known him." The green-haired man turned on his heel and sauntered away. I stuck my tongue out at his back and attempted to flounce from the store in a huff, but I hadn't had enough coffee to flounce or huff. I settled for slamming the door to A's Shoe Ambrosia, but it swung both ways and merely flapped in its frame.

Both symbolic and unsatisfying.

"First you can't slam a phone down when you're angry and now you can't slam doors. What is wrong with this world?" I shouted and caught the stink eye from a construction man. "What?"

He pointed down and my eyes followed.

My work boots were now coated in cement, and I sighed.

"If I give you money, will you go in there and buy me a new pair?" I asked, but he shook his head no. Tugging on one shoe, then the other, they came out of the cement, but I'd left a literal impression. "Sorry!"

The man growled, so I ran away like a chicken, leaving a trail of cement boot prints on the sidewalk. His creative swearing, though insightful, was best heard from a distance. I also had a sneaking suspicion he was planning on throwing something at me and a moving target was harder to hit.

When I was out of his reach, I turned around and studied my own shoe impression. I needed to work on the whole heel strike business because there was hardly any impression of my toe. The impression was also twice the size of the impression I'd seen near the cigarette butt last night, reaffirming that I had unnaturally large feet and the smoker was short.

"What are you doing?" a man demanded, and I blinked against the sun behind him.

"Tracking," I answered Daniel Kirby, and he knit his brows together in confusion.

"Those are your footprints," he scolded. "In cement."

"Yup, I'm trying to find myself," I nodded sagely and stepped around him. "I'm also trying to find two missing women and dancing corpses... or imaginary corpses... or money. If Retta were here, I'd ask her but she's part of the first group. So if you'll excuse me, I have very important work to do."

I tried to scoot around him but he got in my face.

"You need to stay out of police investigations." He had gone red and snarly. I wanted to offer him a cookie or something like I give Winnie when she gets hangry. "What were you doing in Mrs. Charles' apartment last night? Why is your Jeep still parked behind it?"

"Because I took a ride from your brother, Daniel." I shoved him out of the way and proceeded up the street. At the last second, I called over my shoulder.

"Which reminds me, his car is in my garage, if you know what I mean, but we both know it's there. Definitely not stolen!"

I waved goodbye as he slapped his hands over his ears and started humming. An interesting response from a man whose brother supposedly gets around. My smile faded as I considered what the green-haired man had said.

Was Larry just looking for another lay? Was I looking for another lay? If you lay down with dogs and don't get fleas, does that just mean the dogs are excellent bathers?

My face slammed into something solid, and I stumbled backward as I stared at Mo's bakery door. Pushing with my hand, it refused to yield again.

Mo's bakery was locked at 9AM on a Sunday.

The world was coming to an end.

Wondering if it was a body snatcher's deal, I cupped my hands to look through the window. No coffee in the machine, no pastries in the case... nothing.

The world had already ended.

This was not a body snatchers situation. Mo would have made coffee if the world hadn't ended.

The phone in my pocket alerted, and I answered it without checking.

"Cyn! Where are you?" Mo wailed and I winced at the volume of her voice. Then she sniffled and I braced for tears.

"At the bakery. Where are you?"

"At home," her voice sniffed.

"Are you... alive?" I hated when people cried on the phone... or in front of me... or near me.

"Yes... but..." something fell in the background and she sobbed, thick and wet into the phone.

Sounded like a break-up. A break-up calls for coffee, doughnuts, ice cream, a shovel and a burning pyre.

"I'll be right there."

Armed with coffee, ice cream, and doughnuts, I managed to make it to Mo's in under 30 minutes. She lived in a cottage outside of town, surrounded by more greenery than the local botanical garden. Looking through her window, you could expect butterflies, hummingbirds, and the sideways eyes of old men who thought she wasn't "tending to her lawn". They wouldn't dare ring her bell and say something, however, since her front door was nearly invisible in the foliage, and braver men have perished trying to find it.

Her elusive front door was unlocked and partially ajar, so I nudged it open with a toe and called out.

"Mo? Mo!" I could hear tears and sobbing from the living room to the right, so I veered that way. As I got closer, I heard the murmur of a male voice mixed in with the tears. I made a pit stop at the kitchen to dump my load of feel-good foods and check for witnesses. victims or possible body disposal locations.

Man had some nerve sticking around after what he did.

I stormed into the living room, trying to stuff a whole doughnut in my mouth, arms at the ready. Mo was in the fetal position sobbing into her knees while Chris crouched beside the couch and tried to soothe her. Every time he reached for her, she smacked his hand aside.

"Move away from Mo," I said at the same time she bellowed.

"Don't touch me, you traitor!"

I grabbed Chris's arm and pulled him away from my childhood friend. He looked to be in agony more than satisfied... strange man.

"You're dead to me!" Mo continued and Chris flinched visibly, eyes wild and panicky.

I narrowed my eyes at him, immediately taking her side.

"If you're dead to her, there's no reason for me not to make you disappear in less than mysterious circumstances," I dug my fingers into his arm and searched the immediate area for weapons. Mo was a chef, so there were bound to be some inventive tools of torture lying around. There was a 50/50 chance I'd have the opportunity to try some of the more creative "self-defense" tactics I'd learned in the Army with items never designed for the purpose.

"Any last words?"

"You're crazy! Both of you!" he shouted and I rolled my eyes.

"Obviously. Now... I believe I'll remove that first," I eyed his pants. He covered himself and then thought better of it and shoved me away.

"I asked her to be exclusive!" He was waving his hands in a better impersonation of Italian than the cuisine I'd dined on.

"You..." my brain froze and I stared at my hand. "But that's... Mo?"

She was wailing like a lunatic and I could only deduce he was correct. Nothing says over the edge like having a man you're attracted to ask you to be his one and only.

"If we're exclusive, he'll change his mind and leave me!" My eyes drifted back to him and he was stuck for something to say.

"Mo, do you want to be exclusive with Chris?" I felt like a kindergarten teacher trying to talk to teenagers in the 1950s who just learned what "go steady" meant.

"He doesn't mean it! He's just asking so when I say yes he can say he doesn't and leave me!"

Even though I thought that was nuts, bless his heart, the man tried to reason with her.

"But I'm already exclusively with you!"

"Does *everyone* know that?" she simpered and I smelled a plot.

"Everyone who matters. But if you're worried, we can have a really big party and announce it to the whole town!" Mo's tears had dried up. The cat got her canary and I was a big stupid pawn.

"Can I bake a really big cake shaped like swans with their necks wrapped together?" She was regaining her composure, and I was trying to give him the axe gesture without her seeing.

"You can bake anything you want, baby." He was smiling and I just shook my head. Chris was officially an idiot.

I trekked back to the kitchen, grabbed a chocolate dough-nut, put it in a bowl, and scooped ice cream on top. Then I grabbed her coffee and dumped sweetened condensed milk from her fridge into the cup and walked back into the living room. I gave Mo the coffee, but Chris the junk food. He was going to need counseling for this but all I had was doughnuts.

"First of all, NEVER say she can bake anything. That is dumb and how I ended up eating peppermint glazed doughnuts for a month," Chris scrunched his eyebrows together and I gestured for him to take in the sugar while he could. "Second, she took out a newspaper ad last week declaring you off-limits."

Mo drank her coffee, smiling wickedly.

"Third..." I didn't have a third so I smacked him on the back of the head and he snorted out ice cream.

"Was I just played?" he asked, and I nodded.

"Like a hand-cranked accordion monkey," my brain questioned the analogy along with Chris. My mouth opened but I was saved when *Old McDonald Had A Farm* erupted from my pocket.

"Hey, Larry," I said without looking at the screen.

"Are you sitting down?" he asked quietly, and I pulled the phone away to stare at it. What the heck was up with people today and their drama.

"Spit it out, Kirby," I scolded him, and he took a sharp breath.

"I sewed Winnie up, but there was more than a shoe in there. I found the underwear you were wearing yesterday, half a pair of jeans and something that looks like the plastic tab that keeps coffee fresh. There was too much for the small incision I had planned. She's going to have to wear a cone," I could hear him wince over the line and my mouth worked in horror.

"But, the last time..."

"I know, but we had to widen the incision to get it all out. There's no alternative." My voice was strangled in my throat. Not the cone. Winnie was an asshole with the cone. She'd run it into my leg, into the wall... she even peed on it once.

While it was on her head.

"OK," I sighed, mourning the impending suffering we'd both endure in the weeks to come. "I'm on my way back."

Staring at the doughnut box on the counter, I heard rapid breathing from the other room and decided my need was greater. The ice cream wouldn't last so I put that in her freezer and turned on the coffee pot.

She was probably going to need caffeine for round two.

"I'm taking the doughnuts!" I called without looking into the room and made it back out to my car without any new naked visuals of people I love. I was a mere two miles from Dr. Kirby's Critter Care and I stuffed a doughnut in my mouth before turning the engine over and making the short drive. With a conscious effort, I tried not to imagine what I'd say if I'd been Mo and Chris had been...

But I didn't have a Chris, so I ate another doughnut.

Brianne was standing out front, vaping something and looking exhausted.

"You know that can kill you, right?" I told her, passing over a doughnut.

"You know these can, too?" she countered, and I tapped the doughnut I pulled for myself against hers.

"To dying happy then, I guess," and went inside.

"Larry?"

I heard two loud barks and a man cry out.

"Damnit, Winnie!"

Following the voice, I walked into Larry's office to find him flat on his ass against the desk with my 90-pound monster attempting to maul his face with her cone. Though her teeth couldn't reach his face, it was probably the visual that plagued the nightmares of victims past.

"Winnie, come!" She turned rapidly and started bounding toward me, nose and eyes trained on the pink box in my hands.

"She can't have any food!" He warned and at the last second, I managed to transfer the doughnuts to Larry before Winnie could devour the box. He climbed to his feet, dashing around his desk to create a physical barrier between him and the beast.

"Go lay down!" I instructed.

She whimpered.

"Well, when you eat not food, you can't eat actual food for a while. You need to be more discerning about what you put in your mouth." She grumbled and threw herself to the floor in protest. "Let that be a lesson, young lady."

Larry was smiling at us from where he sat behind his desk.

"Are you more discerning about what you put in your mouth, Ms. Sharp?"

He had the doughnut box open and the sight of a man with doughnuts was almost too much.

If only he had coffee, I'd have been a goner.

Shrugging, I walked around to lean against the desk, facing him and plucking a sprinkle doughnut from the box. He took out a second one for himself.

"Problem, doctor?" I asked and he polished off the bear claw in two bites. I licked my lips, and he moved out of the chair.

"Not at the moment," he stepped between my legs, and I knew what I wanted more than a doughnut with sprinkles. I looked down... he was definitely on the same page.

"Can I help you?" I asked, setting the doughnut down as his hands looped my waist and he pulled my lower body against his very revealing scrubs.

"Yes."

He dropped his mouth to mine and our tongues touched. Exploring every inch of my mouth, he slid his hands up my shirt and ran his fingers over my very excited nipples. His pelvis ground against mine until I let out a needy moan and clutched the front of his shirt.

"Yes." I whispered and then my shirt was gone. His mouth replaced his fingers, and I took a sharp inhale at the warm flicks of his tongue. My nails raked his back through the scrub top, and he pulled his mouth away just long enough to ditch the top so I could explore for myself. We joined again at the mouth, and I grabbed the string on his pants... Finally, someone was going to finish what he started.

On a desk no less, cross that off my list.

His desk phone rang.

"Ignore it," I said into his mouth. My cell joined his in ringing.

"Ignore it," he echoed, and I slipped my hands down the back of his pants, the phones rolling to voicemail. My hands grasped his very firm...

Both phones started ringing again and I nearly cried as he stepped out of the V of my legs, tying his pants.

"It's just Joseph." I knew the ringtone I'd programmed for him and pulled the device out of my unfortunately still on pants. Larry kept going to his phone. "Yeah?"

I spoke into the phone as Larry answered his own.

"Cyn, it's Betty," one of the farm hands said and I felt my heart sink as I pictured the Jersey cow I favored at the dairy. I'd met Larry again when he was treating her for an infection. In the three months I'd been home, she'd had several infections, each taking longer and longer to heal. The farm hand must have been on the phone in Joseph's office, and while I knew the voice, I couldn't picture the face.

"Another infection?" I asked, grabbing my shirt from the floor. Watching Larry, he was looking for his shirt as well. Strong probability he was getting the same news. "I'm on my way. Is the calf done nursing?"

"Cyn... she's passed," he said, and my world tilted sideways.

"But on Friday..." I stammered, watching Larry set down his phone. "On Friday..."

The farmhand apologized again, my vision going fuzzy with the sensation of falling.

"She..." Larry gently removed the phone from my hand and bid the farmhand goodbye.

"On Friday..." I tried for the third time and he just pulled me against his chest where I buried my face and cried.

"Betty..."

"I know, Cyn," he whispered through his own tears. "I know."

Chapter Twelve:
Two Funerals and a
Ceremony

I t's not unusual for the end of January to see a snowstorm or two, but the rain was unrelenting. The sky had opened as we walked out of the veterinary office and drove in silence to my apartment. Larry waited while I grabbed things for Winnie and changed into clothes for the farm. My boots, completely solidified in concrete, were sitting by the exterior door and needed to be tossed. I pulled out the new sneakers and put them on, stepping into the pouring rain and staring up at the sky.

"Come on, Cyn," Larry whispered from next to me and I nodded. We got in his car with Winnie and drove to his house next. Betty had already been moved, but we wanted to say good-bye and check on her calf. He was old enough that he should be OK, and cows generally allow other offspring to feed from them, but we needed to see Ronnie for ourselves.

Needed to see where she'd died.

Winnie walked into Larry's and curled into the densely cushioned dog bed. I stared at her cone and her lolling tongue, remembered that she'd just had surgery, and sat beside her to give her a hug. Her nose worked against my pants, and I tried to keep the tears to a minimum. She wouldn't get an infection. She'd be OK... wouldn't she?

Larry moved quickly, ditching his scrubs for jeans and a flannel. He pulled a raincoat from a mysterious closet and tossed a second one toward me.

"Is Winnie going to..." I choked on the words and he pulled me up from the floor into a hug.

"No, Cyn. She is young, strong, and healthy." His voice was as reassuring as his hand that moved in circles on my back. "Do you want to stay here with her?"

I shook my head no, and nudged him away while I wiped off my face. Picking up the jacket he'd tossed me, I slid it on over my hooded sweatshirt and looked down at the logo for his vet center.

"Who named your practice?" I asked, grasping for a new subject as I stared at the childish name.

Larry remained silent, and I looked up to see he was still in the room.

"We should..." he started.

Guilt crossed his face and then embarrassment. "Ex-girl-friend?"

"Not exactly..." he pulled on his boots and grabbed his medical backpack.

"Care to elaborate?" I asked, remembering the words the green-haired shoe salesman had spoken. The green monster in my belly now had respect for his hair. Whatever Larry and I were, she'd always be the woman who named his practice. Whoever *she* was. Maybe it was a he, I hoped. I'm never jealous of men on the other team.

"Not really," he held open the front door and I stared. It was definitely a *she,* and now I wanted Winnie to wake up and take a bite out of his very firm... "Can we not talk about this right now? You look... murder-y."

"Why would I be murder-y? It's not like we're a *we.*" My stomach sank as he didn't disagree. "Right... whatever. Maybe I should just..."

"Amber named the practice," he muttered, and I quit breathing.

"You dated Amber!" My voice rivaled Mo's wail and there was no way to stop it. "You put *that* in *her*?"

I gestured to his masculine bits and he covered them instinctively.

"No!" But he was feeling guilty about *something.* "Her family fronted the money so that I could purchase it, and she made him stipulate that she got to name it in the lease... or loan..."

"The Mayor of Cartersville, Amber Carter's disturbingly creepy, town founder dad, owns your practice?"

"No... kind of. It's a long-term loan without interest." His face was crumbling the longer we stayed on this topic. Amber Carter, my personal tormentor from kindergarten through 12th grade, the woman who tried to marry a fake count and had her cake demolished by Winnie, owned Larry and his livelihood. "When she came to present the sign for the front, she presented herself as well. She'd been watching old movies and had this whipped cream bikini idea..."

My hands covered my ears and I hummed *Whistle While You Work* from Snow White.

"I can't believe you would..."

"I didn't, Cyn. I swear!"

Winnie let out a bark and I immediately dropped to check on her. This was not happening. I was not jealous, we were not having a fight. I was just... emotional. Winnie closed her eyes and I turned to look at the confused man in the door.

"Maybe we should talk about this... later," I started and his face crumpled. "It's just..."

My phone alerted me and I dropped my gaze. The message was from Detective Harpole.

GH: *Andre Gatton funeral tomorrow, noon.*

Me: *I'll be there.*

GH: *Without the gas machine please.*

It was not a question and I scoffed. If Winnie weren't recovering from surgery, I'd bring her just to spite him.

Stuffing the phone back in my pocket, I looked up to see Larry's face. He looked... sad.

"What?" I asked, moving through the doorway being very careful not to touch him. I may never be able to touch him again until he was decontaminated like a level three hot zone worker.

"Was that..." he looked at his shoes and shook his head. "Never mind. It's none of my business."

"Was that who?" I asked, opening the passenger door of his truck, and climbing in. He walked around and slid into the driver's seat, hand not completely steady.

"It's fine, I don't need..." I gave him my best death glare, and he let out a long breath, eyes glued straight ahead, unblinking.

"Was that... Cruz?" He wouldn't look at me, but every inch of him was waiting for my answer. My stomach did a strange flutter. I'd forgotten about Cruz, he'd slipped from my mind like he'd slipped from my apartment. There had only been Larry and his scrub pants.

Now that he'd brought him up though...

My face flushed and I turned away.

"No, it was Detective Harpole. I have to go to a funeral tomorrow." I buckled my seatbelt and felt him relax beside me. I was not relieved. I was so far from relieved I was... struggling to find words. Mo had Chris and I had Winnie. I didn't need him... or Ian... though Larry saved Winnie. He'd cared for her and held me while I cried for Betty.

He was here, where I needed him.

Then I remembered he'd been in the same room as an un-clothed Amber and I growled.

"You're thinking about the whipped cream bikini, aren't you?" He reached a hand over to push the wet hair from my face and pull a ball cap onto my head. His eyes never left the road, but his hand didn't seem to need them. "I'd be happy to wear one for you if it'd make you happy."

A laugh escaped before I could stop it and he took my hand.

"One day, Cyn, you and I are going to finish what we start-ed, and we won't need anyone else again," he spoke quietly...

tenderly... I shuddered. He huffed out a breath. "You're... it for me."

"Because I'm a praying mantis who will rip off your head and eat it once I finish?" I smiled sweetly and he squeezed my hand. My pulse picked up, he wasn't taking the bait and there was not enough air in the car. What did he mean, I was it? Like hide and go seek? "So... Chris and Mo are having an exclusive dating party."

Crap, no, it sounds like I want that.

"It's just so she can bake a cake though. I like ice cream, do you like... ice cream?" I was now sweating through the hoodie and my hands were clammy. I tugged my hand free from his and wiped it on my pants. "Oh look, cows."

"Chicken," he chuckled and pulled into the farm.

"Where? I hate chickens. " I looked around in dismay.

"Sitting on the seat next to me."

I really hate it when he's right.

Ronnie was fine. He'd been fed and was resting happily with the other calves. If he noticed his mom was gone, it wasn't nearly with the same sense of loss the rest of us felt. The farm hands had placed flowers in Betty's stall and though no one spoke, we all stood there remembering her. I could picture her eyes closing as I sang the Taylor Swift song that shared her name.

Betty I was riding on my skateboard when I passed your house, it's like I couldn't breathe.

The worst thing that I ever did was what I did to you.

I swiped at a tear.

"Do you think there's a heaven?" I asked no one in particular. There were four farmhands in the stall, in addition to Joseph, Larry, and myself.

Joseph shrugged and let out a low whistle.

"If there is and there are cows there, they are probably real mad about all those cheeseburgers we eat," he said and I winced. "This is why one should not become emotionally invested in livestock. Between the cows, pigs, and chickens, it would be real great if we all just become worm food or something."

Then he walked back to his office in the rain and shut the door.

"That was cheerful," Larry commented, slinging an arm around me. "Can I buy you a bacon cheeseburger?"

My stomach rumbled.

"Too soon, man. Too soon." But we did need to eat, and the diner was the only place in town to get decent food unless one knew how to cook.

I did not know how to cook.

"We need a taco truck in this town," I grumbled, face palming when I remembered what carne asada is.

"Who in this white-ass town would run the taco truck?" Gerald laughed, and I looked over at the trim African-American farm hand. His usually jovial face was a shadow of his usual humor.

Everyone loved Betty.

171

"Maybe we could coax someone from Southern California to move here?" I offered and he shook his head.

"Too cold and not enough traffic." His coloring improved so I tried again.

"Or... Texas? When was the last hurricane? People probably want to leave there."

"And leave the Cowboys and Astros?" His smile was at full wattage, and I felt my face form one as well.

"I don't think Texas has real Mexican food, anyway," Larry joked, and Gerald gave him fist bump. Having spent my K-9 training days at Lackland Air Force Base, I couldn't argue but it didn't change my point. Someone needed to build a taco house somewhere so my miserable, lonely self could have a damn taco.

Cold and wet, the three of us started to move to the parking lot.

Except only two of us moved.

I was stuck.

"Help?" I said, somehow suctioned into the mud beside the barn. I tugged my left foot and then my right, but I didn't get anywhere. Larry and Gerald came over and looked at my feet. My new, white sneakers were in two inches of mud and I was sinking.

"We were all standing here," Gerald said, struck dumb by my plight. "How did you..."

His voice trailed off. He and Larry each took an arm and tugged, setting me free and leaving my new shoes behind.

"Wait! My shoes!" I reached for them but the rain dissolved the mud around them and they sank like the Titanic.

"Guess we need to hit Main St." Larry laughed, turned around, and pulled me onto his back. My legs wrapped around his waist, I looked wistfully toward the shoes I was leaving behind.

"Today sucks," I grumbled into his neck.

"I know what'll cheer you up." His voice was smiling and he managed to get the truck door open without dropping me. I stretched a foot toward the car, but he kept his hands firmly beneath my thighs until he was sure I wouldn't fall.

"Time machine?" I offered and he leaned over me to buckle my seatbelt.

"Chili," he smiled and my stomach grumbled again. "With cheese and... more cheese..."

My mouth watered and I contemplated begging.

"Where?"

"My house," he said, and closed the door.

The Winnie alarm went off promptly at 7AM.

I was once again in Larry's bed and once again, nothing had happened. I was wearing his pajamas, again. I was touching his bare chest, again. He was very excited for the morning, again.

Yet still, nothing.

"Why do we keep just sleeping together?" I asked, nudging him awake. "They might take your man card if you keep this up."

"Uhn," he muttered against my ear and pulled me back against him. "Five more minutes."

We hadn't made it to the shoe store. Food had taken priority and we'd come straight to his house. He prepped the chili, I raided his cabinets, and we gorged ourselves into a coma watching random episodes of TV shows that popped up in the suggested episodes box. We'd stumbled to the bed, exhausted and full, just before midnight and crashed into sleep. Sleep that was not aided by physical activity.

Le sigh.

Taking stock of the night, it was probably one of the best non-dates I'd ever been on. We'd laughed and shared snacks, never once feeling guilty or awkward if our hands met in the popcorn bowl. He'd put my wet and muddy clothes in his washer, my dog was getting round the clock medical care, and I was getting... nothing.

"You're not getting 'nothing'. " I jumped when I realized I may have said the last part out loud. "You got chili."

He stretched his neck to take a nibble of mine and I had a hot flash.

"Chili is better with hot dogs." My voice came out pouty, and I face-palmed. "This is ridiculous, we are adults."

"We are adults," he confirmed, eyes still closed.

"Adults can do adult things, and we don't need permission."

"Well..." he started, and I poked him.

"Well, what?"

"Without permission, it *is* a crime." His face was in a wide grin. "But if I have your permission..."

Winnie howled and I remembered she wanted food.

"Is she allowed to eat?" I reluctantly pried myself away from the man and stretched. It was silent from the bed and I turned to look at Larry for an answer.

He was asleep again.

"Boiled chicken and white rice it is," I decided for myself and went into the kitchen to make the bland dog food diet delicacy.

"Bon appetit," I said, placing the dish in front of Winnie and opening my phone. My email box was overflowing with spam, so I decided to clear it out while Winnie devoured every last grain of rice. I searched and checked all the boxes for stores that didn't have locations in or delivered to this state. Then emails from the stores I only shopped when I was drunk, it was best to get rid of those while sober because I'd never find them inebriated. Then... an email from Ian Cruz.

Hey Cyn,

I'll be home soon.

Ian

I stared at the email, reading and re-reading the single line. He signed it Ian, had I ever called him that? Where was home? His home? My home? His Army home? My brain worked, my body froze, and my dog shoved her cone into my leg.

"What does he mean, Winnie? Where's home?" I asked her, still staring at the email.

"Home is where your dog is," Larry advised, walking into the kitchen. I stuffed the phone into the pocket of my shorts, that were really Larry's, and tried to look innocent. I was not thinking about another man in his kitchen. My stomach lurched, and I wondered if it was too late to run out the front door.

"Why do you look guilty?"

"I finished the rest of your chicken," I lied and he shrugged.

175

"Store is full of chicken," he scratched his chest and moved us toward the counter. "You know what's not sold in stores?"

"What?" My heart was pounding.

"Something to wear to a funeral." He grabbed the coffee from behind me and moved away. "Do you have anything to wear to a funeral?"

"Crap," I hung my head and my phone rang. "Hey, Mo."

"Cyn! We're getting married this weekend!" she squealed, and I pulled the phone away from my face.

"We are? I didn't get you a ring unless doughnuts count."

"No, me and Chris!" her voice was reaching octaves only Winnie could hear, and the dog chose to leave the room instead of listen.

"You... what?" I guzzled more coffee from the pot I didn't remember making. There was definitely a tear in the space time continuum and I've fallen into a wormhole. "You just became exclusive.... yesterday. Are you pregnant?"

Larry snorted into his coffee, and I watched as some dripped from his nose.

"No, geez! It's not a real wedding. It is a commitment ceremony to celebrate our exclusivity, but we are going to make it a pretend wedding! Won't that be fun?"

"Are you... high?" I asked, confused and disoriented. The woman had fallen off the deep-end manipulating the man into convincing her to have an extravagant party for cake, and now she really wanted to show the world exactly how nuts she was?

"Swan cake, Cyn! I get to make a four-foot high swan cake!" she squealed. "Aren't you happy for me?"

"I am if there's cake," I reached for a newspaper on Larry's counter. I had vague hopes that the world outside Sweet Pea would suddenly make more sense than the world within it.

Personally, I would not be excited about assigning myself a crazy amount of work for a cake. I would be happy to just bake and then eat said cake, but maybe *I* was the weird one.

It was the local paper, published in Yellow Springs, that showed up once a week with news normal people had already read on the internet. On the front page was a beefy man beside an image of a younger boy in front of Sweet Pea Municipal School District, the massive monstrosity that housed all the classrooms for the town's children in a series of prison style structures.

The article read "In Loving Memory" at the top and my eyes stopped on the name.

Andre Gatton.

"So will you?" Mo asked, but my eyes were scanning the article. Graduate of Sweet Pea, served in the Coast Guard... well-loved and would be missed. "Cyn!"

"What? Yeah, of course," I said and she squealed in delight.

"Great! I can't wait to go shopping for your dress!"

"My-" the call ended and I set down the phone, scanning the article. A small quote toward the bottom caught my eye and I barely noticed when Larry came up beside me to read over my shoulder.

"He was a loving son and a wonderful soldier. If only they'd treated him better," his mother, Gloria Charles, 68, said of the deceased Gatton. "I will honor his memory."

"What's this, Cyn?" Larry asked, hesitating and showing me my phone. I looked up at him.

"Mrs. Charles was the dead man's mother." He was unfazed, still holding my phone. "Do you think..."

My voice trailed off as I saw what he was looking at. The email had still been open on my phone when I put it in my pocket. His eyes went from the screen to my face and then back to the phone.

"Care to explain?" he asked, voice mirroring mine from the day before.

"Spam bot?" I shrugged, and the green monster bubbled behind his eyes.

"Try again," he suggested, and I took the phone from his hand.

"I have to go to a funeral," I walked to the front door and clipped Winnie's leash to her collar. "I'm taking Winnie to my apartment because you are out of chicken."

I grabbed the bag that held both of our overnight things and stepped out the front door.

"Forgetting something?" Larry asked, taking in my form.

"Your clothes belong to me now. Buy new ones," I said, slamming the door.

I was halfway down his walk when I realized I had no shoes.

Chapter Thirteen: Rest in Pieces

"D idn't you see the sign?" a green-haired man said from behind the counter and I looked back at the door.

"No?" I asked, quickly grabbing a third pair of the shoes and a replacement pair of work boots while Winnie sat patiently just inside the door. With her cone of shame and heavily medicated state, she looked like a sad drooping flower. If there were any way for her to look more pathetic, it would involve music and cages.

"It says no shoes, no shirt, no service," his haughty voice grated.

"I'm wearing a shirt!"

He stared at my feet, arms crossed.

"Socks are like shoes!"

He blinked at me.

"Take my money, I'll put on these shoes, and then you can ring them up," I suggested, placing the boxes on the register. The door opened behind me, but the green-haired man didn't bother to acknowledge the new customers.

"No shoes, no service," he growled, and I picked up a sneaker.

"I have a shoe!"

"It's not on your foot!" he shouted back at me.

"Take my money and it will be," I countered, trying to insert my card into the iPad. He put his hand over the port.

"No. I'm not selling you any more shoes."

Then he picked up my boxes and put them behind the counter.

"You can't refuse to sell me shoes! This is a shoe store! The only shoe store... seriously Green Bean..."

That was not the best word choice, because then he pulled out a microphone and paged the store manager.

"Fine, whatever," I stood there with my arms crossed and waited for Stella to appear, sell me shoes, and ask after my mom.

Except it was the 20th.

A's Shoe Ambrosia was Amber's Shoe Ambrosia I learned as she teetered over on toothpick stilettos. It was still pouring rain, but she had on a hot pink crop top and a jean skirt that didn't quite cover both of her butt cheeks. The crop top did manage to cover her nipples, but it was precarious and with every jostle I winced.

Someone that ugly on the inside had no business showing me that much of her outside.

"Ew, get out," she said, popping her gum.

"I need shoes. You're a business. Sell me shoes."

"No," she replied and pointed at Winnie. "Get that out of my store. It's a depressing lamp and is scaring my customers."

"What customers? The only person in here is me, and you won't sell me these stupid shoes!"

"My shoes aren't stupid; your furry monstrosity is stupid. She looks like something you'd decorate and bring to prom as a date." Amber snickered and the green-haired man put his hand to his mouth, making the universal "you just got burned" noise.

"Oohh!"

"Winnie is not..." I threw my hands in the air and walked back outside, stripping off my socks. My dog had been insulted, my feet were cold and wet, and now I had to walk home, barefoot, in the rain. Wasn't it bad enough to get a cryptic email, make a man jealous, and only get to have one cup of coffee? Will the day's horrors never cease?

I made it a single street in internal diatribe before a car pulled up beside me. It was a hideous blue classic, and I peered in to see Mr. Elmer Figs.

"Cynthia!" he said, opening the door. "Can I offer you a ride?"

"I'm almost home, Mr. Figs, but thank you," I spoke, looking at the two remaining streets until my building, with the enthusiasm I reserve for mandatory exercise.

"Would you like a ride?" he asked again, and I nodded.

"Yes, thank you."

Winnie hopped into the back seat, shaking her wet fur onto the cloth seats and I winced.

"Nothing new for Blu Belle here. Now, how much of a hurry are you in?" He looked a little too perky for a man driving in the rain. A man driving in the rain with a moldy brown sweater, a hideous color car, and a flair for the dramatics.

"Ummm... I need shoes."

"Got your shoes right here," he said, tapping a plastic bag with two cardboard boxes. "I just need your help for something real small and I'll get you home."

I glanced toward my building, wondering what horrors I'd committed to deserve this. Whatever this was, which still wasn't abundantly clear. I could walk. I could refuse the shoes and walk... except my feet were cold and slightly numb.

"I only need a couple of minutes," he continued and I shrugged.

Better to help a crazy man and get shoes than fight with one and get... Amber-ed.

"Sure," pulling my socks back on, I plucked shoes from the box and removed the stuffing. After checking traffic, Mr. Figs pulled from the curb and began to drive toward the small neighborhood where my parents lived. He was speaking at length about something related to studio satire, and I zoned out lacing up the sneakers.

Hopefully there would not be a quiz at the end.

My phone alerted me with a GIF from Larry.

"What is with you kids and your technology!" he started on a new tangent while I opened it.

It was a chicken clucking on top of a coffin.

"Now you have moving pictures in messages. We used to send letters, have to put words to our thoughts and feelings, and then wait weeks for the mail to be delivered..."

I replied with a cow and a poop emoji because GIFs were too much work.

"Buy a stamp, get an envelope."

I returned to my shoes, still nodding. I had them tied up and ready to go when the car stopped.

"We're here."

The blue car had parked in front of a house that was identical to my parents except for the color and the lawn art.

My parents' house had a small stoop, the Figs had a wrap-around porch. My parent's home was also two stories, except it was blue and my mother kept the American flag outside year-round, adding a celebratory flag next to it at each holiday. The Fig's house was beige, the American flag stood proudly on a pole in the front planter... with a casket on the lawn.

"Why? Just why?" I asked, walking toward it, mesmerized. It was a deep cherry wood, gleaming and flawless, that likely smelled like fresh wood when indoors. When Retta had described top of the line eternal slumber boxes, I bet they looked like this and I was suddenly envious of vampires.

"Wife gets things wholesale. Have to be shipped to the funeral parlors but when they get returned, anyone with access to a code can get one," he was moving casually toward the lawn ornament, and I just stared in wonder. Rain splattered against the box, beading and dripping off the surface without so much as a crater to collect the water on its surface.

"It's flawless," my voice was hushed and reverent. As though a dead body were inside and I might scare it awake. "Why on your lawn?"

"Can't really fit it inside."

"Are they waterproof?" It was my first death box up close and in person. They were both bigger and smaller than I'd expected. It was deep and wide, but not as long as I'd assumed. My hand swiped over the smooth surface, the metal rails making even drips on the ground underneath.

"They'd have to be, they're going in the ground," he rolled his eyes at me and I cocked my head to the side. "Isn't that obvious?"

"Aren't they made of wood to biodegrade along with the body?"

"Not anymore. They embalm bodies. Make everything nice and preserved for some time. Could get up and walk around and you wouldn't know except for the smell. Take a look inside," he gestured to the box.

Curiosity warred with good sense. I wanted to know what it looked like inside, but I also didn't want to open a death box. Especially a yard art death box of a man who thought his wife was haunting him... yet...

Proving again that if I were a cat, I would be dead, curiosity won.

Carefully, I opened the box hoping the interior was similarly weather resistant. The white lining was the softest silk, padded and folded over in precise spacing. The edges were perfectly sanded, stained and varnished so that the whole edge was smooth. I looked inside, and panicked.

Mrs. Figs was in the box. Her skin was grey and shallow, chest unmoving.

"What the hell!" I slammed the lid shut and turned back to the woman's husband, expecting him to point a gun at me and threaten me with death. Elmer Figs just stood there, rocking from his heels to his toes and humming the funeral march. "I'm calling the cops. You're insane!"

The lid flew open, and Mrs. Figs sat upright, eyes wide.

"I'm alive!" she screamed, and then I may have passed out.

"We're so sorry, dear," Mrs. Figs said, pressing a warm mug into my hand. Though I distinctly remember passing out on the lawn, I was now in an old-fashioned parlor with mounted hunting trophies and a record player. When I spotted the TV with bunny ears, I knew that I'd hit my head and was having a *Wizard of Oz* experience set in 1950s mid-west America.

There was no other explanation.

"We like to start Halloween decorating early and the casket was on sale for a steal." Mrs. Figs had been talking the whole time, but I was trying to figure out if the mustard brown flowers on the wallpaper were moving or just mocking me.

I nodded and took a long drink that burned all the way down.

"Geez, what was in that?" I stared at the half-empty cup and felt my stomach turn. I preferred to eat before I drank, but it would seem the Figs didn't care.

"Just a little whiskey. For your nerves," she said, patting my hand. Winnie was beside me, chewing on a toy that had been unearthed from the bowels of the creepy Fig basement. "Now, tell us. Were you scared?"

"No, I have narcolepsy," I said sarcastically and covered my mouth. "I'm sorry ma'am, I don't do well drinking on an empty stomach."

She patted my hand again and shuffled off to the kitchen.

"Mr. Figs said you get caskets wholesale? Where do you work?" I asked, polishing off my mug. I had to go to a funeral today and technically I might have work, but once the initial sting passed, this was pretty damn good.

"Yes dear," she returned to the room with a plate of cheese and bread. "I worked at a mortuary outside of Dayton for years as a grievance coordinator. Now, I mostly freelance and use my connections to benefit under-served families with quality eternal slumber places."

"Where did you work before?" I asked, eating the bread and cheese with only casual interest.

"Vincenzo's Mortuary. I stayed in contact with distributors, and would you believe that there were seven of those beautiful caskets paid for and returned?"

I choked on the bread and cheese in my mouth.

"Do you know Henrietta?" I asked, smacking my chest.

"Of course, dear, best beautician in the business. I always thought she'd marry her high school sweetheart, that Gatton bloke. Did you know they found him dead? Right next to that mortuary," Spoke into space but it felt like a punch to the gut.

"Did she tell you about the caskets?"

"No, an old friend, Vinny, did. He was a little put off by them and tried to get me to help him. When I called the distributor, he was very hesitant to speak on the subject." She was stirring another shot of whisky into her coffee, and I needed to go. "It was so strange that people will be so hush hush about caskets but scream that they'll murder you for cutting them off on the freeway. Vinny has always been a little... off. His poor wife should have cut and run while she could, but the woman already had two grown children so I guess she thought he was better than nothing."

I interrupted her before she took this as an invitation to bring up my own future and children.

"Thanks for... the drink and snacks. I've got to get going," I offered her a hand to shake and she shoved it away to go in for a hug.

"Of course, dear. Elmer will drive you home," and as though she summoned him, he opened the door.

"Stopped raining, great time to take you home, Cynthia."

Returning the cup and plate to Mrs. Figs, I followed Elmer to the car and helped Winnie into the back. If Henrietta was the high school love of Andre Gatton, son of Mrs. Charles... were the women... hiding out together? Why hadn't Retta mentioned any of this?

My work boots were the most waterproof footwear I had, so I paired them with slacks and a sweater in a somber dark grey. The outfit looked hillbilly in mourning, but it was the best I could do. My clothes wouldn't stop getting ruined... or forgotten at Larry's house.

Winnie was sprawled on my bed and half asleep, so I figured it was a good time to leave for a funeral.

Usually, my car is parked on a side-street between where I lived and the block with Mo's bakery. I arrived at the curb to find... not my car. Larry's truck sat there and I dug through my handbag. There were poop bags, Chapstick, pepper spray, and a wayward Oreo which I ate... no keys.

Sighing, I reached into my pocket for my phone. At this rate, I wasn't even going to know how to exhale normally.

"Looking for your keys?" Larry asked by way of greeting.

"And my Jeep. I'm staring at your truck, and I don't have keys to that, either."

"Your Jeep and all the keys are at my house. Meet you at your building in ten minutes," he said... and hung up.

"That was rude," I muttered but Winnie wasn't there to agree with me, so I trekked back to my building and sat outside on the curb. Almost immediately, Larry pulled up in his blue car and unlocked the doors.

"Am I borrowing your car?" I asked, confused.

"You're borrowing me and my car," he said, not meeting my gaze.

"Because?"

"I'm ransoming your Jeep," he declared, and I resigned myself to accepting the ride. The dead man might not notice if I was late to his funeral, but certainly everyone else would.

Whoever everyone else was, considering I didn't know the man.

"What do you need?" I buckled my seatbelt, but he waited until we pulled away from the curb to answer.

"I need a favor," he said to his steering wheel, not continuing for several minutes under the guise of driving in the rain. When we were past the last stop sign in town, he finished his request.

"I need you to come to dinner with me at my parent's house."

"Umm... why are you driving like you think I'll jump out of the car?"

"Because the dinner is for my brother's tenth wedding anniversary and he'll be there," he managed to turn a stop light green as we passed through Yellow Springs.

"I feel like there's more..."

"It's next Saturday."

"Get to the part you don't want to tell me, doctor." Sweat was dripping down my back, and I rolled down a window. His family was going to murder me. Or hand me over to the children... who would murder me. My body braced for impact when he opened his mouth again.

This is it, how our friendship ends. My life, threatened by his family.

"He told my mom we were engaged," he muttered on an exhale and I choked on my spit.

"What the... why?" I tried to breathe around the burning of trying to repurpose my saliva as air.

"I don't really..." I interrupted Larry before he could finish.

"Is it because I told him your car was in my garage suggestively? Because that could mean anything! It didn't have to be a euphemism!"

"You told him what?"

"He was annoying me." My voice was rising in panic. His mom was the church board director and a force to be reckoned with. No way was I lying to his mom after I put her sister-in-law in jail and punched her son in the face. If there was an afterlife, it would guarantee a one-way ticket to the bad place and I had enough red in my ledger. Sweat soaked through my top, and I felt like I lived in Florida again.

"I'll call her and tell her Daniel is an idiot and we aren't engaged. That he was confused because of that time I punched him in the face and all the nights I slept at your house. Actually, I won't tell her that. I'll say... "

Larry was silently watching the road.

"You didn't say it was true, did you?"

His face burned red, and my mouth hung open.

"Why?" my brain was buzzing, and my blood pounded in my ears.

"She... and then Daniel and I..." he stammered but there was no explanation in there. He took a deep breath and tried again. "She and Mr. Carter have an arrangement that if Amber and I aren't married before we turn 30, we marry each other."

"Are you kidding? Did your mom promise him a dowry? Will Joseph give him a cow if he keeps you in stethoscopes and depression sticks? Can Winnie be your best man or did you promise the goat? Mary the lamb is out, Amber won't tolerate anyone else wearing white."

"This isn't funny!" he looked concerned, but the smile ruined it. "Don't make me marry her."

"I'm not your mom, take it up with her. I only want you to take my dog's stitches out in a few weeks, preferably keeping her organs inside but I understand how stressed you must be with your coming wedding. So I'll settle for not getting an infection."

"Keep her organs inside? Don't let her get an infection? What happened to trying to rip off my clothes in front of my staff?"

If he weren't a man, other men would accuse him of being hysterical.

"You need to calm down," I patted his hand in my best con-descending male voice. "It's normal to feel nervous before your wedding and think about other women. If I'd known, I would never have slept in your bed or tried to get into your scrub pants. You need to learn to be more honest about your feelings and intentions, Larry."

"Shut up and tell me your price! I'll give you anything!"

"Will you let me be the ring bearer? Except instead of a finger ring I can bring you a cock-"

"Shut up! You don't want anything else?" he pleaded and I shrugged. Handing him a cock ring in front of a wedding officiant would have been pretty great.

"Maybe if you put the scrub pants back on, I could come up with something..." I scanned his black slacks. "But for now...

just my dog's care, wellbeing, and the permanent scarring of anyone close enough to see the ring."

"Can't you want me to help your dog *and* not marry Amber?" He'd gone up an octave and I cackled.

"You have no leverage in those pants, Kirby. Calm down and tell me what I have to do and I'll tell you if it's worth it?"

"Did you just tell me to calm down? Again?"

"Say it, don't spray it," I wiped imaginary spit from my face. "If you're going to get indignant, I'm not going to-"

"Marry me! You marry me and then it won't be an issue," he shouted, voice still somewhere south of shrill but not far. Apparently telling people to calm down *doesn't* work. Also, marriage proposals are much more effective at getting a person to shut up than telling them to shut up.

We sat in silence.

"Cyn?"

"Yeah?" It was very, very warm.

"Will you?"

"Will I, what?" I watched the farms turn to suburban land.

"Marry me?" My stomach lurched. He was serious.

"For how long? Just until you turn 31 and the deal's off?" I calculated that to be roughly three years. I could maybe marry Larry for three years... it was less time than I'd spent in the Army.

And I wouldn't have to live in Florida.

"Or... you know..." he nodded outside, and I turned to see the cemetery. "Until death."

"You want me to murder you?" I asked, fake horror on my face. "You can't share a casket with the deceased. We'd have to get you your own but I have a source. How long after we get married do you want me to-"

I made the throat slitting gesture and he banged his forehead on the steering wheel. He'd parked on the far edge of the lot, facing the grave site. Easy up tents had been erected over the freshly dug grave, a small collection of chairs and a few pictures beside a flower arrangement.

"I'm serious, Cyn..." he started but I silenced him with my hand. In the light rain, under an umbrella held by one of the parking lot attendants, was Paddy in a suit. His hand was tucked in his pockets, face clean-shaven, and hair neat.

"Is that..." I got out of the car to look closer and Larry followed me, pulling up an umbrella of his own while I tried to shield my face with my hands.

"Is that...your homeless guy?" he finished and I nodded as Detective Harpole approached Paddy. The other two parking attendants stood a respectful distance to the rear of Paddy, while the one with the umbrella remained stony faced. Scanning, I found the fourth attendant at the top of the stairs to the building, shaking hands and playing host, but his eyes never left the old man. The detective reached into his pocket, pulled out a paper, and passed it to Paddy in a brief handshake. The two men nodded at each other, and walked in opposite directions, Paddy's entourage going with him.

"Did we just witness a drug deal?" Larry asked, and I shook my head.

"That was a one-way transaction."

"What did we just see then?" Larry had moved beside me so his umbrella covered us both.

"I... don't know," we stood there staring, until the church bells rang for the service to begin.

Chapter Fourteen:
Aliases

I scanned the crowd from the back-row graveside. Paddy had left, and I managed to conveniently avoid the questionable detective by running into the bathroom every time he looked like he might be walking towards me.

"You're acting suspicious!" Larry declared as I re-emerged seconds before the church service ended. "He's going to think you're on to him."

"No, he's going to think I have a bladder infection," I whispered back, and Larry rolled his eyes.

"He's not bright enough to think it's medical."

I watched the too-smooth detective staring too intently at the backside of a man in a kilt. When the Scotsman turned, Harpole walked into a poster of the deceased on an easel that was saved at the last second by a pallbearer in a yarmulke. He got the picture righted, but a breeze came through and the Scotsman startled a new man into knocking it over completely.

"OK, but he's also not bright enough to think I saw his little transaction either. Why the hell is Paddy pretending to be homeless?" The frustration that I had believed him an intoxicated man with issues bubbled over. "Everything about him said human with trauma and unhealthy substance abuse coping mechanisms. How did I miss that he's some sort of..."

"Drug lord?" Larry offered and I stared at him.

"I told you, there were no drugs! At least not here... He's probably a... Maybe he's..." but I had nothing. No one has people standing behind them at a respectable distance, holding their umbrella and receiving folded notes besides the mean popular girl in movies and men involved in organized crime... and Paddy wasn't wearing pink on Wednesdays.

Unless his undies were pink, but who would know?

Mrs. Charles and Retta shouldn't be difficult to spot and yet no one reminded me of the small bombshell and the two thirds-century alcoholic with lung disease. Every figure that had a similar stature had inaccurate behaviors to go with it.

"Do you think she'd miss her son's funeral?" I whispered, something like regret stinging my eyes. I hadn't even known she had a son, and I was accidentally one of the last people to see him alive.

"I think the service conductor is starting to notice how much you're talking." He squeezed my hand, and I noticed a few heads turning back to the front. A quick glance behind confirmed that they were probably... OK, *definitely* looking at me. The man began speaking, but I couldn't focus on the words. In the second row on the edge, a figure in a long coat was having a soundless seizure.

Inclining my head, I gestured to Larry where I was going and started moving there as quietly as I could. My eyes moved back and forth between my destination and the detective. Harpole was watching a woman in a short black dress now, he hadn't seen me moving and I prayed she carried pepper spray in her cleavage for men like him.

If anyone deserved to be doused in bear mace, it was a man ogling a woman at a funeral.

I stumbled on the leg of the chair and when I recovered, the shaking figure was gone. Two empty seats sat where once a shape was convulsing. My eyes scanned quickly; they couldn't have gone far.

"Don't move." A male voice said, something blunt digging into my ribs. "Come with me."

"I can't not move *and* come with you." It was hard to sound condescending at a whisper, but I did my best.

"Shut up and walk." He nudged me away from the crowd toward a tree at the periphery and my eyes searched for the seizing form, but there was no one outside the general collection of mourners taking refuge in the tent.

"Damn," I muttered, reaching the tree. "Did you see where..."

Standing by the tree was Retta, Mrs. Charles and I turned to face the man who was threatening me with...

"A banana?" I shoved his hand away and leaned in close to his wrinkled and weathered face. "Mr. Lorenzo?"

The Mr. Rogers sweater was gone, but his wire rimmed glasses and hooked nose remained the same. His eyes had two days bags under them, and a check of the two women revealed they did as well. Mrs. Charles was sobbing, managing to keep her coughing to a minimum between gut-wrenching bursts of tears.

"I'm sorry about your son," I murmured, but her body just continued to tremble. "Are you... OK?"

She shook her head and I looked at Retta.

"This isn't what was supposed to happen," her voice was thick with spent emotion, and she sighed. "Andre... he..."

The two women wrapped arms around each other, and I turned to the old man who was now eating his banana.

"I need the potassium," he insisted, and I rolled my eyes.

"Now what are you going to use to threaten people?" I snarked and the man reached for his pants. "Stop! I'm kidding. Keep your... weapons to yourself. Why are you here?"

"We need help," Retta spoke from behind me, and I turned so I could see all three at once.

"I was trying to help you. Now I have mysterious notes, smashed bottles of moonshine, and an unfortunate visual of my parent's in your bed."

I nodded toward Mrs. Charles on the last and she cracked a smile that faded quickly when her eyes drifted to the casket.

"I didn't know when I asked for your help that it would be..." her voice trailed off again, and Mrs. Charles came into her usual air of confidence.

"Cynthia, this is my husband, Vincent." She gestured to Mr. Vincenzo Lorenzo and I made a face. "Don't judge a book by its cover, girlie, he's packing..."

"Stop!" Retta and I shouted at once and the two older people laughed.

"Does that mean your last name isn't Charles? Are you... Gloria Lorenzo?" it sounded weirder when I spoke out loud.

"Don't be daft," the man responded as though I'd punched him. "Vincenzo Lorenzo isn't a real person."

"The man..." I glanced back toward the congregation, scanning for Larry and Harpole. "He had a DMV photo, your picture and that name."

The man formerly known as Vincenzo Lorenzo but might actually be Mr. Charles looked around me to his wife.

"I thought she was smart?"

"No, I said she had experience," Gloria countered, and my eyes caught sight of the tall, dark haired man standing in front of Larry. The veterinarian was conveniently blocking the man's view of us behind the tree but he wouldn't succeed forever.

Gloria saw him trying to sneak past Larry, and rolled her eyes, smacking her husband in the arm. He followed her line of sight and shook his head in dismay at the woman in the short dress.

"I told you, we shouldn't be here," he hissed at his wife and Retta looked as confused as I felt. "Girl will be the death of us."

"It's your fault! Bringing me 'on-sale' alcohol and stealing product from *that* man. You're just lucky little Mary O'Connor found it," Gloria shot back.

"Why did you steal back the moonshine?" I asked, another puzzle piece sliding into place. The drugs, booze, mortuary, and man were connected... somehow.

"Because, my idiot husband said he knew a distributor who could get it on the cheap, except he took the case without permission and it was full of..." he put his hand over her mouth and her eyes widened. Apparently they did not think I knew about the drugs... useful if idiotic.

Glancing back, Harpole was around Larry and closing in, the woman in the short dress trying to distract him.

"What am I looking for?" I asked the trio, who had started to move away.

"You're looking for the damn caskets, girl," the mortuary man said. "They weren't ever supposed to exist, just shell purchases to wash the money. Someone changed the plan. Find the damn caskets."

The trio retreated quickly, making it to a four-door SUV with all markings removed. Retta took the driver's position and the two seniors climbed in the back. Retta floored it, jumped a curb, and made a left turn into traffic just as Harpole and Larry appeared beside me.

Probably for the best, since I could guess what the "powdered sugar" was and it did not bode well for the Charles's that he'd stolen a criminal's drugs.

"What were you doing back here?" The detective had lost some of the boyish charm he'd radiated the night I met him.

"I needed to pee," I adjusted my pants as if to make a point. "Bladder infection. Need to stop for juice. Larry?"

He nodded, took my hand, and escorted me back to the car.

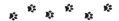

"Yes, can I speak to Detective G. Harpole?" I read off the unofficial business card he'd given me. It was my third transfer in fifteen minutes. It would seem the Dayton Police Department's online directory was lacking. While there were numbers for perfectly normal areas like fraud, burglary and axe murderer reporting, there was no "I think I met a fake detective" hotline where you could verify employment.

"No, Harpole. Like a tadpole with harps?" I paused and watched Larry raise a brow. "No, harps. The musical instrument."

I was placed on hold again.

Winnie let out a long sigh and I rubbed her ears.

"Do you need more drugs?" I asked her, checking her stitches as the line clicked to life. It was the fifth time I'd asked her and the fifth time Larry had rolled his eyes.

Apparently human doctors weren't the only ones tired of people who thought Google counted as a medical degree.

"What was that, ma'am?" a surly woman demanded.

"My dog had surgery. I was asking if she needed medication. Did you locate a Detective Harpole? Or maybe an Officer Harpole? Or a janitor-"

I was back on hold.

A new voice picked up.

"Professional Standards," someone wheezed into the line.

"Hi, I'm looking for a Detective G. Harpole," I said and waited to explain the name again. Winnie let out a grumble, and I held my finger to my lips. We needed to be quiet in case...

"Hello?" I said, convinced I had been hung up on and would need to start again.

"This some kind of sick joke, lady?" he asked and I thought I could hear something clicking in the background.

"No, a man came to ask me about the Gatton murder, he said his name was..."

"I don't care what that man said, who the hell are *you*?" The gruff, now angry man insisted. It was hard not to picture him as the detective in Who Framed Roger Rabbit, a washed up drunk in suspenders and an old-fashioned hat.

"Cynthia Sharp, Cyn, U.S. Army retired. I was near the mortuary the night in question and a man introducing himself as Detective Harpole showed up at my home with-"

"What did this man look like?" He was shuffling paper on his desk.

"He looked..." I glanced down at Winnie. She lifted a brow and yawned. "Like a man? Dark hair... face... two eyes... Harry Potter!"

He let loose a huge sigh from the other end of the phone.

"It was early! He was young, tall, wearing clothes that looked like but were not a uniform, and his hair was... on his head. He was at the Gatton funeral today! He was ogling a woman in a short dress."

The pen scratching paper stopped.

"Ogling?"

"Yeah... with his eyes?" Winnie wiggled her brows and I shrugged. It was a valid word. "Does he work there? I mean... he had crime scene photos and evidence, so he has to work there somewhere, right?"

"What evidence?"

"He had a paper I gave a homeless man, with my name and number for if he saw the death boxes... someone had added to it... said they'd be in touch," but my brain was fizzling. That paper was only evidence if Paddy had somehow dropped it. What if he didn't drop it? What if it wasn't even the one I handed him but one of the two-hundred other ones printed and out in the world.

"Sharp!" The man brought me back and I stroked Winnie's tail.

"Yes, sir?"

"Did the man claiming to be Harpole give you anything?" He was all business.

"A card," I tapped it on Winnie's nose. "A business card. Detective G. Harpole #2319, Dayton PD, Crime..."

"Crime what?" He barked and I hesitated.

"It's whited out after crime. I'd never noticed before. So he doesn't exist?" I clarified, prepared to chuck the card in the garbage now that I knew it was all fake. Minor relief that there was not a crooked cop on the payroll, but it was just another dead end.

"We have a Detective Harpole, or we did..." the man started tapping his pen on his desk.

"What does it mean that you *did* have one?" I climbed off the couch to grab snacks from the kitchen.

"It means a house burned down, the officer was supposedly inside, but no one ever found a body."

He let out a cough and a chair squeaked underneath him.

I set the card on the counter and waited out the man's silence. The card suddenly looked smoky, yellow, and faded at the corners. Optical illusion or not, I was no longer willing to touch a card for a dead man.

"Detective G. Harpole was a solid cop. Promoted to detective after two years, served honorably for ten. Bright cop... very bright. Probably should have questioned more why someone that smart would want to be a cop, but it was nearly fifteen years ago and no one questioned much then." His breath hitched and I pictured him taking a hit of coffee... or gin. He seemed like a gin man.

"Do you have a picture of the former detective?" I leaned against the counter and Winnie flopped to the ground beside me.

"Yeah... somewhere," the chair squeaked again. "What's your email? I'll send it over if I find it."

I gave the man my email and he scratched it out onto paper.

"It'll probably be tomorrow. Day's done for me. Nothing's missing here, Sharp, what are you investigating?" He blew his nose into the phone and I gagged.

Maybe mentioning caskets to someone who sounded this close to dead was a bad idea, so I tried another tack.

"Gatton was murdered?" I asked and he confirmed with a grunt. "The man who was operating the mortuary... is he missing?"

"Yeah, some man pretending to be Vincenzo Lorenzo. Place is linked to fraud and some other shit, pardon my language. Tax records say.... nevermind, that's part of a police investigation." He was moving around more and spouting the department line.

"Just... who owns the mortuary?" I was desperate for something that could lead... somewhere.

"Holding company... Patterson, Anders, Davidson, and Elias, Inc. I gotta go, but if you can save that card for me... I'd like to see it."

I wrote the company name in a column on the back of the card.

Patterson
Anders
Davidson
Elias

"Yeah, no problem," I said, staring at what I'd just written. We disconnected and I looked down at Winnie.

"Apparently, Paddy is an acronym."

She wiggled her brows and I nodded.

"Yeah... I don't know what it means either. But something stinks."

A *pooft* escaped from behind her and I fanned my face.

"That, too," I sighed.

Chapter Fifteen:
Flawed Friends

"**N**ot a chance, Mo," I said to the mountain of pink taffeta in front of my friend's face. I held up my coffee cup in defense as a weapon. While wasting coffee was a crime, permanently ruining whatever *that* is may balance the universe. It was massive, fluffy and she expected it to touch my body.

The only thing touching my body was coffee on the inside and cotton on the outside.

"You said..." she started to whine.

"Can it, O'Connor. I'm not getting any and you cannot sway me with your cuteness. No pink, no petticoats, no heels, no bows, polka dots or stripes," I held up a finger when she started to interject. I downed half the coffee and stared. No, I wasn't sleeping. This nightmare was real and it had neon green highlights in a garish shade of orange.

"This is a commitment party photo shoot, not an actual wedding or an actual engagement. This was an excuse to bake a cake," my eyes studied her face for a tell over the rim of my cup that this was about more than cake. "Unless you are holding something back, I'm not going to prance and dance for you, woman. Not in that."

My eyes scanned her abdominal section.

"I'm not pregnant!" Mo was exasperated with me, yet she was the one wearing a veil with a flute of champagne in one hand and a chef's knife in the other. I had yet to get an answer as to why she was holding the knife, but the clean white of the fabric in the corner gave me hope that no one had been stabbed... in this room.

"Then why are you going nuts buying stupid dresses and wearing a veil?"

Winnie was laying under the table, her cone of shame folded back so she could judge us.

"Four-foot swan cake, Cyn! When am I ever going to have a chance to make and feed people a four-foot swan cake? I need an outfit and party befitting a four-foot swan cake and as my friend you are obligated to wear whatever I want if you want any of that cake! Now, put that coffee down before you spill!"

I downed the rest of it and showed her my empty cup.

"I put down my weapon, you put down yours. Also, hun, you own a bakery. You can make really big cakes and display them and sell them to strangers for money. Money! That thing with the dead white dudes that pays for food, fabric, and... knives."

"I don't want to dismantle the swan cake for strangers. I want to hack into it and stuff the pieces into the faces of my friends and family! Swan cake is an occasion cake, not something you make and sell to strangers!"

She sounded pretty confident, but I was pretty sure that all cakes were suitable for cutting and selling to strangers so long as you kept out the fur and spit.

"Put down the knife, Mo. Put down the knife and I'll give you a cookie, and we can call a nice therapist to explain to you why you are going through all of this to make a big bird cake."

Her grip tightened on the knife, and I backed up a little farther.

"Swan cake, Cyn! Four-foot swan cake, not Big Bird!"

I checked her abdomen again and she brandished the knife farther.

"I am not pregnant!"

"I was checking for a demon to burst out... or like an alien... you are seriously off your rocker right now. At the risk of my own life, I ask again, why are you holding a knife."

"I'm a cook! I have knives!"

"When trying on dresses?"

It had been a very long three days since the funeral. The articles of incorporation on PAD-E were filed under some sort of special gag order... Not the fun gags, but the ones where I needed a lawyer to explain it to the lawyer I'd asked to explain it to me. In summary, the holding company was a dead end.

Another dead end was the casket supplier Mrs. Figs got her lawn art from. The number she gave me was disconnected, the office listed on the sale was a vacant lot, and when she took me to the location she picked it up from, there was a flower market.

She bought two dozen carnations to decorate her death box, and I got an allergic reaction.

Then there were the actual deaths.

My days at the farm were somber. Winnie's photo spot was getting a makeover, and her cone of shame was turned into decoration that, with heavy medication, she didn't much mind. Checking on Betty had been a major part of my day and without her, there was nothing to do but routine inspections, births, and sanitation checks. With Larry working out of the area this week, there wasn't even any eye candy. Work had been... laborious.

Mrs. Charles's bar remained dark across the street, as did her apartment. Without her, the local nightlife effectively went, too, and the only thing entertaining outside my window at midnight was a pack of raccoons. My email remained blank of emails from the supposed detective, and a Google search about a house fire and G. Harpole yielded only a page four plea for information in a five-year-old circular. The news had been overshadowed by a corrupt government official, and in the absence of a body, the story was far less enticing than the seedy dealings of a deputy governor.

Between dead ends, dark bars, and long lonely nights, murdered for cake might be a relief.

I really needed a hobby.

"Where's Larry?" Mo asked, dragging my mind back to her living room. My lady parts sighed but my face tried to stay casual. The woman was still holding the knife, but she'd lowered it to her side.

No need to alarm the crazy woman.

"He had to go out of town to take care of some ranchers' livestock," I shrugged, picking at the tulle on the nearest purple monstrosity. My eyes caught on something blue and sparkly and I picked it up. "Who did you even buy this for?"

It was a wizard robe like the one worn by the sorcerer in Fantasia.

"I... may have been a little tipsy on some of these orders," she bit her lower lip. "Also, I really need to pee."

I took her champagne, but stayed clear of her knife.

"Take your time, maybe you'll find your sanity in the toilet. While you handle that, I'm going to put some of these back in boxes. Whatever I can't return, I'm setting on fire." I held up an 80's inspired dress with geometric patterns and a bright green under skirt. "Some of these I might just burn on principle. Who was this for?"

Mo shrugged and shuffled off toward the bathroom.

I was halfway through wrestling something grey and fuzzy into a box when Mo screamed from the bathroom.

"What? What's wrong?" I dropped the box and came running. She'd carried a knife into the bathroom. Was there a toilet paper confusion? Some sort of incident with cold water and strawberry syrup?

Mo opened the bathroom door holding a celebrity gossip rag.

"Amber made the tabloids!" She thrust the article at me. I hadn't heard the sink.

"Did you wash your hands?" I looked behind her into the bathroom. No blood shed... I looked at her hand... still holding the knife under the magazine.

"On second thought, I need more coffee. You... try something else on and I'll tell you how hideous it is," I passed Winnie on my way into the kitchen and ruffled her ears. The coffee had gotten cold, so I added ice and declared it dessert. From the other room, I heard Mo's camera phone shutter a million times and I rolled my eyes.

"I told you I'd tell you how hideous it is, what do you need pictures for?" I asked, coming back into the room to see Mo in white lingerie, holding the knife seductively to her cheek with her legs butterflied open. "What the hell, Mo!"

I slapped my hands over my eyes and tried to feel for the door with my butt. It was too late, I couldn't unsee her making the knife dirty... dirty in more than just that she hadn't washed her hands.

"Sorry! That was just supposed to be for..." I found the door and opened it with my chin.

"Mail the dresses back, Mo," I spoke with my back to her. "All of them. I will get my own dress. Anything you give me will be burned and I will show up naked!"

"But, Cyn-"

I slammed the door and ran to my Jeep. The engine was primed and ready when the door opened and Mo stood there, in her teddy and garters, holding Winnie by the collar. I looked into the backseat and confirmed she was, in fact, standing next to Mo. Her cone of shame drooped, her tongue hanging pathetically to the side as her eyes pleaded to come home.

It turned out that in the face of knife-wielding, sexy photo shoots, I would in fact leave a man behind.

The Army would be so disappointed.

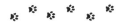

"Clock's ticking, Cyn," Larry said into the phone and my stomach bottomed out.

"What happens when the clock strikes midnight, Cinderella?" I asked, stroking Winnie's ear and watching the microwave turn a bag of oil and organic material into a greasy delicious snack. "Do you turn into a pumpkin? Do all your sperm wither and die?"

"Are you thinking about my sperm, Cyn?"

Crap.

"No..." I was totally thinking about his sperm.

"What's it going to be? The party is next weekend. Are you going to *come* with me?"

We were back to thinking about sperm... well, more specifically its origin...

My body shivered in excitement, and I started panting louder than Winnie.

"Cyn!"

"Larry!" His name came out breathy and it was not on purpose. "Larry! Oh, Larry!"

I think his pants got a little tight on the other end of the phone. It was much better when we were both in the same physically distressed state, though I admit the second time I said his name I was faking. The third time was anyone's guess.

"Stop distracting me," he growled, and I smiled down at Winnie. Distraction was my middle name... along with disaster and dessert. The microwave dinged and I pulled out my popcorn, pouring it into the bowl like a civilized adult before dumping a cup of melted butter on top.

"Don't let Winnie have any popcorn," he warned over the phone, and I took my hand back from almost handing her a piece. The fur baby let out a whimper.

"Just one piece?" I plead her case.

"No, jeez! How did that dog survive four years without me? I have to come home just to save her from your terrible pet parenting." He sounded very smug, so I stuffed popcorn in my mouth and crunched it in his ear. "If you're sharing pieces of something, though, I'd like a piece of your-"

"When are you *coming* home?" I interrupted, face scarlet. Winnie put a paw over her eyes. Apparently, I was embarrassing my child with all this undue emphasis on verbs and innuendo. I pressed my finger to my lips and gave her a small piece of popcorn, making sure there were no kernel husks to irritate her insides.

"Tomorrow. Mo demands I attend the... celebration? Are there going to be actual swans in the cake?" He was just as confused as I was. I glanced at the garment bag on the back of my closet door. After the knife incident, I refused to re-enter her house until she was mentally and hormonally balanced... which means Chris dropped off this bag and I hadn't opened it. Despite swearing to burn it and show up naked, I lacked the motivation to get the necessary permits to hold a bonfire of the size necessary to take out whatever demon lay in that black bag.

Also I liked cookies too much to walk out naked in front of the town. Since the best cookies were made by Mo, I had to do what she wanted to keep getting said cookies. Since what she wanted meant I got to have cake and I loved her, the garment bag remained zipped and away from open flames.

"Did she... instruct you on what to wear?" I gave Winnie another partial piece of popcorn and she licked butter off my fingers. Just in case Larry had friends in Homeland Security, I covered both cameras before letting her lick my other hand.

"No, why? Do you have an outfit?" He was a different kind of excited... great. Giving information to the enemy.

"You'll have to come home on time to find out," I deflected. The longer I could put off opening the bag, the longer I could pretend Mo still loved me.

"Preview?" He was laughing.

"Not a chance. This building could catch fire and I won't have to wear it, so there is no point in acknowledging its existence any longer than I have to," Winnie let out a grumble, and I rubbed her ears with my now butter free fingers. "Winnie would like you to wave a magic wand and heal her."

"Tell her my magic wand only works for her mom." I face palmed. "Also tell her she'll feel better if her mom stops letting her lick butter off her fingers and sneaking her pieces of popcorn."

"I didn't!"

"Liar, liar, pants on fire. I'll have to show you what happens to liars," his voice dropped and the warm feeling in my belly took a dip south.

"Cocky much?" I choked on my own choice of words.

"See? You know what I'm talking about," his response made clear if another man were present they would have high-fived and now I had the visual of two men to occupy my sad, lonely night.

"I have to go to bed," I grumbled, eating more popcorn and letting my imagination go on a wild journey.

"Alone?"

"Nope. I never sleep alone," Winnie confirmed with a low woof. "Later, Larry."

"Cyn," he called, just as I prepared to disconnect.

"Yeah?"

"I'll see you tomorrow?"

"If whatever I'm wearing doesn't make you go blind first, it would seem inevitable," I quipped, but inside I was doing cartwheels.

Stupid Larry.

Stupid lady parts.

"Miss you," he whispered, and I hung up so he couldn't hear me.

"Miss you, too," I sighed and leaned back, using Winnie as a pillow.

The phone alerted in my hand and I dropped it like it had caught fire.

"Oh god, he heard me," I said to Winnie. Her eyebrows danced and I stared down at the offending piece of technology.

Unknown Caller, he hadn't heard me.

"Hello?" I held my breath in case it was a trick.

"Cynthia! Thank god!" a woman bellowed and I moved the phone a few inches away. "I need your help! It's Jake."

"What's little Cynthia going to do about Jake? Call the cops!" A surly male voice said from the background, and I rolled my eyes at the *little*. "I won't have any drug dealers living in my house, Jennifer!"

"Sam, he is not a drug dealer! You've seen the glitter and the costumes. He's a gigolo!" The woman hissed back at him, and I snickered into my hand. "Don't you dare laugh, Cynthia! I need you to find him and save him!"

"Save him from what? The cops? They should get to..." the man's voice moved away from the phone and deteriorated into a sarcastic grumble.

"Cynthia?" The woman sounded desperate and I sighed.

"Start from the beginning," I said into the line, and leaned back against Winnie. Drugs made her an excellent pillow and I might get to meet a gigolo.

The night was taking a positive turn after all.

Chapter Sixteen: Inconvenient Truths

I t was just after 11, and I was wearing jeans, again.

Jeans, and shoes, despite having been happily ensconced in pajamas and nothing.

Winnie and I were two streets over from the fake Italian restaurant that served far too potent drinks. The thrum of the music coming from the establishment promised that if I went inside, I would be reading lips for the weeks to come and somewhere in there was Jake, the drug-dealing gigolo with the fancy wardrobe and glitter. A line of women stood outside, waiting to pay an overgrown man seated at a podium to enter the establishment. Most were in their 30s and 40s, had the recently toned look of a divorcees with revenge bodies, and midlife crisis blue streaks in their hair.

"If you wanna go in, you gotta get in line," the bouncer sounded bored. I followed his gaze and realized he was talking to me.

"I really don't want to go inside," I whispered. "Is this a brothel or a drug den?"

The two blondes at the front of the line tittered and the soccer mom behind them sprouted a look of horror. Jake's mom had given me the rundown on his job as a pilot. The man was making very good money, and had just announced to his family that he was buying a house, with cash, and moving out in two weeks. Jake's dad, a man I pictured looking like Yosemite Sam after being informed his name is Sam, had done a credit check.

This brick building with a neon sign proclaiming it Pickles, was the address his son worked at. There was no airport nearby, and his mom claimed the building was abandoned and her son was using the address as a front.

Apparently, Jennifer had never been out this late in her life, because the building was far from abandoned.

"What the heck, lady! You can't just go flinging accusations!" The blondes tittered again at his use of 'flinging' and the soccer mom lost another shade of color.

"Here's the deal," I decided to take the direct approach. "I need to find a man."

His eyebrows shot up and the peanut gallery in line went off again.

"Not like that," my eyes rolled into my hairline. "His mom thinks he's a prostitute posing as a pilot, his dad thinks he's a drug dealer flying planes for the cartel, and I think it is way too late in the day to be wearing a bra and actual pants without elastic. Do you know this man?"

I turned my phone and showed him a picture of Jake that his mother had sent me.

"Yeah, I know him."

"Does he work here and is his work illegal in any way?" The bouncer made a face at my question and gestured with his head toward the door.

"Twenty bucks and you can go see for yourself," he replied and I blinked.

"Do I have to? My dog is in the car and..." a woman reached around me and handed the man $100.

"Let all of us in and you can keep the change!" It was one of the giggly blondes, dragging the soccer mom. The second blonde tugged my hand into darkness and noise. It was a train tunnel, funneling us toward a patch of light and the sound of screams. Everything smelled like sweat, booze and...

"Pickles?" I asked as we emerged on the other side to see ten men on an elaborate stage, wearing nothing over any place that counts.

"Oh dog, no!"

Turning tail, I tried to run, but the bouncer had just let in another wave. The tide of women, desperate to see the show, dragged me forward until I was standing beside a projector in the middle of the room. To my left was a man wearing a fire hat, beside him a man wearing Dalmatian ears and a tail. They were doing a choreographed dance that involved using their anatomy as fire hoses near strategically placed confetti cannons.

"No, no, no," I started backing away, terrified that if I turned and ran someone would hit me with a glitter bomb. There was no way to get glitter out of your hair, I'd rather be covered in pickle juice. I was feeling for a wall, and my hand grabbed something smooth, warm and rigid. "Eep!"

I screamed, tried to pivot and slipped on spilled pickle brine. My shoe flew into the air, landed mid stage with a thunk, and all eyes turned to me, lying on the floor.

Apparently if you tell the universe glitter or pickles, it will come through.

"You OK?" the flawless Adonis asked from above me, but the undercarriage view was not ideal. The man was only wearing a hat with a tie and pilot wings, meaning I was looking up at squirrel food.

Impressive though it was, this was not the best angle for intros... or IDs.

"Jake?" I asked, trying to sit up and slipping in what was either vomit or a pina colada. My hand gave out, and I was once again upside down between his legs. "Please don't be Jake, your mom didn't give me a picture to identify you from this angle."

Two hands lifted me upright, and I was pressed against the pilot.

"Dear god, no," he muttered and quickly we were in a room that brought the noise level down by 10. "Please tell me she didn't?"

Jake had put on a robe and I got my first look at his face without the aviators I'd missed from my previous angle.

"Yes. She did. Drugs?" I asked, eyes dropping a little, and he shifted uncomfortably.

"No... I uh... like..." he stammered and strategically placed his hands in front of him. "How was the Army?"

I moved in closer and studied his hazel eyes.

"Holy cow, Jacob Weissman? *Those* are your parents?" My horror magnified as I realized I had just seen the penis of a childhood friend who was four years my junior. "That was your..."

"Lets... uhh... not," he said sagely and I nodded.

"Right. So... kind of a pilot?"

"Kind of a pilot," he confirmed, and I stared at my feet.

"Think I can get my shoe back?"

"I'll see what I can do," he said, turning around to drop the robe and strut back onto the floor. He had a dimple in his left butt cheek and that combined with his family jewels was going to ruin my childhood.

Just as the door swung shut behind him, it flew open again.

A dark-haired man in a gun belt and a police hat walked in.

"Are you kidding?" I hollered, staring at the fake Detective Harpole.

"What the-" he took off back out the door and I followed.

"Come back, we need to..." I reached for the belt and missed, colliding face first with my Kindergarten teacher Mrs. Zuber.

"They don't like when you touch them, dear," she whispered and pointed to the stage. "It's pretty good just to watch though."

A glance and I saw that my shoe was in the hands of a caveman, and the faux suede would never be the same.

"Come on, I'll pay you!" I pleaded with the child on the corner. He screamed and ran as fast as he could toward a woman with a stroller. "It's not that serious, ma'am!"

That boy was the first person to walk by in 20 minutes and I was expected at the gazebo in less than an hour. Just ahead loomed Amber's Shoe Ambrosia, and a sign on the door specifically banned me from entering. It wasn't so much a sign as a full color poster featuring an image from a karaoke bar in Germany where I was preventing a drunken soldier from assaulting a beer maid and took a bottle to the head. The image had made the local news in the area, but how Amber got a copy... my eyes were wild, my hair three days past needing a wash. Someone had torn off the sleeve of my shirt, and the broken glass had left a gash in my shoulder that made a stark red stream of blood flow down my arm.

Now, mothers crossed the street when they saw me *and* I needed a new pair of flats.

"What are you wearing?" Larry asked from behind me, and I turned in frustration that quickly turned to a gaping look of lust.

"You... suit..." I stammered and he pulled me in for a hug. His body shook with laughter against mine, and I got a wicked idea that would mean my shoe problems were no longer problems. "Home?"

Winnie nudged my hand and Larry and I both stared down at the depressed pup. Mo had sent flower accessories for decorating the dog's cone so that she could have a beautiful lakeside garden. Mo swore she wouldn't need more than the cone she already had to wear. Sadly, what that actually meant was drooping purple petals, a green bandana, and spring-loaded daisies on top of her head.

It meant Winnie would probably eat Mo's shoes the next time we went over. Given what I was wearing, that would be never because I might have to burn down her house like an Army base in Florida.

"Will you please go buy me shoes?" I held out my credit card and looked up the block as another mom with a stroller looked at the picture, then down the street at me, and crossed at the corner.

"It's out of context!" I shouted and Larry threw an arm over my shoulders.

"I think the shoes you have on are fine. Let's go see Mo," he kissed the top of my head and I sulked into his suit jacket. He smelled like the forest after a rain and mint. The suit was a dark grey, his tie a deep blue. "Maybe she'll take pity on Winnie and we can both watch you strut your stuff."

I let out a whimper and refused to look down as he tugged me along.

Why hadn't I thought anyone would make a dress like this outside of Vegas? Why had the swan cake not been a clue to the horrors that awaited me?

Why had I not demanded payment in cake upfront?

It was a strapless, sea-foam green fit and flare style. The fitted bodice had built in support and flattered my assets. The boning pushed my breasts to impressive angles of observation, and the soft silk kissed my skin. I looked like Barbie with human appropriate proportions and felt like a beauty queen.

Then... then there was the skirt. It was layered faux feathers in a high-low cut, showing off that I was once again sporting my khaki boots from my service days, with a foot-long train that was already filthy... and molting.

"If you get really drunk in this dress, you can always find your way home," he laughed and I looked at the trail of feathers leading back to my building.

"Shut up, Kirby," I grumbled.

"Hey, I never had a thing for Big Bird, but I'd make an exception for you." He slipped an arm around my waist and guided me more firmly toward the gazebo and away from Amber's Shoe Ambrosia. With a last glance, I declared Army boots could only enhance the look and we rounded Main St. toward the gazebo on the edge of the downtown park.

Except the gazebo was gone.

"What the he-" but someone screamed for me.

"Cyn! What do you think??"

Mo flew toward me in another feathered number looking like a swan princess on fire. What was once a perfectly ordinary gazebo had been re-made into a bird's nest. A million twigs adorned the outdoor structure, and I could only marvel at how long someone must have spent on that. Behind her, I saw two women I'd never met in sky blue and lavender versions of the dress I wore. Lavender was Asian and her thick dark hair draped

224

in waves over her shoulder, showcasing flawless bone structure. Sky Blue was a dark-skinned beauty who had chosen to wear her beaded braids secured at the back of her neck with a floral ribbon.

They were all, also, the same height as Mo's five-foot two self. Once lined up, we were mother duck and her three ducklings. Standing between the women of reasonable height, I looked like a Sesame Street "One of These Things is Not Like the Other" song. Between the Army boots, the feathers, and my height, there were so many options for the children to guess.

To make all of it worse, I was stone cold sober.

"Where's the cake?" I asked, and lavender gestured toward the far end of the park where a small crowd of ordinary, non-bird people had gathered.

"No cake until we dance," sky blue confirmed, and I dropped my head.

"Where did you get your boots? They're..." lavender started, but couldn't find a genuine polite thing to say. "Sturdy."

"Army. I lost my cute shoes in a strip club last night." Larry choked from where he lurked behind me, and I felt the first trace of a smile since losing the fake detective in a swarm of hormonal women.

"You went to a strip club?" he whispered and I shrugged.

"You weren't here. A woman has needs," I smirked and walked toward the nest. If I wanted cake, I had to hatch and prance like a swan. Shuddering, I nearly missed the audience beside the park. Jake the stripper and...

"You're not a detective," I said, changing course over the objection of my fellow birds. Everyone wanted cake, no one wanted to keep wearing these dresses. I was the only one smart enough to run away faster than they could stop me.

I pointed my finger at the nose of my disappearing stripper cop. It was one thing to fool me in the early hours, but how had I missed his obvious lack of professionalism and maturity in the light of day?

Twice?

His wry smile showed a dimple and I re-judged his age to be about twenty-three.

"No... I am not. But... the gun belt *is* loaded," he waggled his eyebrows and Larry cleared his throat behind me. "Sorry man, it's hard to turn off."

"Start talking, impersonating an officer is a crime," I activated my phone's recorder and stuffed it in the front of my dress to get everything. Three sets of male eyes followed the phone and I face palmed.

Big Bird must have moved off Sesame Street because they wouldn't give him pockets.

"I wasn't impersonating, I was acting!" He swallowed hard, staring at the phone peeking between my breasts. "I was hired. She said it was like a singing telegram, and she'd give me all the props. She even gave me a red and blue light to put in my car and a badge. It was sweet! I already had the costume, so I thought I'd try being a cop for real!"

"She who?" I asked, narrowing my eyes. There were so many things wrong with this. "Don't you mean he? The man at the funeral you were passing notes to?"

"Nah, that was another gig! She paid me to meet with and hand that man a paper. I needed to look tough and say little.

Got lucky with a lady from that gig." He looked to Jake for a high-five but the man politely declined. It was yet another mask, but I couldn't figure out what lay beneath all the personalities. "It was pretty badass, I felt like a guy in a mob movie."

Hideous dance music started behind me, and I turned to see the birds of many feathers dying gracefully at Mo's feet while she cocooned Chris in feathers.

This relationship would either last forever or he was leaving her in the next five minutes.

"What is your name?" I asked, thinking it was an insult to law enforcement to refer to this kid as anything even loosely associated with a department. His eyes shifted again, another mask... I was getting a headache with all of his personalities.

"Joey," he stuck out his hand and I accepted it. The hand was real and the face was honest. His name really was Joey.

"Joey, did you put a basket of rocks outside Sharp Investigations?"

"Nah, the rocks were kinda cool, though!" He nodded enthusiastically in time to the music. We were back to idiotic stripper. Jake gave me a hopeful smile and inclined his head to speak to me privately by the benches in the square. Joey had added gyrating and flexing to his nodding. Another glance at the elegantly dancing geese and I decided I wasn't necessary for these shots and Joey wasn't exactly helpful depending on who he was "acting" as. Maybe I would be forgotten altogether and I could still have cake.

All of this would be worth it for cake.

We sat on the bench and watched for a moment as Joey tried to insert himself into the nest. First, he photobombed from the back, then peeked from the sides, before finally ripping off his top and turning himself into the tree for all the swans to perch on.

"Is he..." but I paused. Brain fried on illicit drugs seemed a bit harsh, but if we were in California he'd be wearing tie-dye and a beanie on Venice Beach.

At least... this version of him.

"We think he was dropped on his head as a baby. Can't work at the club if you party, they don't want unreliable dancers," I looked over to see Jake studying his hands, squeezed together in his lap. "Did you tell my mom about Pickles?"

My face burned red.

"I told her you were a themed bartender at a club and they tip very well. I couldn't bring myself to inform her... of the full Monty," I winced as I remembered what the underside of that Monty looked like... and the back. "Please don't tell her I saw you naked. She seems like the type to ask for details and proof and then marry us off and demand babies. No offense, but you're way too hot for me to ever want to be naked near."

Jake laughed as my phone dinged and I pulled it out of my dress to check the display.

I had a new email.

Sgt. Patterson from the City of Dayton PD had sent an attachment labeled: Detective Gretchen Harpole.

"Gretchen?" I said out loud, opening the attachment, gaping at what was inside.

"Hey! That's the lady!" Joey had come up behind me and was looking at the phone. "I thought you didn't know her!"

"This woman gave you money to pretend to be a cop?" I turned the phone to clarify and he nodded.

"Yeah, and that card I left you, the paper with your number and the clothes, explaining them was all me." The idiot was beaming and I went back to staring at the image to not throw something at him. I wish the

"And the note in my shoe?" I asked, looking at my phone. He'd said the basket wasn't him, but he seemed like the type to need the contents considered individually. An itemized list to check off, if you will.

"No, that was weird," his wide eyes reminded me of when I first saw the napkin. It had been something legitimately interesting. Even now the idiot mask was slipping, he wanted to know about the napkin too. "I tried to give her the napkin, though, like maybe it was a test of my skills. Couldn't find her."

Jake looked over my shoulder at the picture; curious who would give Joey money to keep clothes on.

"Hey, I know her. She works at the Italian place that serves stupid food."

"Yeah, that's what I got too," I sighed, and looked up the number to the restaurant.

It was Britney from Mi Asiago Prego.

Guess she was the "fuzz" after all and now I had to go back a third time.

Chapter Seventeen: Death Threats

"What do you mean she was fired?" I was standing in Larry's kitchen barefoot, the ghastly dress on his bedroom floor. Also on Larry's floor were Winnie and her wrecked flower costume, a demolished pizza box, and Larry's pants.

Larry, however, was not home.

"Yes, I realize that you said she no longer worked there, but your voice said she was fired," I answered the man on the other end. I was about to chew a hole in my cheek to not chew his head off. My cake induced sugar high had worn off, and as punishment for ditching the photos, she wouldn't let me have any of the leftovers. Immediately after dumping the dress on the floor, I made coffee. The very large, very strong cup of coffee beside me was doing nothing to make this man and my lack of cake more tolerable.

I'd need an IV of Columbian pure dark roast to tolerate this guy.

"Look, you can tell me what happened, or I can come back with my friend and she can vanquish another dragon and a bottle of wine in your dining area," I threatened and prayed to not have to follow through on the threat. Mo snored when she was drunk, and I would be responsible by proximity. The door opened behind me, but I remained standing in the kitchen, listening to the man shuffle paper on the other end. He sniffed and shuffled more paper.

"She did not show for work and did not call in for three days, grounds for termination per policy," at last, he spoke.

"What days?" I asked, staring down at my feet. I'd stolen one of Larry's shirts and forgone pants.

"Two days ago was the official termination," he replied… and hung up.

"Thanks for your help you condescending, arrogant-"

"Why are you in my son's home without pants?" a prim voice said from behind me, and my body folded in on itself. "It is inappropriate for a woman to be in a man's home half-dressed while he is engaged in Christian pursuits."

I snorted and tried to mask it with a cough.

Larry's "Christian pursuit" was finding a baker that was not Mo to make a dirty cake for Chris. A photo based on a picture of her boobs that Mo was unaware Chris, and now Larry, had. Which means the large amount of cake I consumed may be the last cake I get from that relationship. Though with the feathers she'd made him endure and the bird nest she'd made him build, maybe they were even and she could enjoy a piece of her own breasts.

Ah, love, a game of punishing one another 'til death or lawyers do you part.

"Hi, Mrs. Kirby," I smiled sweetly at the woman and tried not to gag at her holier than thou expression.

"Where are your pants, young lady?"

"In my apartment," I shrugged and opened Larry's cabinets. The man usually had bachelor food, which was known on occasion to include marshmallows and I wanted some.

"Why aren't you in those pants, in your apartment?" She sniffed and I rolled my eyes into the shelf of dry pasta and rice. No marshmallows. So I closed that cabinet and opened a different one.

"I asked you a question, Cynthia," Mrs. Kirby tapped her foot in impatience. I found a box of Lucky Charms and that was good enough, so I ignored her and poured a bowl. "Cynthia, do not make me call your mom!"

"Mrs. Kirby, I found my mom in our shed, naked, using a flogger on my dad. I highly doubt my desire to not wear that dress or pants would even register on her scale of concerns. Frankly, I don't know why you're upset. This underwear are practically shorts," I had managed to put milk into my cereal and find a spoon while watching the horror on her face continue to intensify with every moment...

Probably my family was going to be either heavily prayed for, or the mob was due at midnight to tar and feather us.

Maybe they'd go to Mo for feathers and I'd get some sort of warning.

"Because, my son is engaged and you will not take him away from his prospects," Her tone, admittedly, was the reason I decided to be stupid.

"He's engaged to me. I thought Daniel told you, mom." I smiled and ate my crunchy marshmallows while watching her go pale, turn on her heel, and march through the door at a beaming Larry.

Which meant that I, also, went pale.

"I was just..." My voice was high pitched and stammering. "I didn't mean..."

Larry walked into the kitchen and pulled me against him, lifting me slightly so he could prop me on the counter and stand between my legs.

"No take backs," he said against my jaw and alternated kisses and nibbles to my ear and back down.

"I... uh..." but all my blood had headed south and marriage can't be that bad, right?

My phone blared and I reached over to silence it. Larry chose that moment to press himself closer and my hand trembled.

Trembled and answered the stupid phone.

"Cyn, I need your help," a woman said, and I pressed a hand to Larry's chest, pushing him back to pick it up.

"Who is this?" I said into the phone while Larry looked two seconds away from throwing the device at the wall and carrying me away. Something ¾ of my body desperately wanted.

"It's... Gretchen, well, Britney, but Gretchen Harpole," her voice was all business.

"The not dead officer, ex-waitress?" I confirmed, and Larry stopped massaging my inner thigh in an effort to get me to end the call.

"It's... complicated. Will you help me?" she asked and my gut said I should.

"What do you need?" I asked, sliding off the counter and grabbing Larry's butt as I exited the kitchen. He returned the favor and finished my cereal.

"I need you to meet me at a warehouse," she rattled off an address and I stared at it.

"I've been there, it's a flower market."

"That was... bad timing. Please?"

"Give me twenty minutes," I said, stealing black sweats from Larry's pajama drawer.

Winnie whimpered at the sight of the warehouse, and I stroked the fur along her back. The last time we'd been in a warehouse, we were in Florida and Winnie had a bit of a complex.

"I know, girl. But there probably aren't any alligators in there," I whispered, and she curled up on the seat. I saw the small indentation in her tail from our last warehouse adventure and gave her a treat from the glove compartment. We were "on-call" when the call came in about a possible explosives bunker in a warehouse. While I'm fairly certain a private called in that fake bomb threat to get out of PT in the sun, no one would rest until Winnie and I checked it out. The place was dark, humid, and full of alligators. While no one should have been keeping ten live gators in a warehouse. It was not actually a crime... at least not in Florida.

The dent in Winnie's tail served as yet another reminder that Florida really is the worst.

Armed with a cup of coffee and my borrowed clothes, I was just this side of human. It was after five, and I had been forced to pose as a dead swan, see Larry's mom while in my underwear, and give up a sure thing to investigate... whatever this was. All while sober and improperly caffeinated.

I finished the first iced coffee and stared at the second one, contemplating the consequences of leaving to get more when headlights filled my truck from behind.

A jet-black Corolla pulled up beside us, and Britney/Gretchen got out. In the setting sun, her figure was somehow curvier, the dark clothing letting her blend into the night. Everything except the blonde bob sitting crooked on her skull.

"You don't look as good blonde," I said, exiting the Jeep. Winnie climbed through the door behind me but stayed low to the ground, nose working. Britney/Gretchen looked up at her head, blew out a breath, and pulled the crappy wig off and tossed it into her car.

"It's not my favorite. What's she doing?"

"Checking for alligators," I shrugged and walked toward the warehouse. Winnie followed, nose the ground, scooping dirt into her cone. Just before the door, she made a sharp left and I followed.

"Where are you going?" the former detective said, but she went silent at the sound of voices. I placed a hand on Winnies back and she slowed. We were moving around the warehouse toward the concrete wash that cut through the center of this part of town. Voices echoed from all directions, but I could make out one that was familiar.

"Where is my product?" all traces of an alcoholic slur gone.

"Sir, they were here. But we had to move them when-"

A crack echoed from all directions and I flattened myself against the wall, hand groping for Winnie's collar. The sound of water rushing in the wash filled the silence following the shot, and I held my breath. The sky was clear, but the smell of rain remained, and the racking sobs of the prisoner indicated he was still alive.

"That was a warning shot. Where is the last one?" Paddy's voice was robotic and dangerous. We got to the corner and I tried to peek but the space was too wide open. Gretchen moved around me and pulled out a small camera on a metal coil rod, recording but we were blind in the moment.

"They're all inside. All of them," the second man was crying, Winnie let out a soft whimper at the same time a grunt of pain echoed from all directions and I chanced a look. Paddy with his three attendants stood in front a man on his knees, clutching his abdomen with a stream of blood beneath his nose. One attendant was wrapping his hand while the other two kept the man on his knees. The man wasn't a lightweight. He had thick muscles and skin patchy from too much time in the sun. The fading light put his age and nationality at anyone's guess, but I was leaning toward thirty and white.

"They are not all inside. One is missing. I want it," the anger emanating from each syllable. "You think any member of this team can lie to me?"

"That's all of them. I haven't moved any!" The pleas were feeble and terrified. His body looked capable of easily over-powering the two men who held him, but he wasn't trying to. "Please, I didn't know you wanted them. It's my business, but you paid for seven and there are seven. We gave you all your money back."

"These aren't the seven," he gestured for the man wrapping his fists to hit the man again, and I made a poor decision to order Winnie to speak.

"Woof!" her bark echoed off the wash, warehouse, and the buildings nearby. Paddy looked nervous, glanced around, and halted his minion.

"Dispose of him over the edge," he said and the two men nodded. They remained perfectly still until Paddy trod off around the building. As his shadow disappeared with the rest of him, the footsteps becoming muffled, the two goons started struggling to drag the man over toward the wash.

"I can't watch this," I whispered and took off, ordering Winnie to stay safe with her cone of shame. Larry was already pissed. I was letting her walk so much... as though the dog didn't do whatever she wanted. My boots slapped the pavement, but the pleas for mercy drowned everything out until I was nearly upon them. Attendant one let go of the hostages arm and spun with a right hook. I bobbed, weaving to the side, dropped down and executed a sweep. Male attendant one went down, the second looked torn between his assigned job of witness disposal and vengeance for his fellow thug. He had one moment to decide before a fist collided with his face, attached to the arm of Gretchen. Attendant two's head rocked backward and blood gushed from his nose. As soon as both arms were free, the prisoner shot to his feet and ran.

"Hey!" I called out, Winnie taking that as her cue. She stood, let out a growl, and the man stopped just as attendant number one came up behind me and wrapped an arm around my neck, constricting my airflow. I had a few inches of height on the man, and he used the leverage to tilt me backwards. Unfortunately, I had about fifty pounds on him. Using that as I leverage, I bent my knees and braced his body against my back, flipping him over my shoulder. I brought up my knee and jammed it into his nuts, sending him into a state of pain and paralysis. A glance showed Gretchen's man was still down, and Gretchen had taken off after our damsel in distress.

A dog yelped in pain and part of me died.

Panicked, I ran back the way I had come as fast as possible. Winnie was lying in a heap and whimpering. Her sutures had opened and without pausing, I scooped her into my arms and kept moving. She may be ninety pounds, but I'd lift a car for her. I ran with her in my arms, knowing Gretchen and the hostage were out there somewhere, but not caring in the least.

I laid her gently in the back seat, climbed in and floored the Jeep.

Chapter Eighteen: Flying Solo

"You can't keep me from her!" I wiped snot from my face. "She's my partner. I'm responsible and..."

"No." Larry pulled the crate from the bed of his truck. Winnie was inside, still sedated. Her staples had been replaced. She had minor internal bleeding and bruising indicating someone had kicked her. Not hard, she would heal, but she was on strict mobility limitations.

I was murderous and shaken.

"You can't-"

"Stop." He said, setting Winnie down in his living room. "Just stop. You are not responsible. You are not a good dog mom. She should have stayed here and not gone out with you on a mission. This is going to add weeks to her recovery. Winnie deserved better, Cyn."

"I don't go on missions without her." I sniveled into my arm. His words had hit harder than the punches I'd taken in the attack. She was my best friend, my back up, and I had let her down. There was never a reason to take her out injured. Not anymore, and I'd known it.

"Well, now you are going to go home without her," he said, walking back out to the truck and slamming the tailgate closed. It was nearly four in the morning. He had worked through the night while I paced his waiting room. My clothes were still splattered with blood from her ruptured stitches, but she was better now. Larry had promised me she was better.

"Can't I-"

"No, dammit. I'm so mad at you right now, Cyn. You risked her life over missing boxes that hold dead bodies. Winnie should be more important than all of that. You can't treat a dog in stitches like the only thing that's different is she has a cone on her head! You messed up, bad."

Sobs shook my body, and I sat down hard on the sidewalk. The whole drive to his clinic I'd clutched her paw, promising her pup cups and treats. Larry had met me at my Jeep, scooped Winnie out, and gotten to work without so much as a word in my direction. The silence from him was nothing compared to the ache and the chill of my car without Winnie beside me.

"The couch?" I sniffled with hope.

"Your keys are in your Jeep when you're done having a pity party," Larry said, and went into his own house, locking the door. My hands shook, and I stared at the blood, dirt, and grime. I'd fought two men, saved a third, and he kicked Winnie. Kicked her in her stitches; my brain seethed and my blood boiled over.

Anger was more productive than sadness anyway.

My phone alerted for the tenth time this hour and I growled into it.

"Hello?"

"Is she OK?" Gretchen asked, and I stared at Larry's locked door.

"No, but she will be. No thanks to me," I swiped at the various fluids on my face and stared at my shoes. The anger had flared quickly and died at the sound of her voice.

"I caught up with the man who was being held. He's... difficult. So far, I have that Benjamin Bates is the man in charge, and he has no reason to file charges on the assault. He claimed his name is Scooter, but I doubt that's even a nickname."

My shoes doubled as tears spilled down my face. I had risked my best friend to save a man who not only didn't want our help, but kicked her. Winnie was locked in another person's house where I couldn't see her because I wanted to play the hero.

"What do you want from me?" I asked, and she let out a long breath.

"I need to find my mom. As far as my information goes, you're the last person to see her alive... and my dad."

"What does your mom have to do with... anything?" I asked, wondering why the heck the bad guys had to be related to the normal people. Couldn't the bad guys just be bad guys?

"My stepdad was working at the mortuary. The debts piled up, he took an offer he couldn't refuse, made the deals that put this whole thing in motion. My mom could lose the bar, everything, if I can't make this right. My step dad... could die."

"I thought your last name was Harpole?" My tears dried up as my anger bubbled and my brain worked overtime.

"It is... But my maiden name is..."

"Charles?" I asked. Just what I needed, another family member attached to a dead man, death boxes, a bar, and a mortuary. One that had also, technically, died in a house fire years ago.

I totally owed my mom an apology. Her date nights were normal.

"It's actually Gatton. I'll explain later. Please, Cyn, I know this is a lot, but I have to find them. I need to know what's going on," her voice was kind, scared. My heart, however, had its own fears, and I didn't have room for anyone else's. "I used sources and deep cover, but I couldn't get any information and no one would talk to me. My mom kept saying I was a narc and dead to the family. My step-dad saw my brother at the mortuary, but neither of them would give me anything to help them get out."

"I can't help you, not right now. Find another person to send on your fool's errands," I yawned into the phone and got to my feet.

"Please, where did you see them last?" she begged, and I stared at my shoes.

"Last I saw them was at your brother's funeral. They drove away in an unmarked SUV at the sight of a woman and your hired help. Didn't Joey tell you all of that?"

"Did they tell you anything else?"

"Aside from your step-dad being well endowed, they said to find the caskets. But I don't really care anymore. I'm going to bed."

Ending the call, I stared at the dark quiet house.

Maybe Winnie was better off without me, but I would be better off if Retta had never walked into my office.

"Come get your dog!" Larry shouted into the phone, and I could hear her wailing in the background. It was a combination of whimper, bark, and Wookie noise that had managed to make a war zone unpleasant on my Afghanistan tour. Despite the very real chaos she'd caused, the dog had a way of getting what she wanted. She had used this same sound to end her solitary kennel time seven days early after destroying a mess hall.

I'd be proud if I wasn't so damn tired.

"You were right, I was wrong, please!"

It was six in the morning. I had been asleep for all of fifteen minutes, and my injuries were reminding me that I was almost thirty and not physically capable of enduring the level of abuse I'd previously tolerated. I'd sat on my couch drinking coffee and crying for a half-hour before the desire to sleep won out over my desire to cry.

Also, I ran out of coffee, which meant either I had to go get more or cry over that.

I'd chosen to sleep over the fifteen-stair descent to my office where the back-up coffee was.

"Ahshrawtz," I said into the phone and my pillow. It had been thirty minutes since I decided I'd rather have sleep than trek downstairs for more coffee, and it was already biting me in the tail like an alligator in Florida. At this point in my life, it should not be surprising that every decision I make is the wrong one, but here we were.

Awake, without coffee, talking to people.

Larry cut into my downward spiral of negative thoughts.

"Now, Cyn! I have surgeries to do today. She started howling the second you left and she hasn't stopped. Not once. Now, she's pacing the crate, she's not resting... It's actually safer with you than without you. Apparently, the Army put you two together because you are both stubborn, pig-headed pains in the..."

My phone beeped a call waiting so I hung up on Larry and his unflattering descriptors. Just because I was wrong didn't mean I needed a list of why.

"EL-O?" I managed, wondering who these people are who dared to need me at six in the morning. I mean really, this wasn't a war zone. People should be allowed to sleep.

"Cynthia Natasha Sharp, how dare you!" My mom shrieked into the phone, and I considered "accidentally" hanging it up. I hadn't heard my middle name in a decade. I'd convinced the Army I didn't have one so people wouldn't turn my initials into another word for butts. Cyn the Determined was nothing compared to the years everyone spent saying "check out CANS".

No one wants to be called Cans, especially in the Army.

"Winnie's fine, mom. Everyone's fine. Go back to bed," I yawned and the phone sagged against my body.

"Do you hear my voice, Cynthia? Everything is not fine! My youngest daughter got engaged and didn't tell me! I had to find out from a hostile soon to be mother-in-law demanding I order you back into the Army. Why didn't you tell me?"

From there it deteriorated into a re-cap of all the things I "didn't tell her". Like breaking my arm, not making it onto the school basketball team and pretending to go to practice, not telling her when I did make the basketball team when everyone else was sick with mono before the finals and I got to actually play... poorly, but I played.

Then burned down the school gym... kind of.

"Ma, it's..."

She kept going over my objections and I stared at the ceiling. At this rate, there would be no sleep.

Call waiting alerted again.

"Gotta go, ma," I said and hung up to take the new call.

"Are you coming over?" Larry demanded over Winnie' howls of despair.

Call waiting beeped again and I hung up.

"Did you just hang up on me?" my mom was losing her voice from yelling.

Call waiting again.

"If you don't stop-"

Beep.

"I swear to God, Cynthia-"

Beep.

"Ms. Sharp?" a new voice said into the phone, and I peeled my eyes open to read the display.

"Yeah?" I yawned into the phone.

"We need to meet," he said. His diction was clear and crisp. Authoritative with a wisp of somewhere overseas.

"No," I rolled over and put my pillow over my head as call waiting continued beeping fervently.

"No?"

"No. I'm not leaving this bed for anything less than life or death. Are you dying?"

"No, but-"

"Is someone in my family dying?" I spoke over him and he took a sharp inhale of offense.

"Not your family, Ms. Sharp, but members of Retta's family are in danger. I think you can save her son." His anger mixed with formal English made him sound like a Don in a third rate mafia movie. My stomach tried to work up concern for an arbitrary stranger, but I was too tired.

"Prove someone is in jeopardy or you can go kick rocks," I said and hung up. My phone alerted a text and a glance showed it was from the same unknown number. I opened the attachment to see a small child, somewhere between 5 and 12, seated on a chair with a tear-stained face. Beside him, a beefy man was bloody and injured. The text was simple.

Unk Num: *I want my casket.*

I stared at the message. Tired and cranky, I made a hasty reply.

Me: *Maybe if you die, you can have one for your death day.*

Unk Num: *Final warning, Ms. Sharp. Find my box or you find two dead bodies. Twenty-four hours.*

My reply came back undeliverable.

Well... that sucks.

Resigned, I got out of bed and stuffed my feet into shoes. Larry was going to have to endure Winnie torture for just a while longer. Apparently, I was not done chasing empty caskets.

Chapter Nineteen:
Blind Sided

The warehouse was deserted.

There was no flower market, no death boxes, no goons beating a man... there was nothing. I sat in my Jeep staring at the building, windows down. The wash roared on with torrents of water, more rain having fallen in the night.

It was quiet and I nearly decided it was a good time to take a nap when my phone went off again.

"Kirby, for the last time, if you sing to her, she will sleep," I lied into the phone.

"That doesn't sound honest," Gretchen said, and I climbed out of the Jeep.

"It's not, but my choices were limited," I answered her, walking the building. Litter covered the ground, and the whole area was overgrown with grass. It would be a fire hazard in the summer, but for now it was just ugly.

"Where are you?" she asked, and I heard muffled talking behind her.

"Warehouse. Did you find them?" I asked, hoping the voices were her family.

"Yes, but..." a woman screamed in the background, and Gretchen moved through a door and the other sounds were muffled. "Retta's family?"

"With... Ben Bates. They looked OK in the picture I got, but it's not time stamped." I stood in a small patch of blood splatter and looked in all directions. In the light of day, I realized I was on the street between the faux Italian restaurant and the mortuary. If I leaned, I could see both structures in my peripheral vision.

Think, Sharp. I coaxed myself, taking in the area.

"Why were you working at Mi Asiago Prego?" I asked, interrupting her statement that I hadn't been listening to.

"It was a job," she shuffled. "I guess it was an assignment."

My eyes caught on a ladder that ran up the side of the building, and I decided to try a new perspective. I climbed up, careful not to slip on the wet rails, the phone tucked into my bra on speaker.

"Why did it end?" I asked, arriving at the top and taking in the view. Paddy's parking lot, or rather Ben Bates ground operations, were completely visible. The back door to the mortuary where the confrontation occurred in complete visibility.

"My target became complicated," her voice held hesitation.

"You're not a detective, but you're not a civilian," I walked to the edge and studied the ground. A casing lay discarded on the rooftop. Probably this was where Gatton had been shot from. "Was Gatton your half-brother?"

"No, full brother. Mr. Charles, Vincent, is our step-dad. He and my mom married two years before I 'died'." I pictured her making air quotes around the last word. "I'd introduced them by accident. I was investigating him for Dayton, but then it got bigger and worse. My reassignment to the FBI meant I needed to cut ties with my family."

"So, you burned your house down?" I found another casing beside the first. It was corroded. People had been using this vantage as a sniper point for more than just the Gatton murder.

"No, the fire was accidental. The department... was asked to embellish. I was connected to Vincent, so I could reasonably investigate him from a distance and not be suspicious. They didn't want him, a man with debts who made poor choices. They wanted the man he was working with." Her statement made sense on a federal level, but on a local level it seemed idiotic. "I really just wanted to be part of my own family. My mom liked the booze too much and Andre... got lost."

"Why were you at the Italian place?" I asked, seeing a stack of napkins for the establishment beside empty take-out containers. How does a woman grow up to be in The Bureau with a family that screwed up?

"Ben Bates owns it. He owns... all of the buildings," she clarified, and I looked in each direction. I was in Paddy's crow's nest, able to see threats from all directions. "He owns Pickles, the mortuary, the restaurant, the warehouse, the parking lot... he owns half this damn town."

She sounded like she might want to punch something.

"What about your brother?"

"Worked for him, but I was trying to get more information when he died. My brother... wasn't well after being in the Coast Guard. Not that he was especially normal before. We knew the leader was laundering money through the mortuary, but we wanted to know where it came from." Her tone indicated that had not been achieved. "We haven't even found the money, but thanks to the moonshine, we know drugs are in the mix."

"We being... the Bureau?" I found the tent that once lived in the parking lot packed up on the rooftop. Beside it a few electronics, older and outdated, but protected with a tarp. A sleeping bag, an old duffle bag. A foot locker sat at the end, and I opened the box. Photos, dog tags, and socks. A younger, slimmer version of the man I'd seen at the back door graced the image in fatigues. His eyes were hooded, dark. He wasn't in all of the pictures. No one stood out as being in all of the pictures as a bunch of men loitering in places around the world shifted by, in image after image. They showed a life of friendship and camaraderie. One that I had lived, but never really a felt part of. Looking at the images of Gatton each time he appeared, I got the impression it was the same for him.

"Yeah," she continued speaking but I wasn't really listening. Shuffling through the stack of photos, I stopped on a picture with Gatton and a man that looked familiar. Unlike the others, it was a close-up selfie. Gatton was brooding, and the white man with freckles was beaming. I closed one eye and screwed up my face.

Maybe?

"Can I text you a picture?" I asked, interrupting her. She seemed indifferent to the act and confirmed. I hung up, sent the shot and called back. "Is that 'Scooter'?"

"Yeah..." her phone was away from her face, but I could hear her. "It says his name is..."

She was trying to read the name patch on his shirt, but I'd not been able to read it either. Deciding the conversation wasn't helpful anymore, I hung up the phone and picked up the other items.

I stared at the dog tags, squinting and trying to change the angle of the light. The name was practically worn away, too worn for someone who had maybe been out of the military for a half decade at most. Taking a page from Sherlock Holmes, I rifled through the belongings until I found a pencil and paper in the military kit that was standard issue but mostly pointless.

No one ever used the stupid paper and pencil.

Closing the footlocker, I sat in front of it with the dog tag dead center. The thin paper was even thinner than I remembered, but it held as I pressed it into the tag and ran the pencil over it lightly to reveal an impression.

Except there wasn't an impression.

The letter S came through and the number 76, but that was it. The rest of the name was gone. Gone... but not pointless, I thought, staring at the S. There was no S in Andre Gatton.

My temples throbbed and I rubbed small circles, staring at the tags and impression on the footlocker. He hadn't lived here, but whoever had, knew him... or he had someone else's tags. The throbbing turned to stabbing, and I set it all aside, for now.

Real police would have to look into this, but I just needed to save a little boy and his dad.

I also needed more coffee and a nap.

I prayed at least half of those would happen soon.

Moving on from the camp, I stumbled on a skylight and looked down. It was dark in the warehouse, only the low glow of an emergency exit sign brightening a corner. Filthy, but completely intact, the skylight held as I pressed my weight against it trying to peer down into the depths and discern... literally anything useful. My left hand reached to swipe away some grime, caught on a latch, and the window titled down, folding inward.

Hanging on fingertips, I clutched the frame as it swung in, and I was dangling inside the building. Clawing for purchase, my hands slipped and gripped so many times I wasn't sure whether falling or holding on was more painful. To the left was a rail along an iron catwalk and a series of doors. Stretching a foot, I was just inches shy of reaching it.

"This is so stupid," I muttered to myself, throwing my body-weight backward, forcing the window to swing on its hinge back and forth. On the second swing toward the catwalk, I let go. The rail slammed into my chest and I leaned forward to fall gracelessly onto my back, gasping for air and choking on dust.

"I need a new hobby," I said to no one.

After a minute of contemplating the ineptitudes of my life and determining I probably hadn't broken a rib, I hauled myself to my feet and started checking doors. Each one was unlocked and led to a room that housed dust, spiders, and nothing. Not even a metal folding table. The rooms had never been used, and

I tried to remember if there had been anything up here during the flower market, but I'd never looked up.

I had a flashlight in my pocket, but the daylight streaming through the windows was decent enough. As my eyes adjusted, I could see more of what was down on the floor below as the sunlight and exit signs reflected off the smooth lacquer surface of... Caskets?

Carefully descending, I looked for security cameras, alarms... there was nothing obvious. There were maybe a half-dozen caskets; all gloss wood with gold rails in various shades of brown. The room held the smell of flowers and fresh cut wood. I ran my hand across the smooth surface, somehow finding the death box beautiful in the filtered sunlight.

My hand caught on the latch and I released it to open the lid, swinging it soundlessly open.

Inside, the lining was in tatters.

There were cuts in every fabric, every seam torn to shreds. I moved to the next one, and the one after. They'd all been cut and searched. Each box had cuts in the wood, indicating a large knife had been used. No care had been shown for the craftsmanship, the box, or the meaning behind it.

It was storage for something besides bodies... or it was supposed to be.

The level of desperation was evidently increasing as each had been searched. Following the carnage, I identified a pattern that showed which was the first one he'd searched and which was the last. Based on the fact the lid of the last casket was unhinged, shattered and across the room, he hadn't found what he was looking for. I shone the flashlight under and around the death boxes. The ground was littered with leaves, flower petals, and something that looked suspiciously like the powdered sugar in Mo's pantry that was probably more drugs.

My phone dinged, and I saw a message from Gretchen.

GH2: *Find anything?*

I replied with a picture, including the "powdered sugar" and shattered death box.

GH2: *Creepy. But I have an idea where to start on finding Ben Bates now.*

I agreed without response and did one last sweep with the flashlight. The hum of an electric motor filled the room and light poured in from the opposite side of the building. Exposed, I ran to the emergency exit and crouched. I was half behind the smashed lid of the last box, and I strained my ears for a sound.

"What a mess," a woman spoke, her voice older but sharper than any I'd heard before. "Honestly, why do we do business with this man? Discount or not, these linings are going to take days to repair."

"Problem with the merchandise?" A voice I knew entered the conversation. It was stronger now that he wasn't crying and being pummeled. I chanced a glance and saw the same frame from the other night, and a surge of anger flooded me.

That man had kicked Winnie. I saved his life, and he hurt my best friend.

"Who are you?" he shouted, and I realized I was on my feet and moving toward him.

"You don't remember me?" my mouth had gone on a mission separate from my brain but in agreement with my feet. "Let me return the favor you showed my partner."

His eyes widened as I got closer, pulled my arm back, and smashed my knuckles into his face.

Blood surged from his nose and he collapsed as my whole arm sang in pain. I looked over at the woman, she was fit but dressed somberly. Legitimate funeral owner, at best guess.

"I don't know what you paid for these, but the wood is damaged in addition to the lining, and also this guy is a dog kicker. Maybe get a refund," I shrugged and walked out of the open bay door, shaking my arm out. Once in the Jeep, I blasted the radio.

"I am a warrior, I will never stop. What doesn't kill me, makes me stronger. I am the wolf, I am the hunger," I sang, exiting the driveway and gunning the engine toward the highway and home.

One street over, I heard an engine rev and tires squealing.

A truck rocketed up behind me and I saw Scooter, blood dripping from his face, behind the wheel. I gave the Jeep more gas and took a turn on two wheels. He missed the turn and I circled back to the warehouse, heading home in a different direction. My eyes were glued to my review mirror, knowing that when the truck reappeared, I'd need a plan or a defense.

I passed the business district and it turned residential. Residential gave way to farms, but the truck didn't reappear. Apparently, Scooter was as un-motivated to get his revenge as he was to save his life.

My body relaxed as I left the suburb and moved into the country. I took my first full breath at a four way stop, looking all ways before drifting through the intersection. A car came up from the left and I moved more deliberately. It came faster, and

I tried to will my Jeep to go faster, but I'd shifted to neutral and the clutch wasn't where it should be. I stared at my feet, pumping the pedal and shifting. I gassed the engine and... the truck collided with my rear quarter panel. I spun twice, disoriented, my Jeep was nose to nose with the Dodge pickup.

It was Scooter's truck.

He backed up, repositioned, and floored it driving straight toward the side of my car. The brush guard collided, dented the door, and he braked. The truck stopped, but I rolled over. In a nauseating tumble, I barrel rolled down the side of the road, through a fence, and ended tires in the sky beside a cow. The truck sped off and my eyes drifted closed to the sound of a soft mooing beside me.

The radio stuttered, and Taylor Swift filled the car.

"No there ain't no doubt, somebody's gotta catch him now," Taylor sang into the car, and my mind went fuzzy. "No body, no crime but I ain't lettin' up til the day I die."

Hopefully that isn't today, I thought and passed out.

Chapter Twenty: Un-buried Treasure

"Uhhn," my throat made noise but my mouth didn't move. I tried to lick my lips but there was something in my mouth that was sticky and felt like sandpaper. Reaching for my face, I tried to feel for my jaw as my eyes hadn't yet decided opening was a good idea.

My fingers brushed something that felt like stitches, moved toward my face, across dry lips, and grabbed the sticky sandpaper in my mouth.

It was my tongue.

Half of my right eye opened, and the blinding light was an insta-headache.

"Uuhhhn..." I moaned again and a shadow moved to block the sun.

"Water?" A voice asked, and I tried to nod as a plastic straw poked my lips. After a long drink, the cup slurped empty, and the shadow moved. It was back in another moment with more water. "I can't believe nothing is broken."

An eyelid slid back and there was a sandy blonde nurse there. He wore neon green nail polish, rings in each ear, and hair in a neat ponytail on top of his head. His scrubs were black, his shoes were pink, and I couldn't remember if I'd seen him before or It was just that all hospital employees look the same after you've visited this many.

"Where?" I croaked and he gave me more water.

"Yellow Springs," he answered, and I nodded at his beaming smile.

"Bright," my voice rasped at the end and I decided it was my last attempt at speech. He adjusted the light, and my eyes settled closed as he checked my vitals. As though proving I was not some sort of super soldier, he seemed hell-bent on poking every bruise my body had to offer. Then, as a sick joke I assume, asked me if it hurt.

"Die," I hissed and he patted my arm.

"Usually I only get death threats when I work in the PT unit," he laughed, referencing the Physical Therapy unit. Having been in one of those, I questioned his humanity at torturing injured people for money.

"Must be your bedside manner," I smacked his hand away from the bruise across my chest left by the seat belt... Or maybe slamming into the rail when I jumped through a window... It's so hard to keep track of where the bruises are coming from.

"Speaking of bedside, there's a man here to see you," I could feel his eyebrows wiggle but I kept my eyes closed.

"No thanks. Discharge papers please," I held out my hand and he tutted.

"You can't just leave..."

"Papers, please, or face my wrath," it lost some effectiveness when I choked on my spit and had to sit up to get air. "Seriously, I need to find a stupid casket."

"Why? You'll live," he laughed, jotting something on a clipboard and walking out of the double bed room. A glance at the window said it was no longer daytime, but in January that could mean anywhere from four thirty at night to seven in the morning.

A cart squeaked to a stop outside my door, and I looked over at the plump, round woman in pink rose bud scrubs.

"Book?" she asked, turning around and then nearly dropping the magazines in her hands. "Cynthia! I heard you'd come in a few hours ago but I couldn't find you! How lucky you crashed into the back side of the dairy and Joseph found you!"

Mrs. Figs walked over and started looking at my injuries with motherly disapproval. She touched every bruise, making noises and exclamations that were as concerned as they were unintelligible. While her concern was endearing, I was ready to punch the next person who probed my bruises.

"You know, I'm not ready to give up my casket, young lady. You better not be trying to get your hands on it by dying."

I started to laugh, choked again, and she patted my back. Refilling my water cup, she placed the straw near my mouth and I tried to drink without inhaling, failed miserably, and spat water down the front of my gown. It soaked through and seeped down to my skin, the icy liquid forcing a mangled scream from my mouth.

"Do you need the nurse?" She pressed the nurse summoning button against my objections and brought me a towel from the bathroom. I blotted at my face and gown, pressing the cold water deeper into my clothes and bruises until I couldn't decide if it was worse to be wet or try and dry myself.

"Can you cancel..." the nurse appeared as I attempted to un-select the button. "Accident, sorry, I'm fine."

He took in the towel, water dripping from my face, and Mrs. Figs' serious demeanor.

"Honestly, I thought Steve was joking. Now..." he rolled his eyes and walked away.

"Stop talking about me, you gossips," I shouted at no one. Steve had been one of the urgent care nurses who treated my broken arm in November... a few times. His husband had also re-casted my arm. Today, my arms were cast free. A glance at my reflection in the window showed the stitches looked minor. Also in the reflection, I saw a bag of belongings tucked under my bed. Getting up, I pulled it out and started dumping the contents. Deciding to start from the bottom, I pulled up my cargo pants, checking that my phone and flashlight were still inside. I'd foregone a bra today in the interest of personal comfort on a rescue mission, so this next part would be awkward with Mrs. Figs standing there but...

"Could you turn around?" I asked, and she huffed out a breath.

"I have children, Cynthia. I also have boobs. It's not new," but she turned around, arms crossed beneath the boobs she had just mentioned. I swapped my gown for a T-shirt, tugged on my socks, and grabbed my shoe.

"Where's my other shoe?" I asked, dropping to my knees to look under the hospital bed. Wires, wheels, a couple spiders, no second shoe.

"Everything gets put in the bag. Maybe you weren't wearing it?" Mrs. Figs had turned back around and was eyeing me skeptically. "Why are you getting dressed?"

"She needs to find a casket for her next 'accident'," the neon nailed nurse sneered, and I rolled my eyes as he handed me a few sheets of paper.

"Cynthia! I was joking! Are you..." she dropped her voice, looking cautiously around the room, "suicidal?"

My eyes landed on her and I stared. Joking about caskets... why would she joke about...

"Is that death box still in front of your house?" I asked as my mind caught up. It was the same style as those in the warehouse. They were all identical caskets. Identical... and connected? "Can I go see it?"

"Why do you want to visit my casket, dear?" She still looked concerned, but it was mingled with a helping of suspicion. I knew where I ranked in her priorities.

"I need to check it. Please? It's life or death... not mine!" I added as I put my name on the hospital forms. "It's just... it's really important. Is it in front of your house?"

"No, we put it in the shed. It's too early to put on the lawn full-time," she looked at me as though I was an idiot and I marveled. The woman bought a wholesale coffin, displayed it on her lawn, but I was crazy for thinking she'd leave it there.

"Great!" I said, stuffing the forms back into the hands of the nurse. "I'll just drive over there and then..."

I looked down at my sock-only foot.

"Where's my Jeep?" I asked no one.

"It's dead. Maybe you can find it a casket," nurse neon nails laughed and danced out of the room. I sucked my lip into my mouth and chewed on it.

Mrs. Figs was speaking behind me, and I turned around to ask her to repeat herself when she held up a finger.

"Elmer, we owe her after the incident with my death. Get over here, now," she angrily pressed the end call button and gave me a weak smile. "Elmer will be here for you in a bit. Magazine?"

I accepted the Times and went to wait in front of the hospital.

The car ride to the Figs' household was more painful than my car accident.

Today's old man gripe was about ungrateful Millennials.

"Buy them shoes, they crash a car..." my eyes drifted closed as another breeze attempted to freeze off the toes on my sock-only foot. "Now they demand to be picked up. After 18 years, it should be my…"

Probably it would have been less painful to walk.

After seventeen years… or twenty minutes, we pulled into the drive, and I climbed out before he could put the car in park.

"Thank you, Mr. Figs!" I said and ran for the storage shed. Much like my parents, the unit had been outfitted as an extension of the house rather than a storage facility for tools. Whereas mine had turned theirs into an outdoor pleasure dungeon, the Figs had made theirs into a storage facility. The space paid homage to every holiday in coordinating storage totes and eerily discreet speakers played music from each holiday on an arbitrary loop.

Dead center was the gleaming cherry wood death box.

As "This is Halloween" gave way to an Irish jig, I inspected the flawless surface and smooth metal. The casket had no nicks, tears, or indentations in its exterior. The metal was cold to the touch, but clean and cared for. Though not actually for dead bodies, the Figs had taken great care of this one.

The lid swung open at the lightest touch, and I studied the lining. It was smooth, white, and heavily padded. Surprising, based on the lack of stuffing scattered around the warehouse. Perplexed, I pressed down to feel a very firm interior. I pressed again at the top and the bottom. It was firm, flat, and completely un-yielding.

Level with the box, I dropped my arm in and compared to the dozen I had just seen. The interior was shallower. I walked in a circle, checking the bottom and the sides for an indication that the box was less deep than its friends, but it was exactly the same. Yet, my arm stopped ten inches from the bottom of the box.

Curious, and not inclined toward destruction, I traced the seams of the lining, willing the fabric to show me clues or explain the irregularities that made this one special. The stitch work looked impressive, the careful draping folds of the side were flawless, every button rivet perfectly centered. Except... I reached for a button that wasn't sitting flat. Turning it left and right, it refused to sit in the socket carved for it. I pressed as hard as I could, and there was a thunk as something dropped to the ground and dust plumed up.

Hacking on the dust, I tried to keep my mouth and nose from taking in more while still maintaining air. It took ages, or minutes, for the dust to settle back into place, and I peeled my eyes open. There was wrapped wire hanging from the bottom of the box sides, attached to a motorized pulley. Sitting on the bottom of the box were at least a hundred stacks of large denomination bills, each bound in paper tape forming a perfect one-foot thick layer.

"Holy-"

"Move," a man said from behind me and I turned to see Scooter, standing there holding a gun. "You might be hard to kill, but I'm better at this range."

"That's rude, have you seen..." I gestured toward the money. It was somehow more impressive than the man who had kicked my dog, destroyed my Jeep, and pointed a gun at me.

"Move or I'll make sure you never move again."

I rolled my eyes and stepped back into the Christmas decoration alcove.

"Be my guest," I said, stepping back. "Did you kill Andre from the roof?"

"No, I'm not that good. Commander Bates is cleaning house." His hands shook, and I decided he'd be easy to disarm in a pinch.

Also, he couldn't hit the broad side of a barn, but as there weren't any barns, it was best not to test that theory unless absolutely necessary.

He moved to the money, running his hand along the bills when I noticed a loaded duffel beside him.

"Shouldn't that be empty so you have a place to put the money?" It was ridiculous to talk to a mad man, but part of me thought being shot dead in a storage shed listening to Rudolph the Red-Nosed Reindeer would be better than asking Mr. Figs to take me home.

I'd been eerily accepting of death recently and it was probably a good sign I needed therapy... or sex. Either way, I blamed Larry because he was totally responsible for the absence of at least one of those things.

Which was either sad commentary on my home, Mr. Figs, or my morbid association of holiday songs with death.

"Shut up," he hissed, pulling open the bag to reveal identical stacks of cash.

"You're replacing it with fakes?" Now he was just being weird. A dead body by an empty casket was way less suspicious than my dead body being next to a casket full of fake money. This story would be less suspicious if he killed me, took the money, and left nothing.

Though probably I shouldn't think he needs to murder me quite so loudly.

"No, I'm replacing the fakes I put in with real money," he said as a shot exploded from the open door, and he collapsed face first onto the top of the stacks, blood pooling around him.

He didn't move.

Chapter Twenty-One: The Dirty Dozen

P addy walked in, flanked by his four attendants. It was
the first time I'd seen them in a well-lit space, and they
were a far cry from parking lot attendants. Each had a tight
military haircut, muscles, and crisply ironed shirts.

"I've wanted to do that for a decade," one attendant spoke
and I had to look at him twice. He could have been a carbon
copy of Gatton.

"Aren't you dead?" I asked, and he rolled his eyes at me.
"No."

"Your mom was at your funeral," I crossed my arms and
challenged his attitude. "Whose body was in there then?"

"There was no body," Paddy hissed, and I watched him inspect the stacks of money, both from the bag and the false casket bottom.

"So who did the police have photos of at a crime scene?" I asked and Paddy hissed.

"It was staged, damn-it. Shut up! Did you have to shoot him on top of the money?"

"Sorry, boss," Gatton stood at parade rest, hands forming a diamond behind his lower back with feet shoulder width apart.

"Can someone please check Ms. Sharp for weapons?" Ben Bates, aka Paddy, was exasperated, and it was unfortunate I'd shown up unarmed. I probably could have taken out the lot before someone thought of checking me.

A Latino man approached and roughly shoved me into the Christmas display cases. The bright green bin slammed into the bruise against my chest, and I swallowed a scream. In front of me, between two of the bins, was a boxcutter. I slid my hand between them, palmed it, and stuffed it into my back pocket when he spun me around to check the front. He managed to crush the crackers in my right pocket, but missed the pelican light in my left.

The level of incompetence made me wonder how they'd survived the military, let alone participated in a thriving criminal enterprise. Completing his search and missing absolutely everything, the young-ish man shoved me back into the shelving and a box toppled to the floor. All four men jumped, and I rolled my eyes so hard I thought they'd get stuck. Who were these wannabe soldiers? I looked at Gatton and gave an internal shudder.

I guess it *was* the Coast Guard.

Note to self: never live near the coast. It was very poorly guarded.

"Who knows you're here?" Paddy asked, and when he turned, I saw the intelligence and hatred in his eyes.

"I don't know," I shrugged, hoping Mr. Figs had gone inside to watch Game of Thrones.

"The old man is on the couch half asleep," he practically read my mind, and I tried not to think about the knife in my pocket in case he had some sort of extrasensory perception.

"He drove me here from the hospital... so..." I shrugged, and Paddy looked me over from head to toe.

"Where is your shoe?" Gatton asked and I narrowed my eyes at him.

"I don't talk to dead people." He leveled a black semi-auto at me, and I caved. "That man ran me off the road. I only had one shoe at the hospital."

"Is that what happened to his face?" the Latino man asked, nudging the body face up off of the money when Paddy gestured for him to remove Scooter from the money.

"No," I answered and smiled at my handy work. Then I saw the bullet exit wound and bile rose up into my throat. Yes, the world was better off without a dog kicker, but that was... a lot of blood... and muscle tissue.

"She's turnin' green, boss." Gatton spoke, and I gave him my best death glare.

"I was in the Army, I'm always green," I snapped back and studied the men. Gatton was armed, the Latino man didn't appear to be, and the third man, a straw haired carbon copy of the newly deceased... looked like an idiot.

I just couldn't tell if he was an armed idiot.

"Yes... the day they let women in the military, it lost some of its charm," Paddy said, inspecting the difference between the real money and the fake bills. From here, they were indistinguishable... except the fake money was covered in blood and the real money was clean... mostly. "Women have no business anywhere but, in the kitchen, and legs-spread in bed."

Anger bubbled over, and I had a bad idea.

"Because you're gay?" left my mouth before I could stop it, and Gatton landed a kick to my gut that sent me doubling over and gasping for air. "There's nothing wrong with being gay."

It was true, but they were just asshole enough to be baited by the statement.

Paddy turned and kneed me in the face, knocking my jaw shut on my tongue so my mouth filled with blood.

Apparently, they were not going to be donning rainbow frocks at the next parade, but I'd achieved my goal. Bleeding on the ground, I watched the men relax. They turned back to study the two stacks of money and decide whether or not there was value in the fakes. Everyone had their back to me, having neutralized me as a threat.

At least I wasn't the only one making bad decisions today.

It was much easier to attack from the ground when all you have is a flashlight and a knife. No one works as hard to protect the ankles, but everyone needs an ankle. Sliding forward, I worked my way closer to the trio, prepared to look in agony if they noticed me. The low crawl was made challenging by the blood coating the floor, but it would make my story more believable.

"He has only half of the real amount here," Paddy muttered, shoving the money back into the bag. "What did he do with the rest of the money?"

"Hookers and beer?" One of the men suggested and another gave him a high-five.

Paddy's leg shot out in anger, toppling the casket that splintered on impact.

The henchmen stopped laughing.

Under the noise, I pulled the box cutter from my back pocket, stabbed it into Gatton's ankle. As expected, he screamed and dropped the gun. I scooped it up and pulled the flashlight from my pocket while standing. I swung out with my right arm, the flashlight connecting with solid flesh and bone. The straw haired man went down, and I squared off with Paddy and the Latino man.

"Better odds," I said, relieved until the Latino man unearthed a gun from his pants and Paddy did the same.

"Drop the weapons," the old man said calmly, evenly. "In case you haven't noticed, I'm not afraid of sacrificing team members."

"He wasn't your first then?" I asked, stalling. The gun was aimed at the ground. I wouldn't be on-target before one of them fired on me and I could only shoot one if they missed. Studying their hands, I resisted the urge to sigh.

Steady as a rock, neither of them would miss.

I dropped my gun and he smiled.

"Smarter than the men I recruit. Yes, there were more. There were twelve initially," he slid his hand into the handle of the bag, switching the gun to his non-dominant hand. Paddy surveyed the mess, straw haired man still out cold, and Gatton trying to stem the flow of blood from his Achilles tendon. "These are the last of my dirty dozen."

Without preamble, he lifted his gun and fired into the Latino man at point blank range. He fell back, comically slow, as the mess spread across the Halloween decorations behind him. It was a millisecond of horror, but a lifetime of trauma and aversion to flan after seeing brain matter up close. I tried to run, but slipped on the blood, landing face first onto the floor.

"All I wanted was to bury some money for the future. Instead," he fired a round into the straw haired man on the floor. "It was a flawless plan. Pretend to kill someone, bury my money..."

I'd landed on the gun I dropped. It was slick and sticky, the trigger sliding under my finger. It was impossible to aim through the horror show caking my face. Paddy leveled the gun at Gatton.

"I want you to know that it would always end this way," his cold voice indifferent to the anguish etched across Andre Gatton's face.

"Don't," I sputtered. "Just stop. Take your money and go." My hand slid out and my face nearly collided with the floor again. Slipping, using the one shoe I was wearing to gain traction, I forced myself to unsteady standing, gun behind my thigh.

"The job isn't over, princess," he said, turning the gun toward me as I raised mine to him.

"I say it is." We were in a standoff and Gatton was losing blood faster than my pounding heart could calculate. "Just leave."

"Do you know who founded the Coast Guard, Ms. Sharp?" I heard a car door close in the distance. We were in the middle of a residential neighborhood, and no one had called the cops when gunshot after gunshot rang out.

That, or Daniel Kirby had stopped to order a pizza.

"Alexander Hamilton, I've seen the play." I kept my gun level, waiting for him to lose focus for even a moment to get the advantage.

"What is his line, Ms. Sharp?" His smile was growing. I heard footsteps moving around. "I'm not throwing away my shot."

The door flew open, and Winnie bounded in, cone of shame bouncing on the tops of her ears.

"Fu-" he started, but she lunged forward, sinking her teeth in his arm.

"Winnie, out," I commanded. She let go, he dropped the gun, and I kicked it under the storage shelves. I kept mine trained on him, and he slowly raised his hands to applaud as the room filled with Law Enforcement from every alphabet agency in the country. Paddy was slammed to the ground, my gun taken by Gretchen, while the area was secured for medics to enter.

"There's another gun under the shelves," I gestured to where I'd kicked the Latino man's gun, feeling the pain of my accident and getting kneed in the face. A male agent cuffed Paddy, pulling him up to standing. The agent pushed him toward the door, and he stomped on my bare foot so I'd scream. Winnie growled and the agent moved him toward the door.

"You're nothing without that dog behind you," he sang in an impersonation of the Thomas Jefferson character from the play. I reached down and ruffled Winnie's ears. She leaned against my leg and I dug out the crushed cheese crackers, ripping the package open and giving her some from my palm.

"It is nice to have a Winnie dog on my side," she licked the cheese crumbs from my hand.

Chapter Twenty-Two: Swan Song

"Excuse me, but there is a sign!"

It was just after 9AM, I hadn't slept more than fifteen minutes in 24 hours. Well, theoretically one could argue that being unconscious in the hospital counted as sleep, but it only counted if you got to stay there and no one kicked you in the face when you left. The green-haired man was flirting with death. He was just as haughty, surly, and unpleasant at this hour as he was at any other I'd been in this store.

Except now he was unpleasant with a name badge and a caramel macchiato.

"Yes, Terrance, here's another one." I stepped to the side, and Gretchen moved forward. She was wearing a suit, her FBI badge clipped to her pants, and she gave him the once over pausing on his manicure.

My eyes followed hers, acknowledging it was a killer manicure.

Unlike me, Gretchen hadn't been forced to sit in a room being questioned by agency after agency. She'd gotten to go home and shower. She had gotten to witness Retta reunited with her husband and son.

She... was wearing two shoes.

"Terrance," she confirmed from his nametag and he huffed. Gotta give him credit, he was not badge shy. "I need to speak to your boss."

"Eh, whatever," he stalked to the back of the store. I went to the rack holding a pair of the shoes I now only had one of. Then I meandered to the flats section and picked out a perfectly ordinary pair in black. When I got back to the counter, Amber was walking up swiftly.

"You are not allowed in here!" She pointed an angry finger at the door and I smiled, clutching the shoes. "Put those down and leave!"

"Amber? Amber Carter?" Gretchen asked and the angry brunette turned her weak death glare on the federal agent.

"Yeah, what's it to you?" Her eyes dropped to see the badge and she paled a little.

Interesting.

"I'm here regarding the poster in the front of your store. The news photographer owns copyrights on the photo, and when I contacted the photographer, they said you hadn't paid for the use and they did not put the picture in the public domain. If you don't remove it, I have to arrest you," she said. A look of relief washed over Amber until another man in a suit came up behind Gretchen. "Also, this is Agent Bolt with the IRS, and he has some questions regarding the tax forms filed to purchase this facility."

Amber lost all shades of color, eyed the man, and ran.

She shoved through the counter opening, displacing a stack of plastic bags. One wrapped itself around her ankle, but she kept going as fast as her feet could carry her.

Unfortunately, she was still wearing stilettos. Her ice pick heel caught on a rug and she face-planted into a display of children's light up footwear. The lights blinked blue and red, Amber screamed, kicked off her shoes, and barreled into Terrance, who was filming the whole thing.

"What are you doing?" She shoved him away and crashed through the back door, a plastic bag flapping in the sudden burst of air. Terrance followed after her calling out questions like the paparazzi, until the fire door slammed shut and blocked out all sound from outside.

We all stood quietly for a single beat... and then another. The neon green exit sign flickered, but no one banged on the door. No one came around the front. An engine revved, tires squealed, and then silence.

No one came back into the shoe store.

"I guess I'll ring up my own shoes," I shrugged and operated the point of sale while Gretchen removed the unflattering poster. Terrance's abandoned caramel coffee catastrophe looked sad and lonely, so I dropped three dollars on the counter, scooped it up, and guzzled like my life depended on it.

"Does she owe taxes or something?" my eyes widened as the sugar hit my system. I could easily make it another 20 minutes awake now.

"No idea," Agent Bolt shrugged and took off his sunglasses.

"Are you kidding me?" I said to Joey's jaunty grin and Gretchen shrugged, holding the poster.

"The department technically has him on retainer as an informant, actor... witness..."

Her eyes slipped from humor to sadness and I followed her gaze. In front of her was a display of work boots featuring a caricature of a soldier.

"I'm sorry about your brother," I said and she nodded.

"He'll get help. I can visit him, but my mom..." she let out a breath and shrugged. "We all make choices. Then we have to live with those choices. I knew something had happened in the Coast Guard, I just didn't think it was a manipulative jerk who made him a pawn in a drug scheme."

"So... it was just drugs?" I asked and she shook her head. Her face didn't break, tears shimmering in the corners of her eyes.

"Drugs... murder, booze, intimidation, fraud and a sex parlor. The man had his fingers in a lot of pies. Andre deserved... better. He was a normal kind of weird before he joined, believe it or not."

She pulled out her phone and showed me a picture of them, as children. His arm was thrown around Gretchen's shoulder, heads thrown back laughing. They were wearing swimsuits with a beach behind them. None of the anger and darkness lining Andre Gatton's face in his service pictures was present.

Joey placed an arm around her shoulders, and she rested her head on his shoulder.

"We'll look out for him," Joey said softly, putting a kiss on the top of her head. "Maybe I'll feign an interest in his rock collection."

My head dropped to my left shoulder, an imitation of confused Winnie.

"What? Oh, he's my husband," she clarified, wiping her tears on his shirt. He held her tight and gave me a small smile. "I thought you realized that at the funeral when I tried to get to you."

"You were at the funeral?" I asked and tried to summon an image... "Killer dress."

"Thanks... that kilt was the real show stopper," I nodded sagely and then a buzzer went off in my head and I stared at the man in the grey suit.

"Joey... Harpole?" I asked, mouth working like a deep-sea fish. He smiled, normal, and I had to guess his age back at thirty.

"I'm an enigma," he winked and walked out the front door with a little hip wiggle for my benefit. Larry raised a brow, standing outside with Winnie, and I smiled. The man was in jeans and a T-shirt and he looked... yum.

Following Joey, I turned around and gave the store one last look. No Terri or Amber... I checked the door, finding keys in the lock. I walked out to the sidewalk and locked the door, handing the keys to Larry.

"What am I supposed to do with these?" he asked and I shrugged.

"She's your wife, I'm just keeping it in the family." I hip-checked him, and he pulled me close against him. Winnie wrapped us in her leash, and my body plastered against his.

"That couldn't possibly be your final answer," he whispered against my neck and bit the skin beneath my ear gently. "I'm willing to beg... on my knees."

A shiver ran up my spine and I smiled.

"I've spent a lot of time being interrogated... are you planning on asking me any questions?" I asked, my tired brain waging war with the need in my lady parts. The sugar rush from the caramel only took me so far, and now it was up to Larry.

"No questions," he brought his mouth to mine, tongues tangling together, my hands fisting into the front of his shirt. I was definitely not tired anymore.

My breath joined my heart rate and I panted.

"Your place or mine?" I whispered and he bit my lower lip.

"Why don't we try out both and go from there?" he smiled. "We'll start with mine... it's closer. Plus, I have a dress I think you're missing."

My face paled.

"Not the sea foam swan dress!" my eyes widened until I resembled an owl.

Larry moved his lips along my jawline to just below my ear where he took another small nibble.

"Yes, that one. I plan to completely destroy it by ripping it off you," his voice tickled my ear and sent tiny bumps sprouting on my skin.

"Then... I can burn it?" I panted, hands exploring various pieces of his person.

"Then... you can burn it," he said with one final, lingering kiss to my lips. "Then, after, we can have coffee."

"I think I might love you," I whispered. With a small laugh he took my hand, Winnie's leash pressed between our palms.

"When I'm done, you won't have to think about anything at all," he promised.

Oh boy.

Sneak Peek of Book 3: Digging Through Dirty Laundry

Chapter One: New Ride

"What the hell is that?" I stared in horror and simultaneously needed to blink repeatedly to stave off the brightness.

"It's your new Jeep," Larry responded without hesitation. Rubbing the sleep from my lavender eyes and shoving back my messy tangle of blonde hair, I tried to orient myself to what I was looking at. My eyes took in the Jeep, the sidewalk, and my feet in their yellow Crocs six feet below me... Everything was real... Real and...

"It's pink," I gawked as a group of middle school girls stopped in front of the car and took selfies with it. They threw up peace signs and tried to look cute but sexy, disturbing for pre-pubescent girls, but middle school was like that.

"You like pink," he countered and I narrowed my eyes at the Jeep. I'd been happily sleeping in my own bed when Larry had let himself into my apartment, pulled me out of bed, and after a few inappropriate gropes, brought me outside. My apartment was on Main St, a small single room affair that sat on a third of the library lot above a small office. The office and the apartment belonged to a couple local seniors who let me live there in exchange for investigative services donated to the town.

"It has a giant Hello Kitty on the hood!"

"So do your underwear, Cyn," the middle school girls giggled, giving Larry sly glances. Hard to blame them, really, Dr. Larry Kirby was tall, leanly muscled with messy brown hair and flawless skin. Sometimes I just stared at him and giggled too.

Just not when he was talking about my underwear on a public street.

"Where did it come from? Why is it here? I have a vehicle."

"No, you were borrowing my truck. The insurance money from your Jeep came in and you left it sitting there for two weeks. So I took it, bought you this Jeep, and now I need my truck keys back," he held out his hand and I rounded on him.

"Why can't I keep borrowing your truck? You stole my money? I'm sooo telling your brother!" I said, reminding both of us that his brother, Daniel Kirby, was local law enforcement. Incompetent law enforcement, but still technically tasked with upholding the law. He had been the hottest guy in high school with a reputation for nail and bail. Now he was married, had way too many kids, and the investigative skills of a toddler immediately after reading Sherlock Holmes.

He also had zero sense of humor, at least when it came to reminding him of his own stupidity.

"You would never willingly talk to Daniel. Not after his anniversary party!" Larry's wide smile reminded me of what happens when a bunch of children covered in food and food-like substances stand too close to a German shepherd Malinois with an uncontrollable appetite. The child had been right at Winnie height, waving a hot dog around like a baton. Hilarious in retrospect, the incident may have taken years off her mother's life.

"Winnie didn't eat any fingers, so I think I'm good!" my eyes dropped to the fur monster in question. Sgt. Winifred Pupperson, Winnie for short, and I had been in the Army together. We were military police and served four years with an impeccable record of chaos, destruction and fire. The Army had been relieved when our contract expired and they "accidentally" forgot to mention it so we couldn't re-up. Specialist Cynthia Sharp and Sgt. Winifred Pupperson retired to Cyn and Winnie, Ohio's most competent demolition experts.

Certified only to work at a farm maintaining livestock outputs for sale.

"Molly won't touch a hot dog if she's seen a dog in the last ten minutes!" Larry was now laughing, and I thought of the poor, messy child in her stained dress and muddy feet. She'd pet Winnie for twenty minutes once she stopped crying.

"Ugh, fine. I won't tell him you forged my name on a check, cashed it, and bought me a hideous pink Hello Kitty Jeep that is probably mechanically unsound and filled with bubblegum pop music. But why can't I keep borrowing your truck? I mean I fill it with gas and I haven't hit anything!"

"Seriously? You don't know why?" I winced and shook my head. Innocent until proven guilty works in a court of law, maybe it works in the court of *your lover knows you took his truck mudding and spilled a two-liter of Cherry Coke and McDonalds fries that Winnie ate and then barfed up into the upholstery.* "I saw that, you know what you did, young lady."

I moved really close to him and gave him sexy eyes.

"Yeah, I can hold out longer than you can. We've proved it. You can't have my truck, not after the gummy bears," he tapped a finger on my nose.

Damn, I'd forgotten about the gummy bears.

"Fine," I stepped back from him, and felt his eyes on my pajama shorts as I walked toward the pink abomination. For his benefit, I stuck my head through the window and pushed my butt in the air. It's important to remind a man that while he might be able to hold out longer, the world could see his affliction.

Sadly as I was part of the world and seeing is believing, it was best if I personally didn't look.

As expected, the seats were fluffy pink, the stereo lit up in shades of purple and the steering wheel was covered in glitter. I picked at the wheel with a nail to remove the cover.

It wasn't a cover. Someone had silicone lacquered the steering wheel with pink glitter.

I shuddered as another group of girls came by and snapped selfies with it.

Larry had bought me Malibu Barbie's car and he looked a little adorable for having done it. Hands in his pockets, nervously ruffled hair... he shifted.

"If you really hate it..."

Glancing at the front of his pants I had to smile and gesture to the door behind him.

I walked back to the front of my building and opened it, holding it open for the parade that followed behind me. First Winnie and then Larry came inside, the last locking the door to the office behind him. My apartment was only accessible via a rear fire door and a door in the back of my office. Both led to the same staircase and at the top was cozy living quarters that were plenty for an ex-military working dog and her handler.

Larry just plugged himself in wherever there was space.

"How did you get that here?" I asked, walking into the kitchen. A full pot of coffee sat in the machine, and I furrowed my brows at it. Had I progressed to making coffee in my sleep? I know people did weird things on Ambien, but I was fairly certain I didn't take Ambien. Though if my sleep walking meant I had coffee ready when I was awake walking, seemed acceptable.

"I started the pot before I woke you up because I value my life," Dr. Kirby said from beside me where he set two mugs on the counter. "Also, I fed Winnie for the same reason. You're welcome."

I grabbed his butt in lieu of saying thank you and he kissed my temple before bringing out milk, flavored syrup and sauces. Eyes drooping, I just stared at his butt while he made two cups of coffee and passed me one in a delightful mug with a rainbow and a unicorn that declared I was "F***ing Magical".

"So, how did you get the pink Jeep here?" I asked again after half of the coffee was gone from my pink unicorn cup.

"I drove it," he left the kitchen to sit on the couch and I stared. "What?"

"You... Drove that? It's pink!"

"Yeah and?"

"You're... that!" I gestured the length of his body. Winnie cocked her head to the side on the couch beside him and he mimicked the gesture. "Weren't you embarrassed?"

"Toxic masculinity is what's wrong with America, Cyn. Men can drive pink, glitter, Hello Kitty Jeeps without any loss of manliness," he patted the couch on his other side. I refilled my coffee and plopped on the couch beside him, being extra careful not to spill.

"First of all, toxic masculinity is an international problem. Second, I thought America was anti-vaxxers, systemic racism, lack of respect for nature, a disregard for science, the media..."

"Yeah... it might be a shorter list if we just listed all the things *not* wrong with the world... and America," he mused, following my train of thought. I clinked our coffee mugs in agreement and took a long drink.

"If only the infinity stones were real, Thanos could solve this problem."

"Would you snap away half of the population? Who would grow, harvest and roast your coffee?" Larry wrapped his arm around me, and I leaned against him, drinking my hot bean water as though it could be snapped away at any moment. The question was a little too deep for morning hours and I didn't have an answer.

"You know it's not staying pink, right?" my eyes drifted to the offending vehicle. It was still parked on Main in front of my building and it had drawn the largest crowd of people not waiting in line for food in the history of Maint St. Almost on cue, my friend and local bakery owner, Mary O'Connor, appeared with themed cookies that she was selling to the gathered crowds.

"When do you think Mo made Kitty cookies?" I asked, using her nickname and getting on my knees to look out at her artistry.

Larry was not looking at the cookies.

He also wasn't looking at the car.

"Some people are really into kitty... speaking of which?" he waggled his eyebrows suggestively and my lower body flooded with warmth.

"Depends... Aren't you still allergic to cats?" I asked, studying him over my coffee cup. He took the cup, verified it was empty because he values his life, and put it on the table.

"I'm not allergic to this one," his mouth pressed against mine, parting my lips with his tongue while his hands slid up the pajama shorts I was wearing. "In fact, I think I want to adopt it so it's mine forever."

His fingers found their destination and he swallowed my moan.

"Hello, kitty," he whispered, and I laughed my way into ecstasy.

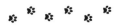

"What the hell is that?" Marvin asked and I followed his gaze through the front window of the shop. Sitting in front was the pink, Hello Kitty Jeep that now shimmered in the sun. The paint had just looked matte pink in the morning light, but at high noon, it was a beacon of mental and visual torture.

Also, the glitter steering wheel trapped heat and my hands had melted on the two-block drive despite the sixty-degree temps outside.

"It's apparently mine. Can you fix it?"

"With matches and lighter fluid," he couldn't take his eyes off the pink Jeep and I started to nod agreement but then remembered I didn't have any other money for cars. Not when I was constantly forking over money to repair Winnie catastrophes and keeping us in snackage.

"I was thinking paint," I told him, and he shook his head. Apparently he really wanted to set something on fire.

"It'll take days for color to get delivered," he tapped into his computer. "Also, you gotta pick a color and your dog ended my sample book."

I looked down at Winnie and she wagged her tail, a few crumbs and a smidge of mustard still on her muzzle.

"Sorry," I said to my shoes.

We'd walked into the body shop and Winnie had been off-leash. Marvin had been eating a sandwich which we interrupted with our arrival, but I was too distracted by the behemoth that was my car. Marvin set the sandwich down on top of a book to help me and the dog in question had jumped onto the counter, devoured the sandwich and picked up the book while holding half down with her paw, splitting the inventory from the ordering section. I'd jumped forward to get it back from her with a stern, *no,* but that became a game of chase faster than Hello Pink Jeep could draw a crowd. A chase ensued, Winnie lunging and dancing just out of reach, straight into the workshop for vehicle restorations. She startled a man working with a caustic liquid that spilled when Winnie dropped the book to shove her snoot into his butt and give him what was likely his proctology exam at the hands of canine.

The liquid spilled, missing the young man's shoes but dissolved the book in less than a minute.

"I'll pay for a new one," I glared at my partner, and she wagged her tail again. "Do you have any... left-overs from other jobs lying around? I'd like it to not be pink until I can pick what color it will be."

We watched a group of girls leave the pottery-painting place across the street and gush over my ride. The begged their moms to take their picture with the Jeep, throwing up peace signs and cupping their hands beneath their chins.

"Literally, any color," I confirmed, and he shook his head in disgust.

"Who would do that to a perfectly good automotive?"

"Who would do that to anything?"

We stared out the window in silence as a bus of Asian tourists arrived, forming a line to take photos with the Jeep on their way into the restaurant next door. The nearest point of interest was an hour and forty-five minutes away, but the Noodle House must have paid someone a fortune to get their establishment added to a tourist itinerary.

A fortune they did not spend on ingredients since I found three-dozen packages of Top Ramen in their trash last week.

It was unrelated to the reason I was looking in the trash but they'd bought my silence with beef and broccoli.

Marvin shook his head as the line slowly dwindled and the car sat alone once more.

"I'll see what I can do. Do you need it today?"

"No, I can walk everywhere I need to go today," a group of teenage boys took the place of the tourists and were now pretending to lick the character on the hood. "Seriously, what is wrong with this town?"

Marvin chuckled and shook his head.

"Lets be realistic, that Jeep is the most entertaining thing this town has seen since you blew up Roger's trailer," he pointed a finger at my chest and I felt my face burn. "Well, and when you managed to get Daniel Kirby stuck in that woman's cleavage."

"Can I blame the chickens?" I asked no one in particular. "The chickens and the rocks and... insufficient caffeination?"

"You can, but no one would believe you. We've all seen the delivery men going to your building with boxes upon boxes of coffee," Marvin tossed me a newspaper from a small stack beside his computer. "Catch up on current events and I'll call you when it's done."

Nodding, I took Winnie's leash and we walked out onto Main St, carefully avoiding the Jeep. There was now a group of seniors, collectively muttering about the nerve of Millennials to ruin a perfectly good car. While I agreed with them, there was something insulting that they thought Millennials would do that to a Jeep. It was not a generational issue; it was a single person with issues that hopefully got help, which is why they sold the Pepto Bismo monstrosity.

To Larry, who arguably also needed help.

Who I was sleeping with so maybe the three of us could get a group rate.

Without anything to do on my Sunday, I took Winnie to the park, plopped on a bench and opened the newspaper. A new column had appeared since I'd been back, Yvette Taylor's *Small-Town Scandal's*. Last week, she'd taken down Amber Carter from Amber's Shoe Ambrosia with an expose on her life's failures that included trying to join the Army. While I hadn't known Amber had tried to join the Army shortly after I did, it was surprising that she failed the medical exam and aptitude tests.

There was also speculation she was adopted and not actually the daughter of Cartersville Town Founder. While it was a stretch considering she was a carbon copy of the man with breasts, watching her refute it for three days was delightful. Winnie and I had brought popcorn and lurked at the periphery of all of her public appearances.

Until Winnie tackled an old lady over some peanut butter, and we decided to make ourselves scarce before we ended up in Yvette's column. The article itself had been brilliant, but it borderline had made me want to defend Amber. Until I remembered she tormented me throughout K-12, and I cut the article out to stick on the fridge.

Usually, I by-pass the front cover as it holds real news which I avoid, but the headline caught my attention.

Gossiper Gossips into an Early Grave

My eyes scanned the article, then I went back and read the whole thing. Yvette Taylor was dead, murdered in her office with a blunt force instrument three days earlier. Many suspects, no leads and a suspension of her column after this week as it had already been written. The article came off a little too light-hearted for murder, but Yvette wasn't exactly a pillar of politeness and she'd exposed her own editor online before the Editor-in-Chief made the woman hire Yvette to raise sales numbers and increase online traffic to the dying papers website. After a check of the by-line, I confirmed that the writer was one she'd ripped to shreds as a two-bit hack for hosting a Dear Abby column and accepting corporate sponsorships for advice answers. Coca Cola had paid big money for Mr. Fred Tannins to tell people soft drinks were the cure to depression and lack of energy.

He also liked to tell women that they would be prettier if they smiled more.

I flipped to page four, curious who Yvette's last victim would be. Though I'd never met her, the woman had made sarcasm and accusatory reporting an artform. While journalism was probably a little better off without her, I would miss the entertainment. Folding back the pages before, I smiled at her last headline.

Law Enforcement's Biggest Loser: Never Solved a Crime

Beneath the headline was Daniel Kirby in his police uniform, looking boyish and charming. A glance toward the shop showed the pink Jeep was gone, taken away to receive a makeover. My iced coffee was only three-quarters empty, so I smiled and settled in to read, delighted for once to enjoy a mystery and a scandal that did not concern me in the least.

About the Author

E. N. Crane is a fiction author writing humorous mysteries and thrillers with plus-sized female leads and their furry friends. She is one of two authors under the Perry Dog Publishing Imprint, a one woman, two dog operation in Idaho... for now. My dogs are Perry and Padfoot, the furry beasts shown above. They are well-loved character inspiration in all things written and business.

If you are interested in joining my newsletter, please subscribe here: https://e-n-crane_perrydogpublishing.ck.page/57 8ed9ab37or on my website, PerryDogPublishing.com

You will receive A Bite in Afghanistan, the prequel to the Sharp Investigations Series, as a thank-you for joining. The newsletter has content from both of my pen names, the other of which rights spicy romance. If it's not your jam, no worries. I only have one newsletter for mental health reasons, but you can follow Perry Dog Publishing on all socials to stay on top of the latest news... and pet pics.

Made in the USA
Las Vegas, NV
10 December 2024

13816953R00166